James A. Wright

Historical Sketches of the Town of Moravia

From 1791 to 1873

James A. Wright

Historical Sketches of the Town of Moravia
From 1791 to 1873

ISBN/EAN: 9783337117375

Printed in Europe, USA, Canada, Australia, Japan

Cover: Foto ©Andreas Hilbeck / pixelio.de

More available books at **www.hansebooks.com**

HISTORICAL SKETCHES

OF THE

Town of Moravia,

FROM 1791 TO 1873.

BY

JAMES A. WRIGHT.

BENTON & REYNOLDS, Printers.

AUBURN, N. Y., 1874.

CHAPTER XIV.

CHAPTER XV.

CHAPTER XVI.

CHAPTER XVII.

CHAPTER XVIII.

CHAPTER XIX.

CHAPTER XX.

CHAPTER XXI.

CHAPTER XXII.

CHAPTER XXIII.

CHAPTER XXIV.

CHAPTER XXV.

CHAPTER XXVI.

PREFACE.

In 1863, some hastily written sketches of this town were published in the Auburn *Journal*, and afterwards in the Cayuga County *Courier*. Those articles are herein revised and enlarged and many others added thereto, containing historical facts, and anecdotes, characteristics of early settlers, statistics, and a *resume* of the present condition of Moravia Village, and other matters, interesting as local history.

The volume is written in a plain, matter of fact way, with the endeavor to arrange systematically, and correctly, and in a substantial form, the history of this Town, so as to be interesting and valuable to those who take our places, as we have taken the places left vacant by the early settlers.

In describing the characteristics of the former generation, we have to deal with, in many respects, a peculiar people ; men born in New England who inherited all the peculiarities of the Puritan character ; industrious and frugal, conscientious, and imbued with a deep religious feeling, often opinionated and prejudiced, but thorougly honest and sincere. They represent a class, and a society, which, on account of the isolation in which it lived and grew, preserved the customs and traditions of New England people, long after such customs had faded from the land where they originated ; a people that had never lost faith in God, Justice and the Bible, and who cherished doctrines which had been either much modified, or entirely rejected by the descendants of the Puritans in the Eastern States. Men trained to certain notions, beliefs, and habits, have a distinct individuality, and this accounts for the many peculiar traits of character which we have alluded to in the following pages, and it also accounts for that firmness, consistency, honesty and piety, for which some of them were noted.

The historical facts are substantially correct and reliable. The main facts were obtained from persons living in the vicinity at the time of their occurrence, or from their immediate descendants. David Wright, one of the early settlers, Isaac Cady, John Stoyell, and William Wade, men well acquainted with the local and general history of the Town, each gave valuable information upon which some of the sketches are founded. Since their first publication the above named persons have all died, and it is a matter of regret that much that would have been of interest historically was not obtained before their departure.

The military portions are not given as a military history, except so far as to follow the experiences of the soldiers from this Town, and especially those who were wounded, or experienced "hair breadth escapes." Probably full justice has not been done some whose names do not appear in this work, but if so, it is because the facts concerning them could not be obtained. The writer has endeavored to give an impartial version of the matters which relate to the Volunteers from this town.

Our thanks are due to Leander Fitts, Cashier of The First National Bank; M. E. Kenyon, Secretary Agricultural Society; S. Edwin Day, Secretary Indian Mound Cemetery Association; R. D. Wade, Clerk of Moravia Village; Henry Cutler, Town Clerk; Will R. Covey, Secretary of Rising Star Lodge; and George N. Shaw, Town Clerk of Sempronius, in allowing the use of the books and records of their several Corporations and Societies, and for information very kindly given concerning the same.

IN MEMORIAM.

"Sketches of the Town of Moravia," as originally published, were written at the earnest request of Mr. Chauncey Wright, the father of the writer. At his suggestion also, the present volume was commenced, and during the last year of his life, he helped to furnish many of the more important facts and incidents of which the present generation had no substantial record. Whatever of personal interest the writer may have had in this work, originated entirely in the desire to gratify the request of the departed,.to whose memory this record of past events, is most affectionately inscribed.

CHAPTER I.

The Al-le-ghans. Irroquois or Six Nations—The Religious Belief of the Cayugas—First White Settlers—John Stoyell—First House Built.

It is now pretty well settled by the authorities in Indian History, that the western portion of the State of New York, was occupied by a race of Indians known as the "Al-le-ghans," who unmolested, roamed up and down on the earth from the Mississippi eastward to, and beyond the *Alleghanies*, during the eleventh and twelfth centuries. They are described as an active, populous tribe, possessing some knowledge of agriculture and the arts. They were however, about the year 1340, after a severe and protracted warfare, superceded by the Irroquois, who were composed of six confederated nations, to wit, the Cayugas, Senecas, Mohawks, Onondagas, Oneidas and Tuscaroras, and compelled to remove westward.

The "Six Nations" as they were called, held possession of the central portions of the State during four hundred years, or until about the year 1790, when they, in turn, succumbed to the advance of civilization, reflected in the countenances of the "pale face," and withdrew themselves to the wilder regions of the Keystone State.

The Cayugas prior to their removal, "owned and occupied," together with the Senecas, as tenants in common, the present County of Cayuga, and consequently the towns of Moravia, Locke, &c.

The first white settlers of whom we have any account, found the forest cut away, and a portion of the land giving evident signs of civilization. Perhaps this was done by the Indians, as a few of them yet remained upon the arrival of the white man, to wit, about 1789. No doubt this valley was a favorite resort, as the surrounding hills abounded in game, and the streams and lake in fish.

The Summit north of the village, known as "Indian Hill," according to tradition, was their burial ground.

The "Cayugas" it is alleged, were a religious race. Upon this point we copy from a treatise upon the "League of the Irroquois," which, while some portions thereof are doubtless overdrawn and imaginary, may yet contain many interesting and truthful illustrations of the Indians' religious belief:

"The personal existence of an invisible, but ever present Deity, was an intuitive belief with the Irroquois, which neither the lapse of centuries could efface, nor human inventions corrupt. If by the diffusion of this great truth, they did not escape the spell of superstition which resulted from their imperfect knowledge of the Supreme Being, and their ignorance of natural phenomena, they were saved from the deepest of all barbarians--an idolatrous worship. They believed in the constant superintending care of the Great Spirit, and that He ruled and administered the affairs of the world, and those of the red race.

As Moses taught that Jehovah was the God of Abraham, Isaac and Jacob, and of His chosen people, so the Irroquois regarded the Great Spirit as the God of the Indian alone. They looked up to Him as the author of their being, the same of their temporal blessings, and the future disposer of the felicities of their heavenly home. To Him they rendered constant thanks and homage for the changes in the seasons, the fruits of the earth, the preservation of their lives, and for their social privileges, and political prosperity, and to Him they addressed their prayers for the continuance of His protecting care."

"Their knowledge of the attributes of the Great Spirit was necessarily limited and imperfect, of His goodness and beneficence they had a full impression, and some notions also of his Justice and perfection. But they could not fully conceive of the omnipotence of the Great Spirit, except through the instrumentality of a class of inferior spiritual existences, by whom He was surrounded.

His power was evidenced by the creation of man. He was also believed to be self-existent, and immortal. The enobling and exalted views which are now held by Christian nations, would not be expected among a people excluded from the light of revelation. In the simple truths of natural religion they were throughly indoctrinated, and many of these truths were held in great purity and simplicity.—Such is the power of truth over the human mind, and the harmony of all truth, that the Indian, without the power of logic, reached some of the most important conclusions of philosophy, and drew down from heaven, some of the highest truths of revelation. While the religious system of the Irroquois taught the existence of the Great Spirit, it also recognised the existence of an Evil One. According to the legend of their finite origin, they were brothers, born at the same birth, and destined to an endless existence.

To the Evil Spirit in a limited degree was ascribed creative power. As the Great Spirit created man, and all useful animals, and products of the earth, so the Evil Spirit created all monsters, poisonous reptiles, and noxious plants. In a word while the former made everything that was good and subservient, the latter formed everything that was bad and pernicious to man.

The immortality of the soul, was another of the fixed beliefs of the Irroquois. This notion had prevailed generally among the red races under different forms and with different degrees of distinctness.

The happy home beyond the setting sun had cheered the heart, and lighted the expiring eye of the Indian, before the ships of Columbus had borne the Cross to this western world. The religious system of the Irroquois that it was a journey from earth to heaven of many days duration. Originally it was supposed to be a year, and the period of mourning for the departed was fixed at that term. At its expiration it was customary for the relatives of the deceased to hold a feast, the soul of the departed having reached heaven, and a state of felicity, there was no longer cause for mourning. The spirit of grief was exchanged for that of rejoicing. In modern times the mourning period has been reduced to ten days, and the journey of the spirit is now believed to be performed in three.

The spirit of the deceased was supposed to hover around the body for a season before it took its final departure, and not until after the expiration of a year, according to the ancient belief, and ten days according to the present, did it become permanently at rest in heaven. A beautiful custom prevailed in ancient times, of capturing a bird and freeing it over the grave on the evening of the burial, to bear away the spirit to its heavenly rest. Heaven was believed to be the abode of the Great Spirit—the final home of the faithful. They believed that there was a road down from heaven to every man's door. In this invisible way, the soul ascended in its heavenly flight, until it reached its celestial habitation. As before observed, the spirit was supposed to linger for a time about the body, and perhaps to revisit it. In consequence of this belief, a superstitious custom prevailed of leaving a slight opening in the grave, through which it might re-enter its former tenement. After taking its final departure the soul was supposed to ascend higher and higher on its heavenly way, gradually moving to the westward, until it came out upon the plains of heaven."*

It is stated that in the summer of 1789, some men from the Town of Genoa, came to the "Flats" for the purpose of procuring a supply of hay. These men were Gideon Pitts, Jonathan Brownell, John Guthrie and Jonathan Richmond. The first permanent resident however, was John Stoyell, who came from Connecticut to Aurora in 1789, and while there became acquainted with an agent of Mr. TenEyck, a wealthy land owner, with whom he bargained for one hundred acres of land, at one shilling per acre, the same to be located on lot number eighty-three in this town, but which was at that time part of the Town of Scipio. Mr. Stoyell was required to advance twenty shillings "to bind the bargain," which amount he promptly paid, and soon thereafter removed to his newly acquired possessions. Here Mr. Stoyell experienced all the hardships and inconveniences which embarrass, and often times dishearten the early settler. Alone in a wilderness, with no one to counsel with or render the least assistance, he laid the foundation for one of the most beautiful villages in Western New York. After building a cabin and planting some corn and potatoes, he returned to Aurora, where he saw Mr. TenEyck, who had been informed that a "*Yankee*" had purchased a portion of his land. His hatred of the Yankees, and all that pertained to them was as violent as it was foolish, and he immediately gave Mr. Stoyell a verbal notice

---

* Morgan's Treatise on the League of the Irroquois.

to *quit*. No Yankee should settle near *his* land. He would refund the money paid, (the twenty shillings), and the Yankee must surrender the premises forthwith. He knew nothing of Mr. Stoyell, *pro or con*, save that he was a Yankee, and therefore objected to him on *general principles*. But in this instance he had "reckoned without his host." Mr. Stoyell was a young man, energetic and ambitious, and knew that in course of time, his land would be valuable. He had made a fair purchase, commenced making improvements and would not yield to his unreasonable objection and demand. Mr. Ten Eyck, however, after inquiring in the neigborhood, as to what manner of man "that Yankee Stoyell was," ascertained that he was just the man for the place, and by his industry would not only pay for, and improve his own farm, but also enhance the value of his, (Ten-Eyck's) adjoining lands. This so far overcame his prejudices, that he afterward *gave* Mr. Stoyell the one hundred acres which he had bargained for, providing he would use his influence toward starting a settlement there. After procuring the services of a carpenter, Stoyell returned to his farm, and built a frame house, just northwest of the present site of "Jenning's Block." There were but six men present at the raising, three white, and the *balance* Indians, the only spectator being a *squaw*.

This was the first frame house built in the town of Moravia. Mr. Stoyell was an enterprising, business man, and subsequently became the owner of lot number 83, half of lot number 84, and a portion of lot number 93, part of which cost him from $12 to $20,00 per acre. The next settlers in this town were Amos Stoyell, Winslow Perry and Jabez Bottom, who came in 1793, and Gershom Morse in 1794.

CHAPTER II.

Gershom Morse had been to the "Flats" previous to 1794, but only long enough to satisfy himself that it was a desirable locality for a settlement. He bargained with Jabez Bottom, who came the year previous, for the tract of land, which is now occupied south of the village by the Morse family. He built a log house in the garden of the Morse family, near their present residence, the house had but one door, which was upon the south side. When Mr. Morse was married he had no chairs or tables, but these were soon manufactured, the former in the shape of what we call stools, and the table of two boards joined together and fastened by hinges into the side of the house, so that when not in use, it would be out of the way, and hung down by the side of the wall; when wanted, one leg was attached which held up the side unsupported by the wall. A large oak tree was cut down near the house, the stump hollowed out, and used with an iron pestle for mill purposes ; several neighbors came there to pound out their corn, the nearest grist mill being 16 miles distant. The road at that time, ran past the door of their house on the south, westerly across the Inlet south of the farm now owned by Wilford H. Van Etten, and up West Hill, and from Morse's line easterly along the ridge or brow of the hill east of the Fair Grounds and near the Brick Yard, to Mont-ville, and thence to Skaneateles. Another road led from near Morse's, across the "Flats" and Inlet, to near the Dean farm, where it terminated. After-ward the road over West Hill was abandoned, and another course taken, which ran south, just east of the old Cemetery and west of Dry Creek Falls, south to Locke. One day after this change had been made, Mrs. Morse being the only occupant of the log house was *weaving*, the door standing open, when a shadow fell across the threshold, and upon looking for the cause, she beheld an Indian in full Indian costume, with tomahawk and scalping knife. She was terribly frightened, but the door was the only way of escape, and in this stood the Indian with either hand upon the door posts. She however retained presence of mind enough to remain weaving, with apparent com-posure ; keeping an eye out, however, without seem-ing to do so, upon her visitor, who remained motion-less and speechless for several minutes, and then beckoned for her to come to the door, which she did with great show of courage. There was really no cause for fear, for the Indian had lost his way, and merely stopped to inquire the directions, &c. He pointed to the West Hill where the road formerly led, and said, "No see road," "No find." Mrs. Morse pointed in the direction of the new road and to a mark on an adjoining tree, (the roads were marked out in that way) and endeavored by various signs, to give him the proper directions, which he seemed to comprehend, and left, much to the relief of "the woman of the house."

Gershom Morse was Justice of the Peace in 1805, but whether he had held the office previous to that time, we are unable to learn. His Dockets show that he was Justice for many years, and had a thriving business, both criminal and civil. He was a man of large physique and couragous. It is said that he would enter a ring during a fight (and fights were frequent in those days, and savage too), collar the parties engaged, and pull them apart as though they were two dogs, or knock them down if necessary, and fine them on the spot, and in case of non-payment, send them to jail forthwith.

The annexed miscellaneous items are copied from his Docket, showing how legal business was transacted in his time, the fees of officers, and other *cursory* matters.

"APRIL 2, 1807."

Summons given to Asa Little, constable, in favor of E. Patty, against James Powers, returnable the 10th instant, at 1 o'clock, afternoon, a subpœna given for three evidences. The Court called, the parties present ; the plaintiff throws in his charge, which was, James Powers to E. Patty, to damage done to a two year old heifer; done by his dog, for which the said Patty charges ten dollars. The defendant pleads for a non-suit on account of a Sheriff's execution being levied on the heifer, the plea not granted. The above cause taken out of Court and left to three men to settle: Cyrus Powers, Cotton Skinner and John Stoyell, to be tried this day, and all their differences between them to be settled. The parties agreed to leave out Cotton Skinner and Cyrus Powers, and take John Bennett and Gershom Morse, who got together and tried the cause, and brought in an award in favor of E. Patty, against James Powers for five dollars.

Names of evidences: Preserved Gibbs, George Thompson, James Dresser, John Bennett, Zadoc Rhodes, John Hemmenway, Daniel Powers, John Powers, Lizzy Patty, Samuel Wright, Orrin Wright."

The following is a bill of costs in Justice's Court, in which Samuel Atkin was plaintiff, and Ephraim Hults defendant, on Dec. 23, 1808:

Summons,	.09.
Constable fee,	.78.
Adjournment,	.09.
Venire,	.12 1-2.
Constable serving venire,	.37 1-2.
Swearing jury,	.12 1-2.
Subpœna,	.06.
Judgment,	.12 1-2.
	$1.77.
Verdict of jury,	7.35.
	$9.12.

> *"To be paid out of the above judgment*
> *to Cady's Tavern, for one pint of*
> *whiskey,"*   -   -   -   -   -   0.49.
> _______
>
>   . $9.31.

"COUNTY OF CAYUGA—ss.

Be it remembered that on the 19th day of January, 1807, Jeremiah Sabins, of Sempronius, was convicted before me, Gershom Morse, one of the Justices of the Peace of said county, of swearing one profane oath, for which he was fined thirty-seven and one-half cents. Given under my hand, at Sempronius, January 19, 1807.

GERSHOM MORSE,

Justice."

"The above mentioned fine of Jerry Sabins, sent by Cyrus Powers, Esq., to the poor master."

"March 6, 1807.

In open Court :—

Elisha Smith was fined before me, Gershom Morse, Esq., for swearing four profane oaths, one dollar and fifty cents, and refused to pay the sum before mentioned, therefore by warrant, was put publicly in the stocks for two hours, and the warrant returned on March 7, executed by

M. MEACH, *Constable."*

"SEMPRONIUS, January, 1807.

Personally appeared before me, Gershom Morse, Esq., Asa Shadwick, of Locke, and makes oath that, and saith that Abel Meach, Deputy Sheriff for the County of Cayuga, on the 13th day of January, arrested Barnabas Castoline, and set him the said Asa Chadwick over him, and that the said Barnabas Castoline made his escape contrary to his wishes, or knowledge, and that by search he found his track in the snow, but being unable to run could not obtain him. Given under my hand, this 19th day of January, 1807.

GERSHOM MORSE."

Here is a specimen of bodily ailment and spiritual cure:

"SEMPRONIUS, Jan. the 26, 1807.

Warrant issued and served by Towner Whiting, constable of Locke, against James Rice of Locke, on the part of the people, on the complaint of Eli Clark for assault and beating. The said James Rice pleads not guilty."

"January 26. John Bennett on oath says: That on the 26th about daylight the complainant and defendant came to a settlement by leaving out to him and J. B. Van Atta. After deciding the matter both appeared well pleased, and agreed to drop the matter. Jacob B. Van Atta on oath says: That on the 26th, after they got the warrant they were going to swear the constable. When they got to J. Kiese's, the parties agreed to settle by leaving it out to two men, and left it out to John Bennett and himself. They agreed each to pay half the costs, *they then dring't together, and both appeared to be well pleased.*"

Domestic infelicity and general *unpleasantness* resulting therefrom :

"January the 23, 1807.

On the complaint of Caleb King, of Locke, on behalf of the people for abuse, against Jacob B. VanAtta who complains and says : That on the 14th of January, this present month, did abuse his wife Nancy, and for parting them, or trying to part them, did violently assault him, the said Caleb King, and kicked him so that he has not enjoyed his health since, at the house of Wm. Wattles Inkeeper of Locke.

January 27. Warrant returned with the prisoner. After taking the examination of Caleb King, Eli Clark, James King and John Van Buren, collectively together, concluded to discharge the prisoner, Jacob B. Van Atta."

The following scrap was found on a loose paper in one of those old Dockets, the originator of which is unknown, and which is copied verbatim :

"SEMPRONIUS Mch 14, 1807

Jon Aspel aplyde fer lisene too retale speritus lickers."

Here is another :

" Aug the 2, 1810 Esq Maus pleas to send me that munny that is cummin to me Joseph Culver from Peter Bathwick to Joseph Culver by the barerer Joseph Culver"

The Morse family have resided upon the same old farm for nearly eighty years ; the title to that farm is undoubtedly good in the family, they having been in undisturbed possession so long "that the memory of man runneth not to the contrary."— The names of the children of Squire Morse being rather peculiar, are appended for the benefit of families in search of cognomens somewhat uncommon: Solomon, Abishai, Rachael Achsah, Orpha, Lucy, Iza Oma, Ency, Gershom, Laura.

The Morse family belong to a hardy, long-lived race, several members are now over seventy years of age; it has been said that the Morses never die —old Squire Morse is not around now, visibly, but there seems to be no actual knowledge of his death, *he merely passed away.* The family is noted for strict honesty.

CHAPTER III.

Cotton Skinner—David Wright—Characteristics of the Early Settlers.

In the spring of 1795, a valuable acquisition was made to this little company, by the arrival of Cotton Skinner, who built a log house, near the present residence of Peter Robinson; he was by trade a shoemaker, and taken *oæl* in all, was a very remarkable man. Of very feeble health and limited capital, he had by frugal habits and perseverance for years, at the time of his decease, acquired a large property; he was very close in deal, but strictly honest, and the wholesome rule "owe no man anything" was as strictly applied to himself, as to his debtors.

Mr. Skinner was a benevolent man, doing good as he found opportunity, and by influence and example did much to sustain the Congregational Church and Society of which he was a member. By his last will and Testament he bequeathed a large portion of his property to the Theological Seminary, at Auburn, N. Y. A few years after Mr. Skinner's arrival in Moravia, he became a merchant, and purchased his goods and merchandise at Utica, N. Y. Upon one occasion he decided to take with him to that place, his eldest son. Going to Utica was a great undertaking in those days, and produced considerable excitement in the mind of the boy, who concluded, among other things, that better clothes were needed for the occasion, than those worn at home, which, though whole and clean, represented several qualities of materials and various colors; therefore the son immediately suggested to his father the propriety of having a new suit; but receiving no satisfactory answer, he was obliged to wait for a more convenient season. When he again brought his fathers attention to the subject, he received for an answer, "Guess clothes good enough at home, are good enough at Utica." But holding a different opinion from his father upon this subject (and what boy does not,) as the time of departure drew near, he again urged the necessity of his case, when he was very abruptly interrupted by his father's exclaiming, in his own peculiar manner: "Hum, *Wall's! Good clothes don't make a man!*"

In 1796, Samuel Wright arrived with his family and built a log house somewhat north of the farm now owned by L. O. Aiken, Esq. Among others who came in 1797 were David Wright and family. He removed from Otsego County, N. Y., to the "Flats," a distance of about one hundred miles. At the present time this would be a journey scarce worth mentioning, but in those days, with ox teams and heavy roads, it was very unpleasant and tedious, and considered a great undertaking. Mr. Wright was thirteen days on the road, being unable to travel more than four miles per day, for a portion of the time. He stated that, if his memory was correct, there were but two houses and a saw mill in Skaneateles at that time, the former built in "salt box" style. He was obliged to ford the lake at the above mentioned place, carrying across in his arms, one at a time, his mother, wife and child, through water two feet in depth. The child was Chauncey Wright, then seven months old. Mr. David Wright was at that time twenty-three years of age; he settled upon a tract of land, upon the Flats, now owned by Joseph Alley, which he cultivated for several years, and upon which he built a house; his title, however, proved defective, and he lost the farm and money paid therefor, and all improvements. In common with his neighbors, he suffered many hardships, but had good health, and was generally happy and contented; he was well educated, and in his early days occupied some time in teaching school. He kept up with the political history of this country even during the last years of his life, and during the Rebellion was very confident that the Union forces would ultimately succeed, and the Union triumph: he died on August 17th, 1869 at the advanced age of ninety-five years and six months.

The early settlers of this town were mostly of Puritanic descent, and brought with them the peculiar religious views which characterized the noble and self-sacrificing men and women of Plymouth Rock. Their Sabbaths were observed with the utmost strictness and rigid solemnity. Commencing at the going down of the sun on Saturday nights and ending with sunset upon the following day. The intermediate time was occupied during the day largely with attendance upon church service. Three lengthy sermons being the usual allowance, and the *balance* of the time in instructing the children in the Catechism or repeating the hymns of the celebrated Dr. Watts. Saturday nights were set apart as preparatory to the coming day. No secular tales, no bear, Indian, or even ghost stories stirred the imagination or aroused the fears of the little ones; but Moses in the Rushes, Daniel in the Lion's Den, Jonah and his miraculous Sea Voyage, interspersed with short biographical sketches of the meekest, oldest, strongest and the wisest man, answered equally as good a purpose, and ended with a moral, calculated to interest and fix the attention of the youthful minds upon the historic teachings of the Bible.

The early settlers were exact in all religious requirements. They practiced that which they preached, and taught to their children and their children's children, what they believed to be the teachings of Holy Writ. The Sabbath was a day when everything, except so called *serious* matters, was laid aside. Their walk and talk, and faces bespoke the day as certainly as did the family almanac. Children must walk slowly, and older people with solemn stately tread, to the sanctuary; no smiles, no joyous exclamation broke the silence of the house, because "'twas Sunday."

Their religion was a serious thing. It cannot be denied however, that this was a good class of people; honest, reliable, industrious and religious. But it may be doubted whether their manner of observing the Sabbath, and their general deportment upon that day, was calculated to impress upon the outer world a correct idea of the Sabbath or of the religion taught by Jesus Christ, the Lord of the Sabbath and the Head of the Church. The Sabbath "was made for man," not to be desecrated by manual labor, or vain amusements, or worldly calculations and business, but to be enjoyed rationally, in church service, in thanksgiving, in "going about doing good," and in social conversation, endeavoring to turn the minds of men, upon this day of rest, to better thoughts and purposes.

It is not a solemn day to the religious man. He has a right to rejoice and to be happy. He ought to be glad, for upon that day "Christ arose from the dead." He may rejoice always. Let him be of serious countenance and of downcast eye who denies His Master, and tramples upon His laws. Let him fear and tremble who loves not His Heavenly Father, whose blessings unnumbered he has received with thoughtless indifference or unthankful heart. Let him go mourning and with a saddened mien.

> "But children of a Heavenly King
> Should speak their joys abroad."

The early settlers clung with great tenacity to their extreme Puritanic views and practices, even longer than those who remained together in the communities from whence they emigrated.   They were industrious citizens, generally physically strong and long lived, and taken all in all, averaged more than ordinary communities in intellect.

CHAPTER IV.

Miscellany—Old Records—Accidents by Field and Flood—Bounty for Head of Wolves and Bears — Free Commoners — Manumittance of Slaves — Ejectment — A Bad Specimen — First School House and Store.

The following memoranda is copied from an old record, the first page of which bears the following inscription:

"Zadok Cady's Book, 1799."

"February 22, 1807. John Locke died by a wound in his thigh, cut by a knife while killing a hog."

"June 16, 1815. James Dresser's head broke by the limb of a tree."

"September 28, 1812. David Locke accidentally shot. Died the 29, in the morning."

"May 9, 1817. David Johns died by drinking."

"Feb. 20, 1817. Jabez Bradley hung himself."

"April 25, 1818. James Powers' two children drowned, Saturday night."

"July 2, 1818. Jared Weeks died at Auburn, taking laudanum."

"July 13, 1822. Mrs. Stephens hung herself."

"Sept. 25, 1824. Oliver Platt fell from a ladder and broke his neck."

"January 12, 1828. E. Reed killed by a fall from his wagon."

"June 28, 1830. William Vincent hung himself."

"January 11, 1831. Hiram Bishop died. Death caused by liquor."

"Oct. 18, 1836. Abram Selover killed by his wagon turning over."

"Aug. 30, 1837. Petit Smith killed by falling from his wagon."

"June 12, 1842. Mr. Chamberlain killed by his house falling in a hurricane."

"Aug. 24, 1843. Laban Wood killed while running horses."

Obituary and business are sometimes intermingled, as witness the following:

"May 29, 1805. James Croy, Dr.
    To 1 small coffin, six shillings—*poisoned with laudanum.*"

"January 3d, 1805, reckoned with Moses Little, and found due to him two shillings two pence, Dr. to 1 pint whiskey, six pence."

"May 21, 1806 Gideon Wheelock, Dr.
To 1 small coffin, 4 shillings.
1 pint whiskey, 6 pence."

The following is apparently a *running* account.

"May 2, 1805, Moses Little Dr.
To boy to ride horse 1 day 18 pence.
3 pints wiskey, 3 shillings.
Boy to ride horse 1 day 18 pence.
1-2 day horse ride, 9 pence.

1 pint whiskey, one shilling.
3   "   "   3 shillings,
1-2 day boy riding horse nine pence.
1 pint whiskey, 1 shilling.
4 quarts and 1 pint, 1 dollar 12 pence.
2 quarts whiskey, 4 shillings.
1 finger in a cradle, 18 pence.
1 cheese press, 7 shillings 6 pence,
1-2 day boy riding horse, 9 pence.
1 pint whiskey, 1 shilling."

It is said that Luther Wright, once a celebrated brick mason in this town, was accustomed to address his assistant in the following plain language, "Brick, Mortar, Whiskey! *What I call for last, I want first.*"

But it is doubtful whether he could intersperse business and pleasure, with the philosophical precision manifested in the foregoing bill.

Memoranda.—"To find Mr. Howe, turn at Wyncoop's farm, enquire of Esquire Purdy, ten miles from Geneva." Dated 1818.

This old book also bears witness to the state of the weather:

"April 12, 1821, began to snow, on the 16th fell six inches, on the 18 eight inches."

"June 8 and 9, 1823, frost each night.
May 9, 1831, snow fell 10 inches deep.
October 5, 1836, snow fell 6 inches deep."
The following charges will show the price of various articles, labor &c.

"February 3, 1801, making one cherry table and bedstead $4.00.

April 1, 1801, three lbs. butter, 3 shillings.

" " " making pair shoes, nine shillings six pence.

Nov. 12, 1801, 1 days work, eight shillings.

Oct. 1, 1809, 1 bushel corn, 4 shilling.

" " " tapping boots, 2 shilling.

" " " 2 1-2 bushels wheat, 1 dollar.

Oct. 31, 1800, use horse 1 day, 2 shillings.

Aug. 1, 1800, to 1-2 ton hay 12 shillings.

Aug. 1, 1807, 1,000 shingles two dollars."

The following items are copied from the old Records of the Town of Sempronius:

Town Meeting 1799, "Voted that the town do pay the sum of Five Dollars for each head of every grown Wolf killed and taken off in town this year."

Voted "That this Town shall pay One Dollar and Fifty Cents, for each and every head of a full grown bear, killed and taken off in said town the present year."

(The foregoing is rather bear-faced.)

In 1808, extra inducements were offered:

"Resolved that this Town pay Ten Dollars for the head of every full grown wolf that is killed and taken off in this town this year, and Five Dollars for every Whelp Wolf."

(It is said that the latter animal, becoming exasperated at this "unequal valuation," moved over into the town adjoining on the north, and that *some* 'whelps' are to be found there to this day. This however, smacks of the stories of Mark Twain, and should be taken with a grain of precaution, unless the reader has some personal spite against that town, in which case this item can be enlarged to suit the occasion.)

1806. Resolved, "That all Swine weighing seventy weight and upwards, *shall be free commoners with a good ring in the nose.*"

In 1814 the Swine Law was repealed, to wit: "That Swine are not free commoners." (This last vote has a different ring to it.)

Advertisement. — "Come into the enclosure of Thomas Summerton, the first day of November 1805, a white sheep ram. Supposed to be a lamb without any mark."

Aggriculture—"1809, Resolved that every man that suffers Canada Thistles to grow on his farm in this town, shall pay Five Dollars for said offence."

Also in 1818, "Resolved that if any person shall suffer and allow Canada Thistles to grow and to go to seed on his farm, and not cut them down in the old of the moon in August, so as to destroy the seed thereof, that every person so neglecting and offending, shall forfeit and pay the sum of \$2.50 for every such offence."

"Be it remembered that Henry I. Brinkerhoff, of the town of Sempronius, on the 20th day of September, 1811, came forward and had a certain negro female child put on record; the mother of said child is his property; the female child is named 'Jute,' and was born March 19 day in the year 1811. The bill he signed, Henry I. Brinkerhoff."

Emancipation Proclamation:

"Be it remembered that on the 15 day of July, 1820, Aaron Connover did give the following manumittance to Thomas, otherwise called Thomas Smith Johnson, a negro man slave: 'To all whom these presents shall come. Know ye, that I, Aaron Connover, of the town of Sempronius, in the County of Cayuga, have and do hereby manumit Thomas, otherwise called Thomas Smith Johnson, a negro man slave aged about thirty years, and he is hereby discharged from all further liability to me by means of being my bonden slave. Given under my hand, at Sempronius the 15 day of July, 1820, in presence of Wm. Price.   Aaron Connover.

Ejectment, *nolen volens*.

"Be it rembered, that the Overseer of the Poor for this town, has warned Ebenezer Pelton to remove out of this town, together with his family, immediately.   Done this 15 day of March, 1802."

At Town Meeting, 1828.   "Resolved that John VanDyne shall not be paid anything in consequence of, he says, being taxed too high, as setting a bad specimen."

In the autumn of 1798, a school house, sufficiently large to accomodate the children of the neighborhood, was built near the present residence of Dr. Alley, and a school taught therein the following year by Levi Goodrich, and the second year by David Wright.

The first store was opened by David Wright, in the year 1800, in a log house near the "Quaker Meeting House," on what is now known as the Cortwright farm.   The next merchant was Cotton Skinner, who had a store in one part of the house in which he lived.

CHAPTER V.

GAME —BEARS AND FORBEAR—-PANTHERS—-THE MORSE BOYS AND A "CATAMOUNT"—WOLVES—THEIR ATTACK UPON DAVID WRIGHT AND FAMILY—BATTLE BETWEEN MORSE'S DOG AND A WOLF—DEER—MANNER OF CAPTURE—FIRST MARRIAGE, BIRTH, AND DEATH.

Game of various kind was abundant. Bears were less feared than wolves: the former would seldom molest a man unless first attacked and wounded by him—they by general consent gave each other a wide berth.

Upon one occasion, one of the settlers coming through the woods near Montville, found his path obstructed by a large tree, which had but recently fallen across it; climbing upon it, he was greatly astonished to find himself in close proximity to a bear, which had also at that moment raised himself upon the other side of the log, preparatory to getting over. For an instant the man at least, was stupefied: "Stet erunt que comae et vox faucibus haesit." The log had put them at loggerheads. The man could not bear it, nor could the bear; forbearance was apparently a virtue, and the next moment "neither stood upon the order of his going, but went at once," upon the back track, each swearing and roaring in a manner satisfactory no doubt to himself, as distance lent enchantment to the view.

Hogs were sometimes killed by the bears, it was customary to build log pens, in which they were enclosed. A pen however, which was built by Mr. Prouty, near the old red house near the head of the gulf, was entered several times and pigs carried off. Abisha Morse says that when a boy, he saw a bear on the flat now used as a Fair Ground ; but he soon disappeared. Panthers were seen occasionally ; two were killed, one near the "Pinnacle" or "Dry Creek Gulf," and the other upon West Hill. When any of the early settlers were out after dark, it was customary to carry a lighted torch, generally a pine knot, of which all wild animals stand in awe. Upon one occasion Abisha and Gershom Morse were returning home, across the Flat, from East Hill, Gershom in the rear, and being so near home, had allowed his light to go out, when suddenly he heard a rustling and scrabbling behind him, and saw, a few feet back, two glisttening eyeballs, advancing, he sprang forward to his brother, who was a little in advance, crying : "Swing your torch! Swing your tourch!" which he did and forthwith the eyes, with a long body and tail, went up a tree at a bound. The boys always supposed that animal to be a "Catamount," as one was killed shortly after on Dry Creek ; but they didn't *wait* to ascertain definitely at the time.

Wolves were more numerous, and far more bold and daring. Mr. David Wright informed us, that while he lived on the farm now owned by Joseph Alley, he went one night on foot, with his wife and child, to visit their nearest neighbor, who resided near the present residence of Roswell Brown; about midnight they started on their way home, and had traveled about one-half the distance, when the howl of a wolf was heard upon the West Hill, which was immediately answered by one from Oak Hill. Mr. Wright, knowing that danger threatened them, and being entirely unarmed, caught his child in his arms, and hastened homeward, with all possible speed. The howling increased, and from every direction, sounding nearer and nearer, until when they reached the house exhausted, they had but time to close the door before the wolves rushed against it from the outside.

Unfortunately the guns had been loaned the previous day, and no weapons were in the house, so that the inmates were obliged to hear the terrible howling of the hungry animals, around the building, until nearly daylight, when they decamped, with apeptites unabated by their nights adventure. Mr. Wright the next day brought home the guns, and also a large bull dog (which had also been absent on a neighborly visit, for a few days). That night the howling of the previous evening was repeated, but with different results. Two wolves got before Mr. Wright's old "flint lock" and laid down, in their last sleep. Their skin made an excellent bed for the old watch dog. The following night, dog and gun were ready for business, but watched in vain for their enemy; the balance of the pack had left on suspicion.

The same party, one evening just after dark, was coming home from a neighbor's, a few miles out of town, and living north of the "flats," was crossing the woods north of Montville Falls, when he heard wolves not far in his rear, barking in a manner which satisfied him that they were on his track. He therefore made for a crossing with which he was familiar, hoping to get over the creek and up on to the hill, before they overtook him ; but as he reached the creek, he distinctly heard the animals running and panting but a short distance back. As his only safety was to climb a tree, he was anxious to reach the top of the hill, thinking that his cries for help would be heard from his house ; at some considerable risk of being overtaken, he scrambled up the steep bank and never stopped to look around until he was safely seated in a tree top ; here he waited patiently, but no wolves came, and after hallooing in vain for help for a long time, he slowly descended the tree and made for home. The next morning he returned to the creek, and found that the wolves had not crossed the log, but tracks were plenty at the crossing and up and down the creek for several rods.

The Morses give an account of one that came through their yard in the evening, and which was attacked by a large dog belonging to their father ; after a severe struggle the wolf escaped, and the dog came into the house badly used up, a piece of skin being torn off his side as large as a man's hand. Mother Morse thought best to make some salve for the wound, but the "Squire" said no, the dog will doctor that. Next morning the dog dug a hole in the ground, in which he lay with the wound next the soil, and the wound soon healed.

Hunting deer was the favorite sport of the early settlers. One mode of capturing them was as follows: After putting the dogs upon the track, the hunters would hasten to the lake, (Owasco), carefully secrete themselves and await the arrival of the deer, who were sure, after being hotly pursued, to run as a last resort, into the lake, swim around, entirely under water, excepting a small portion of the head, and land at a different point, in order to throw the dogs off the track. Immediately upon the deer entering the lake however, the hunters emerged from their place of concealment, and in rough boats hewn from the body of white-wood trees, start in pursuit, overtake the animal, and after a blow upon the head with a mallet, cut its throat, and tow the carcass to the land. The meat was dried or salted; the tallow manufactured into candles, and the hide into shoes.

The first child born in the settlement was a son of Winslow and Rachael Perry, in the summer of 1794.

The first marriage was of Sally, a daughter of the same, to Jonathan Eldridge, in 1795. And the first burial that of Cynthia A., daughter of Gideon and Hannah Wright, April 5, 1796. She was buried near the present residence of John G. Caldwell.

CHAPTER VI.

CHURCHES—FIRST CONGREGATIONAL CHURCH—ITS
ORGANIZATION—BUILDING—NAMES OF PASTORS.

The Congregationalists are descendants of a people formally belonging to the counties of Nottingham, Lancashire and Yorkshire in England. Desirous of enjoying a purer religion, they separated from the English Establishment in 1602, but persecutions arising against them, they were obliged to flee to Holland, where they remained for a season unmolested, but finally embarked for America and landed at Plymouth Rock, Dec. 22d, 1820. There they were free to worship God according to the dictates of their own consciences, and though in an unknown land, in the midst of dangers seen and unseen, the wild woods rang with praise to God, the anthems of the free. This was the foundation of the Congregational Church in America.

A large portion of the first settlers of Moravia were Congregationalists, and on the 12th day of March, 1806, a meeting was held for the purpose of organizing a Church and Society. At that meeting a Confession of Faith and a Form of Covenant were adopted, and after presenting proper testimonials of members and relating their religious experiences, the following named persons were received to communion and fellowship, as the "First Congregational Church of Sempronius," viz:

John Stoyell,
Cotton Skinner,
John Phelps,
Sarah Warren,
Elizabeth E. Morrow,
John Locke,
Jacob Spafford,
Sarah Stoyell.
Justus Gibbs,
Levi H. Goodrich,
Esther Locke,
Mary Curtis,
Abigail Spafford,
Joseph Butler,
Lois Stoyell,

Levi H. Goodrich was chosen Deacon and Clerk. John Stoyell, Cotton Skinner and Levi H. Goodrich, Trustees.

Rev. Royal Phelps was the first Pastor of the church.

At a meeting of the church, held April 2d, 1808, Mr. John Stoyell was unanimously chosen Deacon in place of Levi H. Goodrich, resigned. Mr. Stoyell held the office until the time of his death, which occurred in 1842, having been a consistent and active member of the church for thirty-four years.

In the summer of 1814, a brick School House was built, and though used for secular purposes, afforded a more suitable and convenient place of worship, than the society previously had.

It appears from the church records, that but few additions were made to the church for several years. Perhaps for this reason, a church building was not errected. The first meeting for consultation in regard to building, was held November 5, 1816, when it was resolved "that we build a meeting house fifty by forty feet with a steeple." A committee to solicit subscriptions was also appointed. In December following, however, the idea was abandoned on account of financial embarrassments. No particular change was apparent in the church until the year 1822, when there was a general awakening among its members, and those connected with the Society, which resulted in a large number of coversions. Thirty-nine united with the church, increasing the whole number to ninety-three members.

The following year, 1823, the building now occupied by the society was erected, under the supervision of Daniel Goodrich, Senior, and Henry King, architects. The very name of the chief builder was a sufficient guarantee at that time, of substantial labor and unsurpassed material, and half a centurie's exposure to the elements attests the wisdom of his judgment, and the stability of his workmanship.—The cost of the building was estimated at seven thousand dollars. The land upon which it was built, with additional for a spacious yard, was donated to the Society, by Deacon John Stoyell, Sen.

The society has been fortunate in procuring ministers, so that since its organization, it has not been for any great length of time without the preached word.

In 1831 forty persons united with the church, and in 1843, after an extensive revival, sixty-five more were added.

Of this last revival, which was not confined to

this church, but in which all the Churches were engaged, Mr. Isaac Cady, then Church Clerk, says:—
"The season of revival just passed has been one of deeper interest than has ever been known before in this town.   It commenced about the middle of March and continued about five weeks in this community and the neighborhood around us.   Probably not less than one hundred and fifty persons in town became the subjects of this glorious work."

The total number of names appearing upon the Church Record is 591.   None of its first members are now living.   This church has been for many years a leading church of this denomination in this vicinity.   At an early day the Temperance Question was agitated, and strong grounds taken in favor of total abstinence from intoxicating liquors.

In 1846, when many churches were neutral, or undecided, this church took a decided stand against Slavery, and Resolutions were drafted, and passed by a unanimous vote, and spread upon the Records of the church, upon this important subject.   One of these resolutions, all of which are brief but pointed, is as follows:

"While church censures for unchristian conduct must be in the light of the circumstances connected with each particular case, yet neither the persevering and determined practice of the principle of Slavery, nor the commission of any enormities connected therewith, ought to be tolerated in any church communion."

These Resolutions are referred to, not only as an

expression of the views of the church at that time, but showing the *metal* of which it was composed.

Sixty-seven years have passed since the first names were inscribed upon its Records. To the people at large, scarce else but the names of those persons remain, and even these may be forgotten. Their lives were simple. "No boast of heraldry, or pomp of power,"

> "Far from the maddening crowds ignoble strife,
> Their sober wishes, never learned to stray,
> Along the cool sequestered vale of life,
> They kept the noiseless tenor of their way."

But as the originators of this church, to its members their names are precious, and will doubtless remain in high repute long after the present generation shall have passed away.

The following is a list of the names of the pastors of this church, so far as the same can be ascertained to the present time, 1872:

Rev. George Taylor, who remained from 1825 until the time of his death, which occurred June 10, 1842.

Rev. S. P. M. Hastings, 1842, 1843, 1844, 1845.

Rev. A. N. Leighton, 1846.

Rev. Luther Conklin, 1846, 1847, 1848, 1849, 1850, 1851.

Rev. A. Austin, 1852.

Rev. R. S. Egleston, 1852, 1853, 1854.

Rev. U. Powell, 1855, 1856, 1857.

Rev. P. P. Bates, 1858, 1859, 1860, 1861, 1862.

Rev. C. A. Conant, 1863, 1864.

Rev. J. B. Morse, 1865, 1866.

Rev. E. Benedict, 1867, 1868, 1869, 1870, 1871, 1872.
Rev. Charles Ray, 1872.

This Society has purchased an Organ, at a cost of
$1,200, and contemplate thoroughly repairing the
church building during the coming year. A heavy,
fine toned bell was presented to the Society, January
1st, 1868, by Mrs. Sophia Jewett.

UNIVERSALIST CHURCH.

The first advocate of the doctrine of Universalism,
was Dr. Chauncey, of Boston, in 1784. Writers upon this subject have been numerous, and great differences of opinion have existed among them; one
portion holding that mankind receive their punishment in this world, and that they are at death immediately admitted to the joys of heaven. The other,
that but part punishment is received in this life, but
that the correction and discipline of the soul extends
into the other world, where it will ultimately be prepared for glory.

In 1815 the Universalists built a house in Moravia,
where for a time, they met for religious exercises;
but the building was afterward used as a dwelling
house, and no other has been erected. It is believed
that this Society adhered to the former doctrine and
belief above mentioned. They have occasionally
held meetings in the village, but no church has been
established.

METHODIST CHURCH.

The Methodists owe their origin to John Wesley,
a man "zealous of good works," who labored inde-
fatigably in the cause which he had espoused. In

this work he was ably assisted by the celebrated George Whitefield, who met with unexampled success in his ministrations. Methodism was introduced into America in 1766, since which time it has gradually increased in power and followers, until the Methodists are now the largest body of professing Christians in the United States.

About the year 1818 or 1819, a Methodist preacher, Rev. John Ercanbrack, visited the "Flats" and preached in the Brick School House. Subsequently arrangements were made whereby services were held regularly once in two weeks. We cannot ascertain that any church was organized at that time, or when a class was formed.

In 1847, a church having been established, a neat Chapel was built, sufficiently large at that time, but which as the Society increased in numbers proved too small, and a new brick building of modern architecture, an ornament to the village and a lasting monument of the liberality of the people, adapted to the wants and comfort of the congregation, has been erected, to wit : in 1872, at a cost of twenty thousand dollars. The Society is now in a prosperous condition spiritually and temporally. There is a degree of open-hearted sociability among the members of this denomination which is attractive to many who seldom attend other churches. The outer portals of the church are always open to those who desire to know if the Lord is good ; while the doctrines of the inner courts cordially welcome to full and equal fellowship all who having proved faithful for a season.

desire to devote their lives and energies to the service of their Master, according to its peculiar teachings and beliefs.   Its membership is large.

The names of the clergymen who have had charge of the Society, so far as the same can be ascertained, are as follows:

David Cobb, 1849.

Sylvester Brown, 1851. ·

E. C. Curtis, 1853.

A. B. Gregg, 1863.

J. B. Hyde.

A. M. Lake, 1863 to 1865.

Hiram Gee, 1865 to 1867.

William Jerome, 1867 to 1870.

Daniel W. Beadle, 1870 to 1872.

Andrew J. Kenyon, 1873.

EPISCOPAL CHURCH.

The first Episcopal Church organized in this country was at Jamestown, Va., in 1608.   We find in the history of this Church in Moravia, that its origin and progress are to be attributed largely to the untiring exertions of Mr. Dudley Loomis, who came with his family to this village in 1816.

It is said that a pebble dropped into mid-ocean starts a wave, which though almost imperceptible at first, is felt upon the coast of either continent; and that our feeble breath sets in motion a current of air whose influence extends to the farthest bounds of atmosphere.   So incidents in the lives of humble individuals are often productive of momentous results, which will be felt throughout ages yet to come.

We copy from a History of this Church, by Rev. Henry Gregory, a very able and devoted churchman, who formerly had charge of this parish:

"It was a favorable circumstance that the individual who was instrumental to the introduction of Episcopal services into this village, was of good report, of blameless integrity, of sound judgment, of steady but unobtrusive piety, and universally esteemed for his plain and honest worth, as a citizen, a neighbor, and a friend. He lived therefore above the suspicion of improper motives, and his example carried with it an influence more steady, and in the end more prevailing than any principle of mere interest or of party strife. He was sincerely attached to the Protestant Episcopal Church, and he believed that the services of that communion would prove to be a general and public benefit to his neighborhood. With this persuasion, and after having several times attended public worship with the congregation at Auburn, he obtained from the clergyman of that place, a promise to visit the 'Flats.' The Rev. Lucius Smith, Rector of St. Peter's church, Auburn, and one of the Diocesan Missionaries, made his first visit to Moravia on Monday, June 23, 1822. On the evening of that day he officiated and preached in the Brick School House, and a second service was held on the next day—the festival of St. John the Baptist —at the Methodist Chapel in Locke. There Mr. Smith preached and administered the Sacrament of the Lord's Supper to six members of the Episcopal communion beside several of other denominations."

The next day, June 25, another meeting was held at the house of Lawrence Wormer, in Locke, when it was resolved to be expedient to organize a Society to belong to the Protestant Episcopal Church. A Vestry was also chosen for the Society, which assumed the title of "St. Mathew's Church," Moravia. Before the meeting was adjourned, a committee was appointed to circulate a subscription, for the purpose of building a church; and at the end of two days money and material for building, amounting in value to Eight Hundred Dollars, had been subscribed. The frame of the building was raised in June, 1823, and the work progressed so rapidly that in August following, religious services were held there, conducted by Rev. Lucius Smith. The building, however, was not entirely finished until 1826, and was burned in 1842. In the following year a new one was erected upon the same site.

It would seem that the organization in Locke, was for some reason defective, or informal, for in 1823 a meeting was held at which a Society was organized under the name of "St. Mathew's Church," at which meeting Dudley Loomis and Warren Rowley were chosen Wardens.

The first visit of the Bishop of the Diocese to the church, was on the 10th day of September, 1826, when the church was dedicated to the service of God, and seventeen persons were confirmed in the obligation of their baptismal covenant.

This church, which has never been large, has shown commendable zeal in sustaining public worship, and observing the general ordinances and tenets upon which it is founded.

The following is a list of the names of the Rectors of the church:

Seth Beardsley, Beardsley Northrop, Henry Gregory, —— Miner, —— Phelps, E. W. Hager, Wm. Paret, John Leach, Martin Moody, Beardsley Northrop, Charles Beardsley, Alex. H. Rogers, Peyton Gallegher, Benj. F. Taylor, Alex. H. Rogers.

BAPTIST CHURCH.

No Baptist church was organized at this place until recently; the members of that denomination attending service at Milan.

On the 22d day of June, 1870, a church was formed, and regular exercises have since been observed at the Public Hall, and latterly at the Congregational House; the Rev. M. H. Perry officiating as Pastor. The Society have purchased a lot on the corner of Aurora and Factory Streets, and propose erecting a handsome and commodious church edifice thereon.

CATHOLIC CHURCH.

An organization of St. Patrick's Church was effected in Moravia in 1872, and the building formerly occupied by the M. E. Church purchased and removed to a lot on Grove Street, and services are now conducted therein semi-monthly, Rev. Father A. Paganini officiating.

It is to be hoped that the influence of this Church may be instrumental in doing much good among the class of people reached by its ministrations.

QUAKER MEETING HOUSE.

The Quaker Meeting House was built in 1822 by Quakers or "Friends," and was occupied by them for holding meetings until the year 1840, when the house and premises were sold to the Methodists, who held occasional services until 1859. The property was then transfered to a Society organized under the statutes of this State pertaining to Cemetery Associations.

At a meeting held February 23, 1859, for the purpose of forming such Association, Thomas Ferguson was chosen Chairman, and W. W. Austin, Clerk. The following named persons were present :—Hiram Hunt, William Parker, Isaac Sanford, Ward W. Austin, Selden Curtis, Andrew Edmunds, William Pressey, John P. Wood, Samuel Burlingham, Watson Wood, Thomas Ferguson, Christian Fritts, William Harris, and Isaac Wood. The corporate name there determined upon was "The Moravia Union Cemetery Association." Nine Trustees were elected, a Certificate of Incorporation was drawn and properly executed, and recorded in the County Clerk's Office of Cayuga County, on March 31, 1859.

At another meeting of the Association, held October 29th, 1859, the sum of $437.50 was subscribed for the purpose of repairing and comfortably furnishing the house.

Among the By-Laws of the Association is the following :—

"The Chapel pertaining to the grounds owned by this Association, shall be free, FIRST—For funerals,

SECOND—For public services of all religious denominations: and the term religious denominations, shall be held to include all acknowledging the supremacy of God."

Services are now generally held semi-monthly, conducted alternately by clergymen from the village, or by special appointment from adjoining towns.

The Chapel is very neatly built, accessible from all points at all seasons of the year, is located in a beautiful section of country, and the meetings held are generally well attended. The original owners, the Quakers, mostly resided west of this town and near Cayuga Lake, while occasionally a family was to be found in this vicinity. But few of that denomination attended the meetings except upon special important occasions, but the world's people were generally well represented.

From this brief synopsis of Religious Societies, it will be seen that from the early settlement of this town, its inhabitants have not been unmindful of the moral and religious influence wielded by the churches.

The organization of one of their number (the Congregational,) was effected as soon as a few families settled within a convenient distance to attend service. Others were established when a sufficient number of the same denomination could be gathered together, and it is certainly a matter of congratulation and of public interest, that these different denominations, now existing here, labored with marked earnestness and success, and are prosperous and increasing in strength and religious vitality.

None of them claim perfection ; neither is the medium of salvation to the exclusion of the others.—The great object of the Christian Churches is to aid in bringing men to "Love the Lord their God with all their hearts, and their neighbors as themselves." All believe in "God the Father, Maker of Heaven and Earth, and in Jesus Christ, His only Son our Lord." They differ in the outward forms of worship and church government ; but these are of minor importance. Religion does not consist merely in liturgies or ceremonials, and is not dependent upon particular church polity. In the essentials of religious worship, the Orthodox Christian Churches are a unit. In spirit and in truth they are one. To be sure unthinking and faultfinding men have endeavored to use as an argument against religion the diversity of the churches, their different forms of worship, their disagreement upon certain minor points of church government, and claim that if there *is* any such religion as the churches profess, all would be united in one body, one form, one creed, a unit in everything. But such an argument is devoid of logic. It is to be doubted whether immediate consolidation of the churches would be advisable, could it be accomplished. There is doubtless at this time, much more strength in the churches as they are, than if but one existed. The time has not yet come when even those "who call themselves Christians" can unite in everything pertaining to the *manner* of worship, and of doing labor in the vineyard of the Lord. The Methodist brother can, or thinks he can, "enjoy religion" best *as a* Methodist. By *nature* he is a Methodist, and a great joy and comfort would be taken from him could he not shout his "Amens" and "Praise the Lord," when he wished and with the utmost freedom. The Episcopalian dislikes this freedom: he observes decorum; he reads his prayers with unvarying exactness, month after month, and year after year; his Amens are as fixed as were the laws of the Medes and Persians. The Congregationalist loves formality and *informality*; freedom *regulated* not by Bishop, Priest, or Synod, but by the "will of the people:" he governs himself and his church at the same time; he is liberal and democratic; he is a Congregationalist in all his sympathies and affections. The Baptist may be cleansed "along side of" the Congregationalist; it has been said (and the expression is borrowed,) that a Baptist is only a wet Congregationalist; he believes in self government; he wants but little ceremony; his forms are few, but those he will most strenuously insist upon having observed to the letter.

Now put these several denominations together, and govern them by one set of rules, adapted to all; reconstruct upon one common ceremonial basis these different and unassimilated elements. It certainly cannot now be done. The writer is not unmindful of the diversity of opinion upon this subject, and is aware that there are intelligent and exemplary members of the several churches who are willing to cast aside all minor considerations, and unite in one body, with one common Creed and Church Polity; but the average churchman is unprepared, and dissents from this. When men all grow to the same height spiritually, when in their likes and dislikes they all accord, when they are educated alike, and think, pray and sing in imitation each of the other, then if any is needed, one church might be established. Until that time, sing on, Oh Methodist, and Shout for Joy! "Upon this Rock," Oh Episcopalian, Repeat your Litany, and Hymn your TeDeum rejoicing. Rejoice, Oh Baptist as ye "go down into" and "come out of" the elemental characteristics of your Faith. Rejoicing all in the freedom wherewith Christ hath made you free. Diverse in ceremonials, in faith, one people, whose God is the Lord.

Let him who desires to become a church member, choose the church in which he can be the most useful, and which seems best adapted to his taste and social relations, and in which he can best serve the great Head of the Church. And wherever he casts his lot, let him remember that Christians of all denominations are of one brotherhood, all laboring in the same cause, and for the attainment of the same object, "laborers together with God."

VALUATION OF CHURCH PROPERTY.

The total valuation of church property in this town is estimated at $50,000. The amounts paid annually for sustaining the several Churches and Societies, from $5,000 to $5,550; and for benevolent purposes annually $600.

CHAPTER VII.

MORAVIA INSTITUTE—FIRST TRUSTEES—NAMES OF
TEACHERS.

The Moravia Institute Building was erected in 1838.
The first Board of Trustees consisted of the following
named gentlemen :

Hon. Rowland Day, *President ;* Calvin Whitwood,
Dr. Hiram Bennett, Deacon John Stoyell, Leonard
O. Aiken, Hon. Ebenezer Smith, Artemas Cady,
Chauncey Wright, Orsamus Dibble, Robert Mitchell,
Daniel Goodrich, Loyal Stoyell, *Trustees.*

The first teacher was Elbridge Hosmer, who was
Principal of the school for five years. The School
Record was burned a few years since, so that it is
impossible to obtain a reliable history of its progress.

The Institute has sent out from its halls a large
number of professional and business men, who have
done credit to themselves and to their Alma Mater.

The names of some of the Principals of this school
are appended :

Elbridge Hosmer, Samuel D. Carr, ——— Livings-
tone, ——— Kinney, William Parett, John Leech,

Robert Mitchell, Martin Moody, Wesley W. Willoughby, J. S. Holbrook, John G. Williams, Miss Amy Frost, Phylander P. Bates, Watson C. Squires, —— Goodell, —— Dysart, Eugene Proctor, Miles G. Hyde, Alex. H. Rogers.

CHAPTER VIII.

In the year 1813 a meeting was called for the purpose of adopting a suitable name for the village, theretofore known only as the "Flats." It was there voted "That this Village be called Hamburg." But it was afterwards ascertained that another town in this State claimed prior title to that appellation, and a subsequent meeting was held, at which Mr. Cotton Skinner proposed the name of "Moravia," which was unanimously adopted.

The first Town Meeting for the Town of Sempronius, which was then a part of the County of Onondaga, was held at the house of Ezekiel Sayles, on Tuesday, the 3d day of April, 1798. Present and presiding, John Stoyell, Esq., Justice of the Peace. The following town officers were elected:

Town Clerk, Ezekiel Sayles; Supervisor, John Stoyell; Assessors, Moses Little, James Brinkerhoff; Road Commissioners, Jacob L. DeWitt, Ezekiel

Sayles, Moses Cole; Constables and Collectors, Amos Stoyell, Isaac Shaver; Poor Master, John Summerton; School Commissioners, John Stoyell, Seth Burgess. Jacob L. DeWitt; Pound Master, Ezekiel Sayles; Fence Viewers, Abraham Johnson, Henry Cuykendall, John Summerton, Winslow Perry, Peleg Allen; Commissioners of Highways, Moses Tuttle, Winslow Perry, Jonathan Eldridge, Zadoc Titus, George Parker, Henry Osterhout, James Brinkerhoff, Peleg Allen; Commissioners of Public Lots, Gershom Morse, Cornelius Burlew, John Abbott.

At the next Town Meeting the ticket was made up mostly of Mr. Sayles, to wit :

Town Clerk, Ezekiel Sayles ; Assessor, Ezekiel Sayles ; Commissioner of Roads, Ezekiel Sayles ; Pound Master, Ezekiel Sayles ; Commissioner of Public Lots, Ezekiel Sayles. He was at the same time Justice of the Peace—making in all six offices.

At the present time fears of a centralization of power would be entertained, under similar circumstances, and from the Records it would appear that Mr. Sayles did not increase in popularity, but that for several years thereafter, he did not at any one time, hold more than *four or five* town offices. He held the office of Town Clerk for only twenty-two years ; Commissioner of Highways, eighteen years ; Pound Master, sixteen years.

Town Meetings were held at the houses of Mr. Sayles, Seth Burgess, and William Satterlee, successively, until 1813, when they were held at the Baptist Meeting House until 1820, and thereafter at the houses of Zadoc Titus and Frederick Pendelton.

The last Town Meeting before the division of the town, was held at the house of Joseph Lee.

We give below the names of all the Supervisors and Town Clerks of the old town of Sempronius, from its organization to the year 1832, when such division was made.

SUPERVISORS.	TOWN CLERKS.
1798—John Stoyell.	Ezekiel Sayles.
1799—Jacob DeWitt.	" "
1800— " "	" "
1801— " "	" "
1802— " "	" "
1803— " "	" "
1804—Charles Kellogg.	Cyrus Powers.
1805— " "	Ezekiel Sayles.
1806— " "	" "
1807—William Satterlee.	" "
1808— " "	" "
1809— " "	" "
1810— " "	" "
1811— " "	" "
1812— " "	" "
1813— " "	" "
1814— " "	" "
1815— " "	" "
1816— " "	" "
1817— " "	" "
1818— " "	" "
1819—Rowland Day.	" "
1820— " "	" "

1821—Rowland Day.	Bliss Forbush.
1822— " "	" "
1823—William Satterlee.	Franklin Day.
1824— " "	" "
1825— " "	" "
1826—George H. Brinkerhoff.	" "
1827—Rowland Day.	William Wade.
1828—George H. Brinkerhoff.	" "
1829— " " "	" "
1830— " " "	Elijah Austin.
1831—Rowland Day.	William Wade.
1832— " "	" "

William Satterlee held the office of Supervisor for fourteen years, and Ezekiel Sayles the office of Clerk for twenty-two years. He was the grandfather of L. D. Sayles, Esq., of this village.

At a Town Meeting, held April, 1821, the following Resolutions were passed by a unanimous vote:

" *Resolved,* That the thanks of this Town be presented to Ezekiel Sayles for his able and faithful services as Clerk of said Town, during a period of twenty-two years.

Resolved, unanimously, That the Town Clerk be requested to record the foregoing vote in the common Book of proceedings of this Town."

The Town of Sempronius, by an act of the Legislature passed March 20, 1833, was divided into three towns, consisting of Sempronius on the east, Niles on the north, and Moravia on the west. By the first section of the act, the Town of Moravia is bounded and described as follows:

"From and after the passing of this Act, all that part of the Town of Sempronius, in the County of Cayuga, being the southwest part, bounded on the west and on the south by the present lines of said town; on the east by the west line of lots number ninety-six, eighty-six, seventy-six, sixty-six, fifty-six, and forty-seven; and on the north by the south line of lots number thirty-seven, thirty-six, thirty-five, thirty-four, thirty-three; and extending west through lot number twenty-six to Owasco Lake, shall be and remain a separate Town by the name of Moravia. And the first Town Meeting shall be held at the house of Asa Little, in said town, on the second Tuesday of April next."

We give below as a matter of statistical interest, the names of all the Supervisors and Town Clerks of this Town from that year to 1873.

SUPERVISORS.	TOWN CLERKS.
1833—Artemas Cady.	Wm. A. Richmond.
1834— " "	Wm. H. Day.
1835— " "	" " "
1836—Daniel Goodrich, Jr.	" " "
1837—Rowland Day.*	A. H. Dunbar.
1838— " "	Orasmus Dibble.
1839—Daniel Goodrich, Jr.	" "
1840— " "	O. M. Welch.
1841— " "	" " "
1842—John Locke.	George Hart.
1843—Daniel Goodrich, Jr.	" "

*Rowland Day had been Supervisor for the old Town of Sempronius for several years.

1844—Artemus Cady.   George Hart.
1845—   "   "   "   "
1846—Leonard O. Aiken.   "   "
1847—   "   "   "   "   "
1848—   "   "   "   "   "
1849—Warren Powers.   "   "
1850—   "   "   "   "
1851—   "   "   "   "
1852—L. O. Aiken.   "   "
1853—Reuben Stoyell.   Josiah H. Stanley.
1854—Daniel L. Wood.   George Hart.
1855—Wm. H. Price.   "   "
1856—Wm. R. Hewitt.   "   "
1857—Daniel Sutphen.   "   "
1858—John P. Wood.   Henry Cutler.
1859—Austin B. Hale.   "   "
1860—   "   "   "   "   "
1861—John L. Parker.   "   "
1862—Benj. F. Everson.   "   "
1863—   "   "   "   "   "
1864—Dwight Lee.   "   "
1865—Hector H. Tuthill.   "   "
1866—   "   "   "   "   "
1867—   "   "   "   "   "
1868—E. E. Brown.   "   "
1869—S. Edwin Day.   "   "
1870—Terry Everson.   Frederick Small.
1871—   "   "   Henry Cutler.
1872—S. Edwin Day.   "   "
1873—   "   "   "   "   "

Moravia Village was first incorporated by the following act of the Legislature, passed May 1, 1837:

"The district of country in the Town of Moravia, in the County of Cayuga, contained in the following bounds, to wit: Beginning at the forks of the road running through the village of Moravia on the north, and running from thence east one hundred and forty rods, thence south two hundred and sixty rods, thence west two hundred and forty rods, thence north two hundred and sixty rods, thence east to the place of beginning one hundred rods, shall hereafter be known and distinguished by the name of the Village of Moravia; and the freeholders and inhabitants residing in said village, are constituted a body corporate by the name of 'The Trustees of the Village of Moravia.'"

The village was reincorporated by an act of the Legislature passed March 15, 1859, with extended boundaries, as follows:

"All that part of the Town of Moravia, County of Cayuga, and State of New York, which is contained within the following bounds and limits, to wit:— Beginning at the east or right bank of the Owasco Inlet where said bank is intersected by the north line of lot number eighty-two in said town, thence southerly along the said bank of said stream at its usual or mean height, until it intersects the south line of the farm now owned by William B. Worner, or lot number ninety-two in said town, to the east line of said lot number ninety-two; thence south on said lot line to the southwest corner of lands belonging to the estate of Triphena Cole; thence east on the south line of Triphena Cole's land, to the east line of number ninety-three; thence north on said lot line, to the lands of Samuel Spafford; thence west to the southwest corner of Mary Day's lands; thence north to the north line of said lot number ninety-three; thence west on said lot line to the center of the spring brook leading from a spring in Dwight Day's land; thence northerly in a direct line to and in such direction that it shall strike the small pond or raceway of the stone grist mill at the south margin thereof, and at a point directly south of the center of the gap cut in the rocks and forming a waste weir to said grist mill raceway; thence from that point on the south margin of said raceway, up and along said south margin and along the south bank of the mill pond and creek as the same winds and turns till it intersects Montville Creek at its junction with Dutch Creek; thence across Montville Creek and Dutch Creek to the southeast corner of John Stoyell's land, formerly known as the Cady lot, and along said Cady lot to the north line of lot number eighty-three, upon or near the summit of the right bank of Dutch Creek; thence west along the north lines of lots number eighty-three and eighty-two, to the place of beginning, shall hereafter be known and distinguished by the name of 'the Village of Moravia.'"

The following are the names of the Presidents and Clerks of the village since the latter date:

PRESIDENTS.	CLERKS.
1859—N. T. Stephens.	A. H. Dunbar.
1860—B. F. Everson.	" "
1861—Benjamin Allee.	Seth P. Hart.
1862—Alonzo Cutter.	Wm. Tallman.
1863—Terry Everson.	" "
1864—J. M. Sawyer.	A. H. Dunbar.
1865—C. E. Parker.	Norman Parker.
1866—Wm. Titus.	George Hart.
1867— " "	R. D. Wade.
1868—S. Edwin Day.	W. H. Day.
1869—Wm. Titus.	" "
1870—J. L. Parker.	R. D. Wade.
1871—M. C. Selover.	" "
1872—J. H. Holden.	W. H. Day.

CHAPTER IX.

Of the first settlers of this Town, perhaps there were none more worthy of mention than Hon. Rowland Day, who came to the "Flats" in 1810, and erected a frame building, in which he "kept store," in after years known as the "Old Yellow Store." He was an excellent business man, and did much to enhance the prosperity and growth of the village. He was Post Master for thirty years, Supervisor for fifteen or thereabouts, and was elected Member of Assembly in 1816. In 1821 he represented this District in State Convention in which important changes were made in the Constitution. He was also a Member of Congress for two terms. Mr. Day did not excel as a debater, but was highly respected as a wise and shrewd counselor. His shrewd management was so well understood in Congress, that he acquired the sobriquet of the "Cayuga Fox."

An honest, upright man, he held the above named

offices of trust efficiently, with credit to himself and honor to his constituents. He was faithful to his party—a strong Jackson man—and bitterly opposed to the dangerous doctrines of secession advanced by John C. Calhoun.

Mr. Day died Dec. 23, 1853, at the age of 74 years.

In 1810 Zadoc Cady joined the little settlement on the "Flats," built a log house, and used the front part as a Tavern. He afterwards erected upon the same site, the frame building known as "Cady's Tavern." This Tavern was a general rendezvous, not only for the town's people, but for those of the surrounding country. It was the head-quarters of a militia regiment, which held a "general training" on the "Flats," which lasted two or three days and as many nights.

"Aunt Cady," as she was familiarly called, (the wife of Zadoc,) had wide-spread notoriety as a cook, and the traveler at any hour of the day or night was sure of a substantial and digestible meal.

Said Mr. Samuel Weller, "Weal pie is a werry good thing, if you knows the woman wot made it." The hungry man, be he ever so fastidious, had but to be told that "Aunt Cady" was at the helm, to be warranted in the enjoyment of a meal fit to set before a king. Upon the sign used to inform the public of the name of the Tavern, was painted the figures 1801, the first three of which were nearly obliterated, so that it was often jocosely remarked that "Aunt Cady" had kept tavern there ever since the year one.

The Moravia Cotton Mill was built in 1831 by a

company composed chiefly of citizens of this town, and contributed greatly toward increasing the business and prosperity of the place; employing when in full operation, about one hundred workmen. The goods manufactured were said to be fully equal to imported stock, and found ready sales at satisfactory prices. The mill was destroyed by fire in 1856, and the following year a Grist Mill was built upon the same foundations, having a reservoir and water power sufficient to run the mill at all seasons of the year. This property is now owned by M. C. and Wm. M. Selover.

Montville Tavern was built in 1813 and 1814, by Walter Wood, at that time first Judge in Cayuga County. The Brick Tavern (now "Moravia House,") was built by Dr. David Annable, about 1820, and Goodridge's Hotel by Lemuel Porter in 1852.

Speaking of Taverns, is a reminder of an incident related as having occurred at a time when the Montville, Milan, and Brick Hotels were in full blast. Upon this occasion a small social party, consisting of Samuel E. Day, John Locke, Chauncey Wright, John H. Hinman, and Isaac M. Cook, familiarly known as "Sister Cook," had been celebrating some special political event by taking a sleigh ride about town, as a matter of course stopping each time around at the several hotels mentioned. The only sleigh procurable, contained but one seat holding but two persons, so that two more were obliged to sit in their laps, while the driver sat upon an empty tobacco keg in front. Cook was the driver, a regular John.   Late in the evening it was proposed that the party should drive to Milan, take a final drink, return to the Brick Tavern, take another final drink, and go home—sober as deacons. Accordingly the trip was made to Milan and return, but instead of stopping at Moravia as agreed upon, Cook put on the whip, turned the corner and went to Montville, where, after some delay, the Landlord was aroused from his slumbers, and informed that the law allowed him to keep open house for the reception of travelers *at all hours*, and the law must be enforced then and there; thereupon the landlord was hustled, without much ceremony, behind the counter, and the bottles and glasses set out. The driver however, was so overcome at the kindness, (as he often repeated,) of their host, "in entertaining travelers and angels unawares," that the tears flowed copiously down his cheeks, while he endeavored to embrace his benefactor, who stepped dexterously behind a post, around which Cook threw his arms with brotherly affection.

Upon starting out again, the ability of Cook to get them safely to Moravia was seriously doubted by his companions, but he insisted that he was the only sober man in the party, and should run no risks by allowing any of them to handle the reins. However all went quietly enough until they arrived near the top of "Skinner Hill," when Cook suddenly stood up in the sleigh and laid on the whip with all the force he could muster; the team immediately became unmanagable, and ran with great violence down the hill, all but the driver comprehending the state of affairs, jumped out into the snow, in all directions, he and the team disappearing down the hill, followed as quickly as possible, under the circumstances, by the balance of the party, who fully expected to find Cook dashed to pieces along the road. The team was found in a huge snow bank near the foot of the hill, and after considerable miscellaneous digging around, Cook was drawn out of the snow wherein he had been completely buried, and so wound about with the reins as to be unable to move; whereupon he was accosted by Mr. Day with "Hallo! Sister Cook! Are you dead or aint ye?" to which Cook with some difficulty and apparent resentment, answered, "Dead? no; but I want you all to understand that *I'm the last man to let go of the lines.*"

CHAPTER X.

FREE MASONRY—ITS ANTIQUITY—ORIGIN AND PURPOSES—SYLVAN LODGE—WHEN FORMED—ST. JOHN THE BAPTIST CHAPTER — REPRESENTATIVES TO GRAND CHAPTER—"SO MOTE IT BE."

Says one writer, "Every since symmetry began and harmony displayed its charms, our order has had a being." Doubtless Free Masonry is of ancient date and origin, but its longevity can hardly be traced to the time of the creation of the world. The original formation of the order was in all respects very crude and uninteresting; aiming to regulate the affairs incident to business relations, and to the duties of practical life; but it possessed none of the imposing ceremonials, or exterior display and grandeur for which it is now celebrated. A few mechanics or masons by trade, formed a league or union, for the advancement of their occupation, the better protection of their rights, and to secure the increased strength and influence which a society or organization generally possess. They were governed by certain simple rules applicable to their business and the times in which they lived. Among their ancient charges was the following, which recommends itself to every one, whether of the order or not, and is worthy of consideration by all:

"Ye shall be true to the king, and the master you serve, and to the fellowship whereof you are admitted.

Ye shall be true to, and love each other.

Ye shall call each other brother, not slave, or any unkind name.

Ye shall ordain the wisest to be masters of the work; and neither for love nor lineage, riches or favor, set one over the other who hath but little knowledge.   *   *   *   *   *   *   *

All the brothers shall treat the peculiarities of each other with the gentleness, decency, and forbearance he thinks due to his own.

Ye shall have reasonable pay, and live honestly."

Once a year they were to assemble for consultation in the interests of the order.

From the pen of a very able historian, we find. "That the Italians with some Greek refugees, also some French, Germans, and Flemish, joined into a fraternity of Architects; they styled themselves 'Free Masons,' and traveled from one nation to another, as they found edifices to be built. They had regular rules and regulations among themselves, fixing their residence in a camp near the place where they were employed. A Surveyor governed in chief. Every tenth man was called a Warden, whose duty was to overlook the other nine."

As to the pecuniary advantages of the ancient order, witness the following:

"St. Albans loved masons well, and cherished them much, and made their pay right good, for he gave them 2 shillings per week, and 3d to their cheer; whereas, before that time, in all the land, a mason had but a penny a day and his meat, until St. Albans mended itt. And he gott them a charter from the king, and his consent for to hold a general counsell, and gave it the name of Assemblie; thereat he was himself, and did helpe to make masons, and gave them good charges."

The laborer is worthy of his hire. For the benefit of those who are interested in ancient writings, and who perhaps have not heretofore had opportunity for their perusal, concerning this subject, we append the following questions and answers, which perhaps, will throw some light upon the character of the order of "ye olden times," and also a note lauding its merits, written by the celebrated philosopher John Locke.

The orthography of the original being somewhat unintelligible, is corrected in some instances to conform more nearly to that of the present day.

"Certain questions, with answers to the same, concerning the mystery of masonry, written by the hand of King Henry the Sixth of the name, and faithfully copied by me, John Leylande, antiquarus, by the command of his highness.

Question. What might it be?

Answer. It be the skill of nature, the understanding of the mighty, that is herein; and its sundry operations, particularly the skill of numbers, weights, and the true manner of forming all things for man's use, chiefly dwellings and buildings of all kinds, and all other things that make good to man.

Question. Where did it begin?

Answer. It did begin with the first men in the east, which were before the first men of the west; and coming westerly, it hath brought herewith all comforts to the lone and comfortless.

Question. Who did bring it westerly?

Answer. The Phonecians, who being great merchants, came first from the east in Phonecia, for the convenience of merchandise, both east and west, by the Red and Midean seas.

Question. How came it in England?

Answers. Pythagoras, a Grecian, journeyed for knowledge in Egypt and in Syria, and in every land wherein the Phonecians had planted masonry; gaining entrance in all lodges of masons, he learned much, and returned and worked in Grecia 'Magna, growing and becoming a mighty wiseacre, and greatly renowned, and here he framed a great lodge at Groton, and made many masons, some whereof did journey in France and made many masons, wherefrom in process of time, the art passed into England.

Question. What arts hath the masons taught mankind?

Answer. Agriculture, architecture, astronomy, geometry, numbers, chemistry, music, government and religion.

Question. How came masons more teachers than other men?

Answer. They themselves have only the art of finding new arts, which arts the first masons received from God, by the which they find what arts Him pleaseth, and the true way of teaching the same.— What other men do find out is only by chance, and therefore but little, I trow.

Question. Do all masons know more than other men?

Answer. Not so. They only hath right and occasion more than other men to know, and many do fail in capacity, and many more do want industry, that is absolutely necessary for the gaining of all knowledge.

Question. Are masons better men than others?

Answer. Some masons are not so virtuous as some other men, but in most part, they be more good than they would be if they were not masons.

Question. Do masons love each other mightily, as hath been said?

Answer. Yea, verily, and it may not otherwise be; for good men and true, knowing each other to be such, do always love the more, as they be more good."

The following is the closing portion of the note referred to above, written by John Locke to the Right Honorable Thomas Earle, of Pembroke, to whom he sent the manuscript.

"I know not what the effect the sight of this old paper may have upon your lordship, but for my own part, I cannot deny that it has so much raised my curiosity as to induce me to enter myself into the fraternity; which I am determined to do (if I may be admitted,) the next time I go to London, (and that will be shortly).

I am, my Lord, your Lordships most obedient , and most humble servant.

JOHN LOCKE."

It will be seen from the foregoing extracts, that Free Masonry originated in the interests of a class of tradesmen, or architects, for their better protection, profit, and better knowledge of their trade, which the order secured to them. From this germ has grown a tree, whose branches extend throughout christendom, and the fruit of which has been gladness and consolation to many in time of weariness and distress.

Latterly, however, the distinctive characteristics of the original order, to wit: the advancement of certain mechanical pursuits and the interests of a class of tradesmen, have become unimportant and obsolete, especially in our own country, where labor in all its branches, is honorable, and the rights of all men are guaranteed by constitutional enactments and enforced by judicial dictums.

The seeming necessity of the organization for the mechanic of the earlier ages, no longer exists or is no longer applicable to those of the present day.— But the order thus established has never ceased to exist, and for the most part flourish. There must be something attractive in this bond of union: something real in this system of brotherhood which has withstood the changes which time has wrought, the turmoil and confusion of revolutions, and the rise and fall of empires. And there certainly is. Masonry with such small and almost insignificant beginning, has outgrown its swaddling clothes, and become a power in the world. Uniting with morality and benevolence, pecuniary means one of the most essential elements of successful operation in any cause. Masonry is established on a firm foundation, to wit: brotherly love and charity. To be a true mason, one must be, to say the least, a moral man, "he is firmly to believe in the existence of a Supreme Being, who will be the Judge of our actions, and reward us according to merit, to pay Him that worship and veneration which is due to Him as the great architect of the universe." He is to be loyal to the government, peaceable and obedient to the civil powers which yield him protection. He is to avoid all manner of intemperance or excess which might obstruct his performance of the laudable duties of the order, or lead him into crimes which would reflect dishonor upon the fraternity. "He is to abstain from all malice, slander, and evil speaking; from all unmannerly, scornful, provoking, reproachful, or ungodly language, keeping always a tongue of good report."

Another important element is the requirement of giving pecuniary relief to those who are needy, especially if they belong to, or are connected in any way with the order, though they are not circumscribed in liberality toward destitution wherever it exists.

It is however but just that the funds received into the treasury of the order should be expended when necessary, upon those who have assisted in accumulating such fund. The widows and the orphans of deceased members of the fraternity, have received aid and comfort from this source when but for this sympathetic and timely action, want and distress would have been their portion.

The assisting and comforting arm of the brotherhood encircles each of its members, and the interests of his family. And here it may be well to say that the idea of which some are, through ignorance, possessed that free masons are bound by their obligations to assist a brother to escape from just punishment, which he has incurred, by his own evil acts, or to protect him in his wrong doing, is a mistaken idea, and in direct opposition to the teachings and the spirit of true masonry.

Thus much of the origin and primary object of free masonry, and its present aims and pretentions. With the faults or inconsistencies of individual members, we have nothing here to do; these are but a disgrace to themselves and not an argument which can with candor be used against the order. Churches have their hypocritical members, but religion remains the same. The general principles of free masonry are correct, and highly moral, and if practically observed, tend to honor the Great Master and to establish peace and good will to men upon the earth.

A lodge of free masons was first established in the United States at Boston, Mass., April 30, 1734, and in the state of New York on September 5th, 1781.

In 1810 a lodge was constituted in Moravia, (then Sempronius,) and named "Sylvan Lodge No. 44," and has been in active operation without cessation, since that date. The names of the members who have held the office of Worshipful Master, which is the highest official position in the lodge, will appear hereafter as representatives of Sylvan Lodge to the Grand Chapter.

A Grand Chapter was organized at Albany, N. Y., March 14, 1798, with DeWitt Clinton as Deputy Grand High Priest. At a Grand Royal Arch Chapter, held at Albany. N. Y., February 5th, 1811, the following dispensation was granted "To Companions John Newcomb and others to hold a Chapter of Royal Arch Masons at Owasco Flats, in the Town of Sempronius, County of Cayuga, N. Y., November 23d, 1810," and thereafter on February 6th, the action of the Grand High Priest in granting such dispensation, was ratified, and a warrant issued as follows:

"To Companions John Newcomb, Cyrus Powers, and David Annable, to hold a Chapter at Owasco Flats, in Sempronius, Cayuga County, N. Y., by the name of 'St. John the Baptist Chapter, No, 30.'"

We give below the names of the representatives of this Chapter to the Grand Chapter, held at Albany, N. Y., annually, to wit:

1812—John Newcomb.

1813—Cyrus Powers.

1814—I. Platt.

1815—Cyrus Powers.

1844—O. M. Welch.

1845—Samuel E. Day.

1846—O. M. Welch.

1847—Orsamus Dibble.

10

1816—Ithial Platt.
1817—Elias Hall.
1818—Not represented.
1819—   "   "
1820—John Newcomb.
1821—Cyrus Powers.
1822—   "   "
1823—Not represented.
1824—Joel Bartlett.
1825—Warren Parsons.
1826—   "   "
1827—   "   "
1828—Chauncey Wright.
1829—Orsamus Dibble.
1830—Ebenezer Smith.
1831—John Locke.
1832—Not represented.
1833—Orsamus Dibble.
1834—Not represented.
1835—Orsamus Dibble.
1836—Henry Carroll.
1837—Orsamus Dibble.
1838—   "   "
1839—Ebenezer Smith.
1840—Chauncey Wright.
1841—William Wade.
1842—Orsamus Dibble.
1843—Samuel E. Day.

1848—Orsamus Dibble.
1849—   "   "
1850—Samuel E. Day.
1851—William Wade.
1852—Nelson T. Stephens.
1853—{ George Hart.
       { William Wade.
1854—   "   "
1855—James H. Wood.
1856—   "   "
1857—William Wade.
1858—Samuel E. Day.
1859—N. T. Stephens.
1860—   "   "
1861—William Wade.
1862—Benjamin L. Avery.
1863—James H. Holden.
1864—   "   "
1865—William Wade.
1866—   "   "
1867—S. Edwin Day.
1868—   "   "
1869—   "   "
1870—John C. Chase.
1871—Henry A. Whitman.
1872—   "   "
1873—Fred B. Heald.

At a meeting of the Grand Chapter, held at Albany, February 8th, 1849, Orsamus Dibble, a very prominent and zealous mason of this town, was elected Grand King for the ensuing year.

The order of Free Masons has now in the United States 4,000 Lodges, and over 500,000 members. Indeed a powerful organization for good, if the virtues of the order could keep pace with its steadily increasing membership. "So mote it be."

CHAPTER XI.

MORAVIA AGRICULTURAL SOCIETY—ORGANIZATION—RULES AND REGULATIONS—OFFICERS, &c.

A meeting of the citizens of this town was held at the "Moravia House," September 18th, 1858, upon the suggestion of H. Alley and Wm. Tallman, (who drew the notices of the meeting which were posted about the village by Mr. Alley,) to consult upon the expediency of holding a Town Fair and Festival.

Gurdon L. Mead was chosen Chairman, and M. K. Alley, Secretary. The meeting then decided to hold a Fair and Festival during the month of October; and a Society was regularly organized with the following officers:

President, Sidney Mead; *Vice-Presidents*, James Thomas, James Thornton, and David Webb; *Secretary*, M. K. Alley; *Treasurer*, E. P. K. Smith.

At a meeting held September 20th, 1858, the following Constitution and By-Laws were adopted:

ART. I. This Society shall be organized under the name and title of the Moravia Farmers' and Mechanics' Fair and Festival.

ART. II. It shall consist of the following officers: One President, five Vice-Presidents, a Secretary and

Treasurer; and after 1858 there shall be a Board of Directors to consist of five members, of which the President shall be chairman.

Art. III. It shall be the duty of the President to preside at all meetings of the Society and Board of Directors, and sign all papers that may be necessary to carry on the business of the Society.

Art. IV. It shall be the duty of one of the Vice-Presidents to preside in the absence of the President.

Art. V. It shall be the duty of the Secretary to officiate as such at all meetings of the Society, and attest all notices and warrants drawn on the Treasurer.

Art. VI. It shall be the duty of the Treasurer to receive all monies belonging to the Society, and keep a correct account of the same, and pay it out only on the warrant of the President and attested by the Secretary. He shall make an annual report to the Society, of all monies by him received, and produce his vouchers for the amounts by him paid out.

Art. VII. It shall be the duty of the Board of Directors to make out a Premium List for each year, appoint the Judges, and make all necessary arrangements for the grounds for the annual Fairs and Festivals.

Art. VIII. The above mentioned officers shall be elected at each annual meeting of the Society for the election of officers, which shall be held on the Third Tuesday of January of each year, at such place as shall be designated by the President.

Art. IX. Any person may become a member of

this Society, and a competitor for any premiums, by paying to the Treasurer the sum of Fifty Cents; and any person not a member may be a competitor for any of the premiums by paying to the Treasurer the sum of Fifty Cents, subject to the By-Laws and Rules and Regulations of the Society.

ART. X. The annual Fair and Festival after the year 1858, shall be held some day or days in the month of September, to be designated by the Board of Directors.

BY-LAWS.

ART. I. All stock and other articles for exhibition shall be entered and arranged before ten o'clock A. M. on the day of the fair, at which time the Judges will commence their examinations.

ART. II. No premiums shall be awarded unless the committee deem the animal, production, or implement offered for competition, worthy to receive the same.

ART. III. All premiums shall be awarded on the Fair Grounds by five o'clock P. M., on the day of Fair, except grain and root crops.

ART. IV. All entries in grain and root crops shall be accompanied by certificates of the management and product per acre thereof.

ART. V. No stock or article offered for exhibition shall be removed from the Fair Grounds until five o'clock P. M., except by permission of the President.

ART. VI. Any person neglecting to apply to the Treasurer for the amount of any premium awarded to him on the day of the Fair, shall be deemed to have donated the same to the Society.

Art. VII. Visitors are to be on the Fair Grounds upon such terms as each annual meeting shall determine."

The Society is also protected and governed by general and special Acts of the Legislature. The following is a list of the names of the chief officers of the Society since the date of its organization:

	President.	*Secretary.*	*Treasurer.*
1858—	Sidney Mead.	M. K. Alley.	E. P. K. Smith.
1859—	C. C. Jewett.	Wm. Tallman.	B. F. Everson.
1860—	G. L. Mead.	J. L. Parker.	H. H. Tuthill.
1861—	No record.		
1862—	John Stoyell.	M. L. Everson.	T. Keeler.
1863—	J. H. Jewett.	"	"
1864—	C. S. Jennings.	Henry Cutler, Jr.	"
1865—	No record.		
1866—	Elondo Greenfield.	H. Cutler, Jr.	H. H. Tuthill.
1867—	"	"	A. H. Livingston.	"
1868—	"	"	"	"	M. L. Everson.
1869—	"	"	M. K. Alley.	C. S. Jennings.
1870—	"	"	"	"	M. L. Everson.
1871—	"	"	M. E. Kenyon.	M. K. Alley.
1872—	"	"	"	"	"	"

The annual Fairs have been generally well attended. Considerable competition has been had between the farmers and mechanics of the several adjoining towns.

The Floral Hall has been well supplied, and upon some occasions literally loaded with farm products and fruits, excelled in kind and quality by none in the state. Latterly large and choice varieties of grapes and small fruits have been displayed.

The premiums offered have been fair, and as liberal, no doubt, as the financial condition of the Society would permit.

While some fault has been found, no doubt upon reasonable grounds, taken all in all the general management of the affairs of the Society has been successful; and this success may be attributed largely to the management, good judgment, and untiring zeal of Elondo Greenfield, for several years past its chief officer.

CHAPTER XII.

ISAAC CADY.

One of the most prominent citizens of this town, was Isaac Cady. Born in Vermont, he came to Moravia with his parents in 1801, and thereafter always resided in this town and upon the premises where his parents first located. His father and mother, Zadoc and Lucy Cady, of whom mention is elsewhere made, were for many years the proprietors of the formerly well known "Cady's Tavern." During his youth and early manhood, liquor was drank very freely by all classes of society, without remonstrance from any source. Mr. Cady succeeded to the business of his parents, which was considered very remunerative at that time, and continued therein until the beginning of the Temperance Reformation about 1830. He became a member of a Temperance Society, destroyed his liquors, and transformed his hotel into a Temperance House. The strong conviction of duty by which he was actuated, will be appreciated from the fact that by becoming a temperance man, he relinquished a business from which he had derived an income which exceeded a thousand dollars per annum. This was a sacrifice of no mean proportions. Worldly policy would have dictated a continuance of this lucrative employment; public opinion would have sustained and sanctioned it. Personal friends threatened to forsake him. His mother predicted financial ruin to himself and destitution to his family. But none of these things moved him. One word answered all remonstrances and reasoning, and quieted the voice of friendly advice or bitter reproach. Duty was at once the guiding star and sheet anchor of his soul ; it was his watchword through life, and characterized all his business, political, and social relations. Like Deacon Stovell, he was at an early day one of the most prominent abolitionists in Cayuga County : his home was well known as a temporary refuge for the slave. At home and abroad, in public and in private. he most strenuously advocated the right of all men to life, liberty, and the pursuit of happiness. Though naturally "a most mildly mannered man," upon the great national question—American Slavery—he was like a lion roused from his lair ; with a righteous indignation he rebuked its advocates. and came down upon their arguments in favor of its continuance, with an avalanche of historical facts and precedents, scripture texts and commandments, constitutional and natural rights which its ablest defenders were unable to withstand. Herein consisted his great strength : His familiarity with ancient and modern history ; he made no statement at random ; he reasoned from correct premises, and assumed no untenable position : if his statements were doubted or denied. his proofs were forthcoming ;

his bookshelves were crowded with statistical reports, sermons, lectures, congressional reports, biblical commentaries and digests, from whence he gathered a vast store of knowledge, ready for use in defense of his principles, and the arguments which he advanced.

In the Congregational Church, of which he was an active member, he stood shoulder to shoulder with Deacon John Stoyell on all questions of reform and church polity. For many years he was the leader of the choir under the "fa, sol, la, and la, sol, fa" regime, and at all times was prepared to sing either from book or memory ; at prayer meetings he was never at a loss for an appropriate verse, or a familiar tune. Of his favorite hymns were the following, of which we append the first verse only :

> "Jesus, I my cross have taken,
> All to leave and follow thee ;
> Naked, poor, despised, forsaken,
> Thou from hence, my all shalt be ;
> Perish every fond ambition,
> All I've sought, or hoped, or known ;
> Yet how rich is my condition,
> God and heaven are still my own."

Also a hymn entitled "Loving Kindness."

> "Awake my soul, in joyful lays,
> And sing thy great Redeemer's praise :
> He justly claims a song from me.
> His loving kindness—Oh, how free."

Also,

> "Alas, and did my Saviour bleed,
> And did my sovereign die ;
> Would he devote that sacred head
> For such a worm as I ?"

Whatever else of early remembrances may by the dust of toilsome years become oblivious, those good old heart songs as sung by Isaac Cady to his favorite metres, will linger in the memory of the writer, growing sweeter and more sacred day by day. He never showed the jealousy and foolish sensitiveness of many choir singers, so despicable, yet so difficult to properly deal with. Although he had been the chief dependence of the church in singing for many years, there came a time when the choir which was then composed mainly of young people, thinking him too "old fashioned" to assist in public singing, gave him a gentle hint to such effect, upon which he gathered up his books and went quietly below into his pew without remonstrance, or show of martyrdom which usually accompanies such summary proceedings. Within two months the choir failing, he as quietly returned to his old position. The same thing occurred several times; but whether in the congregation or in the choir, Mr. Cady was never disconcerted, but always, under all circumstances, ready to "Praise God from whom all blessings flow."

Though eccentric, his peculiarities but more plainly showed his purity of heart and honesty of purpose.

The following incident will illustrate a peculiar characteristic. He sold a horse to a neighbor for seventy-five dollars, which the purchaser considered a very reasonable and satisfactory price. But for several days Mr. Cady was uneasy, and stated to his family "that he feared he had received too much. To be sure the horse was just as recommended, but perhaps he had over estimated his value." He accordingly went to the purchaser and insisted upon returning him ten dollars, although he was entirely satisfied with the original price paid.

Mr. Cady was not faultless—to err is human; but his errors were of the head rather than of the heart. He died August 26th, 1864, aged sixty-nine years.

CHAPTER XIII.

STEAMER ENSENORE—CAPT. KELLOGG—DIVE OVER-
BOARD.

In 1847 Aaron Kellogg conceived the idea of building a steamboat to be used in navigating the waters
of the Owasco Lake, and opening up full and speedy
communication between the city of Auburn and
Moravia via Camp's Bridge. Aaron thereupon invested his spare money and that of some of his friends,
in boards, plank, and other materials, together with
a small steam engine, selected a suitable place for
building and launching his vessel, (which was immediately in the rear of the tannery,) and went to work.
In course of time his vessel was completed, christen-
ed the "Ensenore," and launched with considerable
eclat, into Mill Creek. Horses were then provided,
and the boat dragged and pushed to the Inlet, where,
by Capt. Kellogg's order, the teams and ropes were
taken off, fire built, and the Ensenore started on its
tortuous way to the Owasco. Very soon, however,
it was apparent that some great mistake had been
made in the erection of the vessel. It refused to
obey the Captain's orders, though given with great
promptness and decision. Steam was shut off, and

an examination made, during which the boat was as quiet as a lamb, but at every attempt to "move on," showed a very decided inclination to stand on end. This fault, which seemed as a mountain to those on board, was but a mole hill to the undaunted Aaron, who said it could be easily remedied, and accordingly a few hundred pounds of stone were loaded upon the stern of the vessel, and another effort made to proceed, which failed. Upon further examination it was ascertained that the poor Ensenore, upon receiving its additional weight of stone, had settled deep into the mud! But Capt. Kellogg, still undaunted, went on board with the half dozen men who were assisting him, and assured them that by throwing off a portion of the freight, and putting on a little more steam, he could yet make a start, which being done, a plug blew out allowing steam to escape, which so frightened the Captain that he sprang in terror to the side of the boat, exclaiming, "*Dive overboard boys, or she'll blow us all to h-l!*" and suiting the action to the word, dove into the black muck and water of the Inlet, deeper than the Ensenore with its overweight of ballast. The boiler did not burst, however, but Aaron's steamboat, like certain works of his ancient namesake, ended in smoke.— The Ensenore was a failure, and likewise its owner, financially and as a boat builder; but he could put together a *good raft*.

CHAPTER XIV.

The early settlers in Moravia were all accustomed to the use of intoxicating liquors as a beverage.— They kept and used them in their families; children were helped moderately to whiskey in their infancy, and helped themselves abundantly in after years.— At all times and in all places, it was considered an indispensable household article. Houses were but indifferently furnished which had not a jug of "black strap" within its cupboard.

> So on all occasions—both of Church or State,
> All took their regular drinks, and took them straight :
> At births, in order that the child be frisky,
> Old folks and child must take a little whiskey ;
> At weddings, bless you, at such joyous season,
> One *must* get drunk and put away his reason ;
> And funerals, all other time surpasses,
> For after " dust to dust," *rum and molasses.*

Clergy and laity, publican and sinner, found no cause of disagreement, no bone of contention in this, but with one accord endorsed the sweet maxim, "A little wine is good for the stomach's sake," blessed the memory of St. Paul, and quadrupled the prescription. Custom, which regulates these things more than statutes, allowed all classes to drink liquors, while the deacons and elders of the church distilled and sold them. It is not strange that under those influences, a temperance reformation seemed almost impracticable, or that total abstinence principles found few endorsers; it is more surprising that any were found bold enough to attempt to stem the current of public opinion, by proclaiming themselves temperance men, and opposed to liquor drinking, or its use in any manner.

The masses throughout the country were bitterly opposed to such a project. But it is an historical fact, that all reforms have been begun by a few in the midst of the many, and under almost insurmountable difficulties and discouragements. It is almost impossible to change or eradicate a man's fixed principles and prejudices, especially if he belongs to the majority, and is in the popular current.

But notwithstanding the wholesale use of intoxicating liquors, one man was found who believed that the happiness of the individual, family and country, and especially of his own community, depended upon discarding entirely their sale and use. In 1830 John Stoyell, always the first in any good work, after reading the temperance sermons of Dr. Lyman Beecher, drafted and signed, together with his family, a total abstinence pledge. He then presented it to Chauncey Wright, then and always thereafter an intimate friend, who also convinced that the principle was right, became the fourth signer. Mr. Wright put the pledge into his pocket, went to Cyrus Loomis and quietly broached the "Cold Water Question," (so called,) to him. After considerable general conversation, Mr. Wright asked him if he was not going to sign Deacon Stovell's pledge, to which Mr. Loomis replied, that he thought not ; but being rather closely pressed, and confident of the safety of his proposition, said, "Chauncey, I'm as much a temperance man as you are, *and when you sign the pledge, I will!*" whereupon the document was produced already executed. Fairly entrapped, but true to his word, he placed his signature upon the paper, and in company with Mr. Wright, labored all day in obtaining signatures to this, the first temperance pledge circulated in the town, which at night contained the names of forty persons.

The "Washingtonians," "Sons of Temperance," "Cadets," and various other societies have been organized in aid of the temperance cause, and have done what they could for its promotion.

A Lodge of Good Templars was instituted in this village, in 1857, under the auspices of Isaac Cady, John Stovell, Austin B. Hale, and others, which continued in operation for several years, gathering in a large membership, many of whom but for the influence and protection of the society, would probably have died drunkards.

On June 20th, 1866, the "Rising Star Lodge" was organized, with Mr. Nichols as Worthy Chief, and has now upon its records the names of about one hundred members, and is an efficient, working lodge, laboring for the best interests of their fellow men. The following named members have held the office of Worthy Chief: W. W. Nichols, Jesse M. Frost, A. J. Hicks, Lauren M. Townsend, Horace H. Baker, O. R. VanEtten, Asael Lee, O. F. Rayner, Q. D. Greenfield, Fred Downing, Mark Harris, James M. French, Rowland D. Wade, Miss Edna Dean, and James M. Palmer.

All these temperance societies have done well, and accomplished much good in their day ; but they have not been able to accomplish all that temperance men have wished, or to destroy the influence which upholds and protects the liquor interests of the country. How shall the liquor traffic be regulated ? is a question of great magnitude among thinking men. Can a prohibitory law, if constitutional, be enforced ? or is an excise law well executed, the better plan ? or is it better to allow liquors to be sold freely by every one and any one, until from their deleterious and deadly effects, all men shall unite to banish them from the land ? All of these methods are advocated, and are being tried ; but meantime these temperance organizations are endeavoring to gather in and shield those who are unable to protect themselves. All men are frail, but none so weak as he who has fixed upon him, an appetite for strong drink, and none so worthy of assistance and encouragement as he who is struggling almost against hope, for release from the body of this infirmity. We say, God speed, to every man, woman, and child, and every society engaged in the temperance cause, in saving men from themselves.

But after all the earnest labor of years, men still become drunkards and vagabonds upon the earth. Not only is the use of intoxicating liquors as a beverage the great cause of destitution and misery in the land, and the source whence cometh a terrible catalogue of crimes, but is also financially a heavy burden to the state and to every tax payer within its borders.

All admit that the excessive use is a curse to the user and to all associated with him ; but yet perhaps a majority of electors in the state of New York are opposed to prohibitory or excise laws (unless the latter are very liberally construed), and under such circumstances, no such law, however good and just in itself, can be sustained or enforced. The great question therefore, " How shall the tide of intemperance be stayed?" remains unanswered. A nation of captives to this evil, no Moses has yet appeared to liberate or lead to better hopes and happiness.

The sale and use as a beverage, of intoxicating drinks, is a curse to society and a crime against humanity, and in the humble opinion of the writer, all intoxicating liquors should be banished from the land except for medicinal purposes, and in such cases should be dealt out with all the care and strictness observed in the sale of poisonous drugs and medicines.

But public opinion will not now consent to this summary method of disposing of this matter, and another must be devised. And there is but one other safe course to pursue. The future hope of the nation is in the children : upon their education depends its future honor or dishonor. If taught the principles of sobriety, to detest and shun the wine cup and the resort of the wine bibber, and that there is safety and health only in total abstinence from all that will intoxicate, there need be little solicitude as to the welfare of the nation in this subject. If the children are raised under correct moral and religious instructions, when they are old they will not depart from them—a temperate young man will almost always be temperate through life.

Sad as may seem the philosophy which consigns men to the ruin which continuous intemperance inevitably brings, without endeavoring to save, experience teaches that such endeavors are generally failures. Health, property, love of home, love of friends, are remorselessly sacrificed to this insatiable demon. Scarce love of life, nor fear of death, suffice to turn the drunkard from his downward course. Temperance and Anti-Dram Shop Parties, nor all the paraphernalia and machinery of organizations which benevolent and well meaning men have instituted and set in motion, and efficiently and earnestly sustained for half a century, have more than rescued a small proportion, here and there from the great mass who went down to the drunkards grave. But were the labors of organizations and the magnificent efforts of temperance men and women directed to a strict temperance education of the children, a quarter of a century hence this great question will be solved, custom will no longer tolerate, or public opinion sustain, the sale or use of that which makes a man an enemy to himself and society, and a disgrace to humanity.

CHAPTER XV.

MILITARY—109TH REGIMENT—GENERAL TRAINING—NAMES OF OFFICERS—A COLONEL'S HAT IN THE PORK BARREL—ARE WE ALL CORPORALS—CAPT. POWERS AND LIEUT. LOCKE—I AM BOHEMOTH—BULL SOUND B—PRESENT MILITIA—NAMES OF MEN—OLD 19TH—CO. F.—NAMES OF VOLUNTEERS—SHODDY CLOTHING—TWO YEARS—CONSOLIDATION—3D N. Y. ARTILLERY—GOLDSBORO, NEWBURN, &C.—SAMUEL ANDREWS KILLED—MUSTERED OUT—75TH REGIMENT—CO. A.—NAMES OF OFFICERS AND MEN—FORT PICKENS—DEATH OF LYMAN H. GOODRICH—EXPEDITIONS IN LOUISIANA—DANGEROUS EXPLOIT OF LIEUT. WORDEN—CHARLES H. LAKEY AND JAMES K. GOULD—WORDEN AND GOULD WOUNDED—PORT HUDSON—SHENANDOAH VALLEY—111TH REGIMENT—CO. I.—HARPER'S FERRY CAPTURED—GETTYSBURG—JOHN THOMAS WOUNDED—LEVI WHITE'S NARROW ESCAPE FROM DEATH—WM. H. BIRDSALL WOUNDED—LEVI WHITE WOUNDED—EBENEZER PLATT KILLED—A BLOODLESS DUEL—LEVI WHITE AGAIN WOUNDED—REAMS STATION—CAPTURED—LIBBY PRISON—PRISON FARE—STARVATION—EXCHANGED—CAPTURING A FLAG—HUMPHREY DAVENPORT WOUNDED—THE LAST BATTLE OF THE 111TH—138TH REGIMENT—NAMES OF MEN FROM THIS TOWN—160TH REGIMENT—CO. F.—NAMES FROM THIS TOWN—BAYOU TECHE—GUNBOAT "DIANA"—UNDER FIRE—CAPT. JOSIAH P. JEWETT WOUNDED—JOHN D. CLARK WOUNDED

THE DIANA SURRENDERS — FORM OF PAROLE—JOSIAH E. WHITE WOUNDED—CEDAR CREEK—JOSIAH E. WHITE AGAIN WOUNDED.

About 1810 a Military Regiment, known as the 109th, was organized, consisting of seven companies from the following places: Moravia, Locke, Summerhill, Dresserville, Dutch Hollow, Kelloggsville, and Pennyville, with the following officers:

Col. Zadoc Rhodes, Moravia; First Major Peleg Slade, Kelloggsville; Second Major Daniel Sage, Locke. The following named were Captains: Wm. Foote, Locke; Martin Barber, Summerhill; Eli Atwater, Dresserville; ———— Watson, Dutch Hollow; Luther Fuller, Kelloggsville; Abijah Allen, Pennyville; Asa Little, Moravia. Major Sage afterwards became Brigadier General.

We give the names of other persons who were Captains of the Moravia Company in after years, in the order in which they held the office: Asa Little, Watts Skinner, James Powers, John Locke, Orsamus Dibble, Henry W. Locke, John Stoyell, Laurence Vosburg. Artillery, Captain Isaac Cady.

Captain Henry W. Locke subsequently became Lieut. Colonel, and Captain Abijah Allen, Colonel. The regiment was afterward commanded by Colonel P. H. VanSchaick. Dr. William E. Cooper was Surgeon, and Amasa H. Dunbar Surgeons Mate.

The following is a copy of Mr. Dunbar's commission:

"The People of the State of New York:

To all to whom these Presents shall come, know ye, That pursuant to the Constitution and Laws of our said State, we have appointed and constituted, and by these presents do appoint and constitute Amasa H. Dunbar, Surgeons Mate of the 109th Regiment of Infantry, of our said State, (with rank from July 26, 1838,) to hold the said office in the manner specified in and by our said Constitution and Laws.

IN TESTIMONY WHEREOF, we have caused our Seal for Military Commissions to be hereunto affixed.

(Witness.) WILLIAM L. MARCY, Esq.,

Governor of our said State, General and Commander-in-Chief of all the Militia, and Admiral of the Navy of the same, at our City of Albany, the 16th day of August, 1838.

Passed the Adjutant General's office.

W. L. MARCY.

ALLEN MACDONALD, Adjutant General.

"General Training," or regimental drill, occurred annually, and lasted one day, while officers' drill generally occupied three. Officers in their military dress and large three-cornered cocked hats, made what was considered in those days, a very grand display.

Speaking of hats, it is said that Colonel Rhodes resided in a small log house near the Brick Yard, and like very many of his neighbors of those days, was sometimes rather short of rations. When the

13

new large military hat was first received by the Colonel, having but little room in the house, he was somewhat puzzled in finding a proper place to store so valuable an article, when it was not in use, (it being a Colonel's hat and rather too "hefty" to associate with common furniture), and finally inquired of his wife " Where he had better put that hat," and received the somewhat sarcastic yet truthful answer, "In the pork barrel is the most room." How small a step from the sublime to the ridiculous. Of course the Colonel appreciated the value of a full larder, but it was not an auspicious moment for giving him a reminder in that direction. But the honor of holding office of whatever grade, was generally fully appreciated and participated in by the wives of those fortunate persons, and female society received some sudden convulsions after an election or promotion. Naturally the "gude wife" shared in the general notoriety.

Upon one occasion it is said that Mr. Little came home to a late supper, having just been promoted to "Corporal." Considerably elated, and with all a "little sprung," he and Mrs. Little were congratulating themselves over their good fortune, when a small voice from the trundle bed innocently inquired, "*Mam, are we all Corporals?*" and was answered, "*Oh no, Bub! no body but your father and I.*"

In those days everybody drank liquor, and often upon "training days," and especially at officers' drill, these gentlemen showed great lack of military discipline and knowledge, or inability to perform according to "Hoyle."

At one time after the first day's training, Captain Powers went home at night thinking that his Lieutenant, John Locke, had imbibed rather too much of the ardent; accordingly at about four o'clock the next morning Lieut. Locke was aroused from his slumbers by a "tapping at his chamber door," which being opened, in walked Capt. Powers, when the following dialogue occurred:

Capt. Powers. Good morning friend Locke.

Lieut. Locke. Good morning Captain, out early.

Capt. Friend Locke, to tell the truth, I came down to have a little talk, between ourselves. You see, friend Locke, yesterday you and I got a little over the sea—drank a little too much; we didn't appear as well as we ought to, not as well as we could on drill.

Lieut. That's a fact, that's a fact.

Capt. Now we musen't take anything to-day, we must keep sober and make a good appearance, and set a better example before the other officers and men.

Lieut. You'r right, Captain, right, you'r always right; example is everything. Stay to breakfast, Captain Powers, and we'll talk things all over. Mother's going to cook the snekers.

Thereupon the officers consulted over some preliminary arrangements to be made upon the grounds, &c., after which said

Lieut. Locke. Captain, got up pretty early didn't you!

Capt. Yes, pretty early for me.

Lieut. Let's take some bitters to strengthen your appetite—got some good *tanzy.*

Capt. No, no, friend Locke, we've made all the arrangements—and our example, you know.

Lieut. You'r *right*, Captain, but you aint used to it ; you won't get through without anything all day : you know it's a sudden change, better *start well* any way : try a little of that (pouring out a glass), it gives a relish for the suckers.

Capt. (sipping) You see our example, friend Locke, will be worth everything to-day—off-set yesterday. We had *almost* too much yesterday.

Lieut. You're right, Captain Powers, take another glass of this tanzy to quit on, helps your appetite, you got up so early. Nothing like sober officers, Captain. Let's have breakfast and take a little tanzy to settle it, and go down sober, and set an example.

To which the Captain, having risen so early, consented. An hour afterward these officers were marching in Indian file, with drawn swords, to the Brick Tavern, before which they drew up and formed a "hollow square," Captain Powers exclaiming with authoritative voice, and flashing sword, "I am Behemoth, I trusteth that I can drink up a river!" It is needless to add that those officers had a general training of their own that day, in which Captain Powers told the Lieutenant for the fortieth time, how much he loved his Company and especially his Lieutenant. To which the Lieutenant invariably replied, with index finger pointed at an angle of 45 degrees, "Hark ye! hark ye! Captain, there's a God in Israel." Before night these officers had risen from Captain and Lieutenant to Major, Colonel and General, successively, having been fairly, and as Lieutenant Locke emphatically announced, unana*mously* elected, the Captain putting the vote and the Lieutenant voting, and vice versa.

In those days John Locke was a musician, and his favorite instrument being a bassoon. Upon one occasion returning home from practice, feeling pretty highly elated and full of fun, instead of keeping the highway, he went across the fields, of which a bull was the sole occupant. Whereupon hearing the animal's voice, he took the opportunity to instruct him somewhat in the rudiments of music, as follows: "Hello, bull you got a musical voice; sound high note or low note first rate. I'm a musician. Take the key," and sending forth a moderate blast from his bassoon, said, "There, bull, sound B," to which the bull, approaching nearer, gave rather an unsatisfactory sound. "Oh, modulate your voice—modulate your voice," says Locke. "Your first too low and then too high. Here," coming nearer and placing his bassoon close to Mr. B's ear, "Bull, sound B," gave a tremendous blast, and jumped for the fence, which was close at hand, but partially missing his hold, the bull, with a key note which shook the ground, made double short metre time and landed his musical teacher in a gully near by, while his bassoon became the booty of the bull as contra-*band* of war, and was speedily demolished in his very face and eyes, while Locke, picking himself up almost speechless, rubbing his sides, looking up to the top of the bank, where the bull stood, tossing his head, and pawing up the earth, slowly exclaimed, "Oh you needn't bow and scrape and pretend it was an accident, you did it on purpose, you d——n Dutch bull, your no gentleman, or, or, *musician either.*"

As before stated, almost everybody drank liquor in those days. Captain Powers was a member of the church. In later days Captain Powers and John Locke both became temperance men.

Captain Locke was the best historian in the County, and a shrewd politician, but had no ambition for office, and though one of the best tacticians in his regiment he refused to accept any office higher than Captain, and finally declined that.

PRESENT MILITIA.

" He that kills me some six or seven dozen of Scotts at a breakfast, washes his hands and says, ' *Fie upon this quiet life, I want work.*'

' *Oh my sweet Harry,*' says she, '*how many hast thou killed to-day?*'

' Give my roan horse a drench,' says he, and answers, ' *Some fourteen.*' An hour after, ' *A trifle, a trifle.*' "—SHAK.

In 1870, Company H., of the 49th Regiment N. Y. S. M., was organized, with the following named officers and privates:

Capt. Rowland D. Wade ; *First Lieut.* George McGeer ; *Second Lieut.* Fred B. Heald ; *Orderly Sergeant* Frederick Small ; P. K. Decker, Wm. H. Hike, Wm. H. Secour, Abram Nostrandt, A. W. Marshall, Walter Whalen, Silas W. Austin, Chas. E. Wright, Albert Campbell, Patrick McNamarra, Jabez Lilly,

Wm. A. Davenport, Chas. A. Arnold, August Lehmant, John H. Harris, Edwin D. Arnold, Frank Fittsmartin, Charles Ogesby, Byron J. Lombard, C. Bently, Q. D. Greenfield, James Dolan, Coryden Arnold, Fred Bingham, Dan Royce, Wm. McGeer, Orlando Claflin.

It is to be hoped that the services of these gallant "Sons of Mars" may never be needed at home or abroad, but that their swords may be speedily beaten into plowshares and their spears into pruning hooks.

VOLUNTEERS.

Civil war was inaugurated directly, by the attack upon and bombardment of Fort Sumpter by the Rebels, on April 12, 1861. Three days thereafter, President Lincoln issued a Proclamation calling for 75,000 men to suppress the rebellion and maintain the integrity of the government and the laws. To this call, Cayuga County was among the first to respond. Measures were immediately taken to organize a regiment; and by the active co-operation of the principal business men of the county, in an almost incredible short time the 19th was on its way to the front.

In the formation of this regiment, Moravia was not a whit behind the other towns of the county. Enthusiastic "War Meetings" were held, and a Company formed, which was afterward known as Company F, with N. T. Stephens, Esq., a prominent lawyer, as Captain, and Watson C. Squire, at that time Principal of the Moravia Academy, as First

Lieutenant, and Edward D. Parker as Second Lieutenant, and the following named as subordinate officers and men from this town:

Sergeants.—Edgar B. Warren, Daniel Bothwell, Barney C. Goodrich, and Robert Haynes.

Corporal.—James Mosher.

Drummer.—James Cannavan.

Fifer.—Wm. E. Sanford.

Privates.—Samuel Andrews, George H. Barlow, Charles L. Beitz, Charles W. Brokaw, Isaac Bradley, John Cannavan, Curtis Fritts, Wm. Frier, Daniel Frieze, T. Gordan, Peter D. Greenman, D. Webb Goodridge, Ezra Harter, Joseph Kennedy, John L. LaBarrow, Abner H. Livingston, Dwight Powers, Frank Rowny, Benj. Rockwood, John Tyler, Seth VanBen Scoten, William VanTassel, Upson Watts. R. D. Wade went out as Corporal in Company E.

The regiment was ordered to Elmira, N. Y., and shortly thereafter an election of Regimental Officers was held, and John S. Clark, of Auburn, was elected Colonel, and Clarence A. Seward, of New York, as Lieut. Colonel of the regiment. The balance of the officers were mostly from the city of Auburn.

The regiment having been uniformed, although in a manner very unsatisfactory to themselves and their friends, and in suits the farthest removed from uniformity of color or material, on June 6, 1862, were ordered to the seat of war. Arriving at Washington, they encamped upon "Kalorama Heights," near the city of Washington, where they remained for about thirty days, and were ordered to join Gen. Paterson, and remained under his command during the battle of Bull Run, while Gen. Johnson was permitted to reinforce Gen. Beauregard, and thus decide that memorable battle in favor of the rebel army; Gen. Paterson with a force of 20,000 men, remaining unemployed, when if he had obeyed orders, and forced an engagement with Johnson, the Union forces would doubtless have been victorious, and the government saved the disgrace which followed the retreat to Washington.

The 19th was organized as a ninety days regiment, the men were sworn in as such, and expected at the end of that time to return to their homes; but at the expiration of that term, they were without notice, turned over to the United States to serve out the additional term of one year and eight months. This arrangement, coming so suddenly and unexpectedly, a large proportion of the regiment rebelled, and refused to serve longer. But the "powers that were" prevailed, the contest between the men of the 19th and the authority of the government was too unequal, and the 19th, with a few exceptions, were obliged to submit and return to the ranks.

In September following, Company F. was consolidated with Company A. Capt. Stephens and Lieuts. E. D. Parker and Squires were mustered out, the two former returning home and the latter taking the command of a western regiment.

About January 1, 1862, the 19th was reorganized as an artillery regiment, and was thereafter known as

14

the 3d N. Y. V. Artillery, and ordered to Newbern, N. C., to join the forces of Gen. Burnside.

From Newbern various expeditions were made through the adjoining country. In one of these, on September 5th, 1862, at Washington, N. C., Samuel S. Andrews of this town was killed.

The 3d also took part in the battles of Kinston, Whitehall, Goldsboro, &c. The men were mustered out at the expiration of their term, on June 2d, 1873, and returned home, having been in the service two years.

The ranks of the 3d artillery were soon filled by re-enlistments from Cayuga and adjoining counties, none however, from this town.

The volunteers from this town in the "Old 19th" escaped the very severe fighting which fell to the lot of those of the other regiments from this vicinity, partly for the reason that they were located most of the time in a section which was comparatively quiet, and for the further reason that in becoming an artillery regiment, they were not as a rule, exposed to a close fire from the enemy, which the infantry regiments experienced. But the men were courageous and worthy to be remembered as those who, in the first hours of danger, unhesitatingly left their homes to defend the government, and even its chief citadel, from invasion.

SEVENTY-FIFTH REGIMENT.

The second regiment formed in this district, was the 75th. It went out with John A. Dodge as Colonel, Robert B. Merritt, Lieutenant Colonel, and Willoughby Babcock. of Cortland County, Major.

The volunteers from this town enlisted in Company A., under Captain C. D. MacDougall, : their names are as follows :

David L. Gould, Amos H. Ercanbrack, James O. Davenport, Lewis A. Carr, John Cannavan, William Dennis, David Feek, Lyman H. Goodrich, James Jones, Wm. H. Jones, James E. Mosher.

Dr. Cyrus Powers was appointed Assistant Surgeon of this regiment, and afterward received the appointment of Surgeon of the 160th Regiment of this State.

The regiment was ordered to Fort Pickens, Florida, where it arrived about the middle of December, 1861, doing duty as necessity demanded, but experiencing very little fighting until the following August, when the 75th was sent to New Orleans to join the forces under command of Gen. Butler. While at Fort Pickens, one of the boys from this town, Lyman H. Goodrich, died.

While under Gen. Butler, the 75th made several expeditions through the country adjoining New Orleans,—none, however, of very great importance. After Gen. Banks assumed command, considerable skirmishing ensued in the southern part of Louisiana, at Bayou Teche, and Brashear City, &c., the regiment losing at the former place several good men —none, however, being from this town. In April, 1863, another campaign was agreed upon, which resulted in several severe marches and battles, and considerable loss of life, and in the capture of a quantity of cotton; but otherwise was of little importance, and terminated without any apparent successful operations. During this time occurred the battle of Fort Bisland, which upon the arrival of the forces of Gen. Banks, was occupied by the rebels commanded by Gen. Dick Taylor. Fort Bisland was flanked upon one side by Grand Lake, while upon the other were swamps, underbrush, and low shrubbery and weeds, which made an attack from that side extremely difficult and hazardous, as the enemy could not be seen except at very close range. The rebel works were well built and strong, and were protected by several cannon, and about 11,000 men—Gen. Banks having but 14,000 effective men at the time. A part of this force under Gen. Grover, was ordered to proceed up Grand Lake, while the balance, including the 75th, which acted as skirmishers, were to make an attack from the left through the swamp above described. Into this terrible jungle the 75th advanced with great caution, with orders to discover the position and force of the enemy.

On the 12th day of May, 1863, while slowly advancing, the 75th was opened upon by a terrible firing from the enemy's entrenchments. However, undaunted, the brave men continued to hold their position, while the 160th brought up the right centre. At this point, Lieut. Col. Babcock ordered the 75th to lie down near the banks of a large ditch, while Lieut. Worden, and two or three men should proceed to reconnoiter. It was understood that these men should be followed by the regiment after they had been gone fifteen minutes. The men selected by Lieut. Worden. were Charles H. Lakey and David S. Gould. of this town.

The undertaking was one of extreme danger and difficulty. The thick foliage of the low undergrowth of brushwood. together with more or less mud and water underneath. rendered their progress very slow, while the utmost caution was required. as the enemy were known to be but a short distance from our troops : but just where their batteries were located, or where their infantry might be concealed. was unknown.

These three men. knowing the danger to which they were exposed. undertook to ascertain the enemy's position and report the same to Gen. Wietzel. Unable by reason of the obstructions before mentioned to see more than twelve or fifteen feet before them. slowly picking their way. and even crawling upon their hands and knees. the little party left the regiment behind. expecting it to follow in supporting distance in case of attack. For several rods the enemy were not heard or seen. when suddenly. upon coming into a small opening a few feet square, a rebel picket was discovered and surprised, he being at the moment looking in an opposite direction. Upon seeing the "situation." he threw down his gun and surrendered. Lieutenant Worden accompanied him back to the lines. while the others held their position until their companion's return, when they again moved on as before for about fifty rods to another partially cleared spot, into which they came carefully upon their hands and knees, suspicious of the proximity of the rebels, although none had been seen except the captured picket.

At the opening, they resolved to get a view of the prospect ahead, and accordingly rose to their feet, when a broadside was poured into their midst from the enemy's infantry which was stationed only four or five rods ahead, apparently expecting them. At the first fire, Lieut. Worden was wounded in the hand and arm, and David S. Gould through the lungs. All three fell to the ground, thereby escaping the bullets which flew thickly over them. Mr. Lakey, with great presence of mind, succeeded in dragging Mr. Gould back into the thicket, meantime giving orders for a *charge*, in a loud voice, which doubtless prevented their capture. Lieutenant Worden helped himself to the rear for several rods, to which place Mr. Lakey carried and dragged Mr. Gould, where all three lay several minutes completely exhausted—Mr. Lakey from his exertions, and the others from pain and loss of blood. Mr. Lakey then hastened back to the regiment and procuring help, returned, and the wounded men were carried back to the regiment, and thence to Brasheur City Hospital, where Mr. Gould died from the effects of his wound. For gallant services, Mr. Lakey received a furlough for six months.

Considerable skirmishing was had with the enemy

during the day, and fearing an attack in the rear
from Gen. Grover at Grand Lake, Gen. Taylor withdrew his forces and abandoned the fort, together
with a large number of guns which fell into the
hands of the Union troops.

The 75th was engaged in the siege of Port Hudson,
and suffered severely; also in the engagement at
Sabine Pass. None of the men from this town,
however, were injured.

The regiment took its full share of the labors and
sufferings of the war, not only in Louisiana, but in
the Shenandoah Valley. It was decidedly a fighting regiment of first class men, and made a record
of which the State may well be proud.

ONE HUNDRED AND ELEVENTH.

At the call for "three hundred thousand more,"
another regiment was formed, and part of a company
raised in this town by Sidney Mead, as captain.
The following persons enlisted:

Alonzo Arnold, William Bowen, Martin Booth,
Richard Booth, Andrew Burgess, Nathan Booth,
Sanford Burlingham, William Birdsall, James Bris-
ter, John Baker, Wm. H. Booker, Daniel H. Craw-
ford, Leander Creathers, Orrin Davenport, Alfred
Hoagland, Gilbert Impson, Jonathan Jenkins, Dan-
iel J. Lombard, Alonzo Lilly, Jabez Lilly, Hosea
Munn, Charles Miller, Nathan North, Jr., Morell
Parker, Ebenezer Platt, Tyler Royce, Nathan Stur-
gers, Alonzo Slarrow, John Slarrow, Zenas D.
Stearns, William Shimer, William Sherman, John
A. Thomas, Levi White, Charles White, Wayne

Lester, Amos H. Ercanbrack, Aaron Chase, Thomas Harrop, George Fox, Frederick Moss.

The regiment went out commanded by Colonel Jesse Segoine, with Clinton D. MacDougal as Lieutenant-Colonel, and were ordered to Harpers Ferry, Va., where, with several other regiments under Col. Miles, Commander of the Post, they were captured by the enemy. The following is an extract from "The American Conflict," giving a graphic description of the location of the Union troops, and the incompetency, to use a wild term, of their commander.

"Harpers Ferry is little more than a deep ravine or gorge, commanded on three sides by steep mountains, and of course defensible only from one or more of them. A commander who was neither a fool nor a traitor, seeing enemies swarming against him from every side would either have evacuated in haste and tried to make his way out of the trap, or concentrated his forces on one of the adjacent heights, and there held out until time had been afforded for his relief. Miles did neither. .

   *   *   *   *   *   *

At nine o'clock, P. M., our cavalry, some 2,000 strong, under Col. Davis, 12th Illinois, made their escape from the Ferry across the pontoon bridge to the Maryland bank ; passing up the Potomac unassailed through a region swarming with avenues, to the mouth of the Antietam, thence striking northward across Maryland, reaching Greencastle, Pa., next morning, having captured by the way the ammunition train of Gen. Longstreet, consisting of 50 or

60 wagons. Miles assented to this escape; but refused permission to infantry officers who asked leave to cut their way out: saying, he was ordered to hold the Ferry to the last extremity. Next morning at daybreak, the Rebel batteries reopened from some commanding points, directing their fire principally at our batteries or Bolivar Heights. At 7 A. M., Miles stated to Gen. White, that a surrender was inevitable, his artillery ammunition being all but exhausted; when the brigade commanders were called together and assented.

A white flag was thereupon raised; but the rebels not perceiving it, continued their fire some 30 or 40 minutes, whereby Miles was mortally wounded.— Jackson was just impelling a general infantry attack, when informed that the white flag had been raised on the defenses.

At 8 A. M., a capitulation was agreed to, under which 11,583 men were passed over to the enemy, about half of them New Yorkers, the residue mainly from Ohio and Maryland. Nearly all were raw levies; some of them militia called out for three months. Among the spoils were 73 guns, ranging from excellent to worthless; 1.300 small arms, 200 wagons, and a large quantity of tents and camp equipage. Of horses, provisions, and munitions, the captures were of small amount."

The 111th, although unmentioned, was of the number who surrendered, and after remaining prisoners for two days they were paroled and sent to Camp Douglas, at Chicago, Ill., where they remained five

15

weeks, were exchanged and ordered to Washington, and thereafter to Centreville, Va., where considerable skirmishing was had with Gen. Mosby.

The next serious fighting was experienced at Gettysburg, on the 3d and 4th days of July, 1863. The 111th were in Gen. Hancock's Corps, which on the latter day were on the left of the centre of the Union army. In one of the last engagements, on July 3d, John A. Thomas was severely wounded in the leg, just above the ankle by a minnie ball. He was carried by William Shimer and others to the field hospital, where his leg was amputated. He was afterward sent to a hospital in Baltimore, Md., and being rendered unfit for duty was honorably discharged in April, 1864.

LIFE AND DEATH.

During the latter part of the 3d day of July, at Gettysburg, this regiment was placed in front of the Federal batteries, and about five or six rods distant, and ordered to lie down behind an old dilapidated stone wall which afforded a very slight protection from stray bullets, while the enemy's batteries were located about one mile distant in advance, and somewhat to the right. Lying in this position, shoulder to shoulder, as close together as possible, our boys remained during two hours, while two hundred heavy guns thundered continuously in their ears, and cannon balls shrieked and tore up the ground in all directions. While in this state of awful suspense, expecting death every moment, and nothing to do but *wait*, the man upon the right of Levi

White moved one place to the right, a vacancy having been made there. Mr. White, thinking to better his condition, took his place, while the soldier on the left moved into the position which had been occupied by Mr. White. He had scarcely exchanged places when he was struck and torn to fragments by a cannon ball from the enemy's battery.

William Birdsall was wounded on July 2d, by a piece of shell which struck him in the left arm above the elbow, making a severe and very troublesome wound. He was sent to Newark Hospital, N. J., where he stayed for ten months, and was then transferred to the 21st Regiment Reserve Corps, stationed at Trenton, obtaining recruits. There he remained until the close of the war, and was discharged July 6, 1865.

From the time of the battle of Gettysburg until October 14, 1863, the 111th had but little fighting to do. Upon the latter day, however, while near Bristoe Station, while acting as a part of the rear guard of the Second Corps, the 111th, 125th, 126th and 39th regiments consisting of about 500 men, were attacked by the forces under Gen. A. P. Hill, the enemy being posted in the woods on the left of the Union lines, the Orange & Alexandria Railroad lying between. Very soon after the attack was made, the above named regiments made a charge for the railroad which was reached with some loss, and the men ordered to lie down behind the road embankment. The rebels, who were some forty rods distant, thereupon made a charge in turn for the purpose of dislodging the Union forces and holding the railroad. Our troops remained quiet until the enemy were but five rods distant, when they poured into them a terrific and deadly fire, which caused a speedy retreat. They were again formed in the woods, and another charge made upon the left, which was met as before, when their ranks were again broken, and the attack repulsed with considerable loss. Seeing the result, the Union troops charged after them *without orders*, captured 5 pieces of artillery, and more prisoners than the successful party had numbers. Though this victory was achieved without orders, none of the officers in command were cashiered or the troops reprimanded. "*Not much*," as one of them said.

During the first attack, Levi White, who, instead of firing and then falling down behind the embankment, was standing up loading and firing as rapidly as possible, was wounded by a ball which passed through his thigh, causing an ugly wound. He was carried off the field in a rubber blanket, and removed to Alexandria. The same ball which wounded him, struck Ebenezer Platt in the head, killing him instantly. Mr. White was eight days in the hospital unable to sit up, when an order came to furlough every man able to travel. He was immediately able, or thought he would take the chances of getting home again, and succeeded in getting as far as New York City, when he gave out and was carried to the soldiers' lodgings in that city, whence he came to Moravia, was seized with inflammation of the lungs and was sick for two months.

Upon recovering his health he returned to his regiment at North Anna River, on May 25th, 1864. The 111th was skirmishing nearly every day with the enemy; but the army kept marching on toward Richmond by day and digging trenches by night.

During the campaign, Mr. White being on the skirmish line, was shot at by a rebel, who immediately sought shelter behind a large tree, nearly two feet in diameter, which entirely shielded his person. White took his position behind a small pine sapling only eight or ten inches through, which protected only a portion of his body, leaving the residue a fair target for his opponent, twelve rods distant. *Business was brisk*; some ten shots had been exchanged, the rebel having greatly the advantage of position, and White's gun being a miserable concern, when a ball struck the edge of the tree behind which White was partially concealed, and came nearly through, just breaking the bark in range of his head. Fearing that in course of time the enemy might miss the tree but not the portion of the U. S. soldier exposed to view, said soldier deemed discretion the better part of valor, and skipped along out of range.

Very soon after this occurrence he was again wounded by a minnie ball, which entered his right breast and glanced out through his right arm. He was again sent home on a furlough, and having regained his health rejoined his regiment at Petersburg, August 1st, 1864, in camp, the Second Corps being reserves; meantime the regiment had experienced severe fighting.

The next battle was fought at Reams' Station.—
The following is from "The American Conflict."—
"Hancock returned from the north of the James,
had worked rapidly to the Welden Road, in the rear
of Warren. Striking it at Reams' Station. he had
been busily tearing it up for two or three days, when
his cavalry gave warning that the enemy in force
were at hand. Their first blow fell on Miles' division
on our right, and was promptly repulsed ; but Hill
ordered Heth, under a heavy fire of artillery, to try
again, and at all events carry the position, which he
ultimately did at the fourth charge, capturing three
batteries. Hancock ordered Gibbons' division to re-
take them, but they failed to do so.

Miles, rallying a part of his scattered division and
fighting it admirably, recovered part of his lost
ground and one of his captured batteries.

Gibbons' Division, assailed by a force of dismounted cavalry, was easily driven from its breastworks ;
but the enemy attempting to follow up his success.
was checked and repelled by a heavy flank fire from
our dismounted cavalry posted on the left.

Though but four miles from Warren's position,
no reinforcements, owing to various blunders, reached Hancock until he had been forced to retreat,
abandoning Reams' Station after a total loss of 2400
(out of 8000) men and 5 guns. Hill's loss was also
heavy but considerable smaller."

A large portion of the 111th were among the captured, together with their colors.

On August 23d, 1864, they were taken to Richmond and confined in the notorious Libby Prison ; their room was in the upper story of the prison building, and was 69 feet long by 25 feet wide, occupied by 300 men, who slept on the bare floor with no covering, their blankets, overcoats, and money having been taken away by the officers of the prison. Their fare was as follows : A piece of corn bread two inches square, one and one-half inch thick, twice daily, occasionally a small piece of poor beef, generally partially spoiled. a little bean soup (less the beans) once per day, nothing else. They suffered extremely not only from the cold. but from hunger, and at the end of six weeks confinement, were mere skeletons, so that when ordered from the prison to Belle Island a mile distant. scarcely a man was able to reach the place with out falling down several times on the way. from weakness. On the Island their rations were the same as in prison.   At the end of a week. being the seventh as prisoners. during which time the other prisoners had been removed to Andersonville, an order came for our boys to be ready to start for that place at 10 o'clock that night. Fortunately at 9 o'clock a boat load of rebels who had been sent by our government to be exchanged. arrived, and instead of going to Andersonville Prison. they were exchanged and taken to Aiken's Landing inside the union lines.

The boys of the 111th regarded this as an almost miraculous escape from death by starvation, for of the men sent from Richmond to Andersonville. scarce any ever returned alive.

Most of the men of the 111th received furloughs for twenty days, and came home to regain their health and strength, after which they again joined their brigade and went into winter quarters.

For the benefit of those who are unfamiliar with the general formula and official routine through which furloughs were granted or refused, a copy of a furlough granted to Levi White is annexed.

To ALL WHOM IT MAY CONCERN :

The bearer hereof, Levi White, Sergeant of Capt. Sidney Mead's company of the 111th Regiment of New York State Volunteer Infantry, aged 26 years, five feet eight inches high, dark hair, and by profession a Cooper, born in the County of Cayuga, State of New York, he having received a furlough from the 2d day of May to the 22d day of May, 1865, at which period he will rejoin his Company or Regiment at camp at Buckville, Va., or wherever it then may be, or be considered a deserter.

Subsistance has been furnished to said Levi White to the 2d day of May, and pay to the 29th day of February, 1864, both inclusive.

Given under my hand at head-quarters 111th N. Y. V,, this 20th day of May, 1865.

LEWIS W. HUSK,

Lt. Col. 111th N. Y. V., Com'd the Reg't. Camp of 111th N. Y. V., 3d Brig., 1st Div., 2d Army Corps., April 27th, 1865.

Levi White, Sergeant Co. I, 111th Reg't N. Y. V., makes application for a furlough for 15 days, to go to Moravia, N. Y., for the purpose of attending to important pecuniary matters concerning himself and family.

Respectfully forwarded approved.

Sergeant White is perfectly reliable, good character and prompt in the performance of his duties.

JOHN C. SMITH,
2d Lieut. 111th N. Y. V., Com'd'g Co. I.

Head-Quarters 111th Reg't N. Y. V. 3d Brig.
1st Div., 2d Army Corps, April 17th, 1865.

Respectfully forwarded approved.

Company. Present for duty—14.
"   Absent with leave—none.
"   Absent without leave—none.

Regiment. Present for duty—429.
"   Absent with leave—1.
"   Absent without leave—7.

Applications pending—none.

The applicant has never been absent on furlough.

LEWIS W. HUSK,
Lt. Col. 111th N. Y. V., Com'd'g Reg't.

Head-Quarters 3d Brig., 1st Div., 2d A. C.,
April 27th, 1865.

Respectfully forwarded approved for twenty days. Serg't White is a splendid soldier, has been wounded three times, and a prisoner twice. He supposed he could only get 10 days.

C. D. MacDOUGALL,
Col. 111th N. Y. V., and Brevet Brig. Gen. Com'd'g.
16

Head-Quarters 1st Div., 2d Army Corps,
      April 28th, 1865.
Respectfully forwarded approved.
    NELSON A. MILES,
     Brevet Brig. Gen. Com'd'g.
Head-Quarters 2d Army Corps,
      April 29th, 1865.
Respectfully forwarded approved for 20 days.
    FRANCIS C. BARLOW.
     Brevet Maj. Gen. Com'd'g.
Head-Quarters of the Army of the Potomac,
      April 29th, 1865.
Approved for twenty days.
    By command of
    MAJ. GEN. MEADE.
     F. S. BARSTEN, A. A. G.
Official—T. S. Dodt, Capt. and A. A. G.

Head-Quarters 3d Brig., 1st Div., 2d A. C.
      April 30th, 1865.
Head-Quarters 111th Reg't N. Y. V., 3d Brig., 1st
   Div., 2d A. C., May 2d, 1865.
Official—WAGER H. REMINGTON,
    2d Lieut. and Acting Adj't.

Head-Quarters 111th N. Y. V.
      May 28th, 1865.
I certify that Serg't Levi White, Co. I, 111th N.
Y. V., returned to duty at the expiration of his fur-
lough, and has not been reported a deserter.
    LEWIS W. HUSK.
    Lieut. Col. 111th N. Y. V.
On February 13th, 1865, skirmishing commenced

along the lines, and our picket line advanced toward Petersburg.

On March 29th, the brigade broke camp, crossed the rebel's line, and followed in their rear to Boyington Plank Road, where a charge was made upon the pits, behind which the enemy were stationed. The first man in the pit was Levi White, who captured a rebel flag. He was followed closely by Thomas Sandwich, George Perkins and others.

Levi White, for gallantry displayed, was promoted to First Lieutenant.

Humphrey Davenport, of this company, was wounded in battle at Boynton Plank Road, near Dinwiddie Court House. Va., on March 31st, 1865, by a minnie ball, which entered his right side cutting off two ribs, and lodged in his left side, where it still remains. He was as soon as practicable conveyed from the field to the Division Hospital, and from there to Lincoln Hospital, Washington, where he remained until honorably discharged, on May 25th, 1865, when he returned home. He was also in the battles of the Wilderness, Spotsylvania, Cold Harbor, and Shady Grove.

Another fight occurred at South Side Rail Road, where the brigade made two charges upon the enemy and were repulsed. The third charge was successful, and the Rail Road and some prisoners captured. This was on April 1st, 1865, and the last engagement in which the regiment took part. They remained near there for nearly a month, and were ordered to Washington, and thence to Syracuse, and discharged June 6th, 1865.

138TH REGIMENT.

This was the next regiment organized, and the following named persons enlisted from this town in Company E, with Salem Cornell as Captain, and Arthur W. Marshall and George C. Stoyell as Lieutenants.

Henry Austin, Julius Bush, Dorr Cutler, Wm. Evans, George Fritts, Charles Lee, F. L. Royce, Patrick Lavin, Simeon Stoddard, Richard D. Wright, Dorwin F. Wright, Frederick Allen, Lester Oakley, Thomas Ferguson.

The regiment left Auburn in September, 1862, for Washington, near which place it remained for several months, protecting the city and engaged in building military roads and forts.

We have been unable to obtain information sufficient to give a history of this regiment, but believe that with one or two exceptions, the soldiers from this town died or were discharged during the first year of service.

160TH REGIMENT.

This regiment was organized in September, 1862, and a portion of Company F enlisted from this town, under Capt. Josiah P. Jewett and Lieut. Gideon F. Morey, with the following named men :

John D. Clark, John Stoyell, George Shaver, John Shaver, Dwight Day, Alex. Peterson, William E. White. The remainder of the company enlisted from adjoining towns.

Soon after its formation the regiment was ordered to New Orleans.

The commanding officer, Col. C. C. Dwight, (now a Justice of the Supreme Court, for the Seventh District), although theretofore a civilian, soon became one of the best and most efficient officers in the Union Army; the officers and men under his command, without exception, respected him not only as their superior officer, but as a man of kind heart, social, careful and discreet, possessed of that high moral principle and courage, without which no man, though physically courageous, can become a capable or safe officer.

The first engagement in which company F participated, was in March, 1863, at Bayou Teche, in which the rebel gunboat Cotton was destroyed by the rebels to prevent its being captured by our troops.

On March 28th thereafter, about thirty-two men belonging to Co. F, commanded by Capt. Jewett and Lieut. Kirby, embarked at Brasheur City upon the Union gunboat Diana, which had also received a portion of the 12th Regiment of Connecticut, which, including officers and Co. F, amounted to a force of about 120 men, armed with minnie rifles, while the gunboat carried three heavy guns.

The object of the expedition was to discover if possible the whereabouts of the Rebel gunboat Queen of the West, which had been lurking in the vicinity, and supposed to be in Grand Lake, which was about twenty miles in length and distant ten miles from Brasheur City.

After a very careful search however, in that very crooked lake, no gunboat was found, and if the commanding officer could have been satisfied in fulfilling his duty and obeying orders, and returned by the same route which he came, several lives would have been saved, much suffering avoided, and the government saved from the disgrace of having incompetent men as the guardians of the lives of valiant and worthy soldiers. Returning however, by a different and unknown route, they unexpectedly encountered a large force of the enemy securely entrenched upon the banks of the river, and with several batteries of artillery which fully commanded everything upon the river. Their force consisted of about seven thousand men. The Diana was very soon disabled and completely riddled with cannon balls and shell. The gunboat was under fire two hours, yet but very few of those on board were killed—ten in all, and eighteen in Co. F wounded.

In addition to the dangers to which the men were exposed from land, the enemy had placed torpedoes at short distances in the water, and expected every moment that the Diana would be destroyed from that source.

The men of Co. F were upon the upper deck and consequently received the most injury, the remainder of the force being below. Capt. Jewett was struck upon the head with a piece of shell, a part of which also wounded Corporal John D. Clark who was near him. Capt. Jewett very soon became helpless. Mr. Clark had previously been wounded by a minnie ball which entered his mouth, extracted several teeth and lodged in the right side of his face, from which it was next day extracted.

It becoming apparent that sure destruction awaited them, the gunboat being unmanagiable, an attempt was made to surrender; but the Lieutenant giving the signal was wounded while doing so, and the officer who took his place also severely injured, the enemy's firing continuing, notwithstanding the signal of surrender could be plainly seen. A third time a signal was raised, and the enemy ceased their bombardment, and boarded the Federal gunboat, or what remained of it, and carried their prisoners to the fort, where in a few days the privates were paroled, and returned to their camp, and the officers held as prisoners of war.

Shortly thereafter a force sent out by Gen. Banks under Gen. Weitzel, came upon the enemy at Franklin, and recaptured Capt. Jewett, Lieut. Kirby, and the other officers, driving the enemy northward.

The following is a copy of the parole of John D. Clark :

HEAD-QUARTERS BATTERY FUSALIA.
30 March, 1863.

The bearer, John D. Clark, a Corporal of Co. F. 160th Regt., is paroled on condition that until duly exchanged he will not bear arms against the Confederate States of America, nor in any way give aid and comfort to their enemies.

By order

COL. HY. GRAY, Com'd Post.

ROBERT BRADLEY, Capt.

Mr. Clark was honorably discharged July 7, 1863.

Josiah E. White was also wounded in this miserable exploit. while lying upon the second deck. by a shell which entered the pilot house and burst. scattering splinters in every direction. some of which entered his left hand and still remain there. while others entered his left shoulder and ear. causing very troublesome flesh wounds; he was knocked over back of the stair railing. and finally escaped to the hold below the water mark, where he remained . with several others, until the boat was boarded by the enemy, who expressed great surprise at finding so many alive after such a terrible and continuous bombardment. One officer casually remarking that they didn't *intend* to take any prisoners. and supposed there were none alive.

After being paroled, the prisoners were taken to near New Orleans, and finally to Ship Island. Meantime the balance of the regiment had an engagement at Camp Buland while on their march to Port Hudson. Afterward the part of Co. F paroled were also ordered to Port Hudson, but upon arriving there. were sent back to camp by Gen. Emory. as they had not been exchanged. The balance of the regiment took part in the battle of Port Hudson. but none of Co. F from this town were injured. They were next engaged at Sabine Cross Roads. where the Union troops were beaten and forced to retreat. fighting under great disadvantage, and largely superior numbers, combined with unaccountable mismanagement on the part of officers in command. Our troops finally retreated to Grand Ecore. where they encamped; the enemy being unable to pursue, he having received during the 7th, 8th, and 9th of April severe punishment though obtaining a nominal victory.—The regiment had also engagements at Pleasant Hill on April 9th, 1864, and at Burnett's Bluff, April 23d, after which they received orders to report at Washington, and were attached to the 19th Corps, and were shortly afterward, on July 19th, 1864, engaged in skirmishing with the enemy at Snickers' Ford, after which the regiment had occasional skirmishing but no severe fighting until the battle of Fisher's Hill, on September 24th, 1864, where the Union forces under Gen. Sheridan obtained a very decisive victory over Gen. Early, capturing several guns and many prisoners, and destroyed a large quantity of army stores, wagons, &c.

Soon after and on October 19th, 1864, was fought the battle of Cedar Creek, the circumstances of which have become familiar in almost every family circle, and which virtually used up and destroyed the forces of the enemy in the valley of the Shenandoah.

The 19th was a very prominent corps, and bore the brunt of the battle, both in the disastrous retreat and the glorious and decisive victory which followed.

Josiah E. White was again wounded at Cedar Creek, October 19th, 1864, early in the engagement, in his left ankle by a minnie ball; he laid upon the field during the day and until 10 o'clock P. M., his clothing having been taken by the enemy who were in possession of the field during that day, but driven back that night and our wounded recovered and cared for. Mr. White was taken to Middletown where his leg was amputated by Dr. Armstrong, of Auburn; in two or three months he was sent to Washington, thence to Philadelphia, and thence home on leave of absence; while home he was transferred to Rochester, N. Y., and discharged.

CHAPTER XVI.

TRIBUTE TO THE DEAD—JOHN STOYELL, JOSIAH P.
JEWETT, DORWIN F. WRIGHT, GEORGE C. STOYELL,
LYMAN H. GOODRICH, FREDERICK ALLEN, PROC-
TOR MELLEN, JONATHAN JENKINS, SANFORD BUR-
LINGHAM, THOMAS HORROP, WILLIAM SHIMER,
WILLIAM S. MOSS, EDGAR E. MOSS, DAVID GOULD,
EBENEZER PLATT, THOMAS DAVENPORT, JOHN
SLARROW, SIMEON STODDARD, JOHN S. CADY, JE-
ROME PALMER.

TRIBUTE TO THE DEAD.

"Men die but once, and the opportunity of a noble death is not an
every day fortune.   It is a gift which noble spirits pray for."

The followers of Mahomet were instigated to deeds
of valor in defense of their religion, and taught to
welcome death by the promise that by their swords
they should open the gates of heaven, and that an
immortality of sensuous pleasure awaited them,
adapted to their physical inclinations and desires.—
And at the later day of the Crusaders, eternal salvation was promised to those who should help to fight
the battles of the Lord.

While the bible or the christian religion afford
no grounds for such anticipations, but require the

giving of the heart to God as well as the body to his service, there is naturally a disposition to hold in high esteem those who fought and died, nominally in quelling the rebellion, but virtually for the establishment and preservation of civil and religious liberty throughout the Union.

A majority of the soldiers from this town who died in the army, were brought home for burial. In some cases however, this was impossible, and the graves of a few are unknown.

The following brief biographies are but a slight token of respect for the memories of those brave men who gave their lives to their country, and who will never cease to be greatfully remembered, no matter where they fell or where they were buried, so long as patriotism is honored by their countrymen.

JOHN STOYELL.

The subject of this article was born in this town. Full of the energy and ambition which his father (the pioneer of civilization in this vicinity) possessed, he early became known as a thrifty, enterprising farmer and citizen. Though not an aspirant for political preference, he held various offices of trust with great efficiency and credit to the town.

In 1831, he became a temperance man, and drew up and signed a pledge of total abstinence from intoxicating liquors, presented the same to his friends, and organized a temperance society, which for many years labored faithfully and with considerable success in the cause. From that time to the day of his death, John Stoyell was the leader of the temperance party in southern Cayuga. He was always present at appointed temperance meetings, cheering his fellow laborers with his presence and aiding with his money, which was always free in every good work.

He united with the First Congregational Church of Moravia, and was elected a deacon of the same in 1834, which office he held during life. He was a pillar in the church. Firm as a rock in his religious belief, strict in the performance of duty, not fanatical or unreasonable, but consistent, holding the popular theories and practices of the day, and in fact all things else subservient to the one great first principle of his life, — the glory of God.

During his membership, the duties of the officers of the church was very perplexing and the burdens heavy to be borne, but when others shrank from the duties and responsibilities which the emergency demanded, Deacon John Stoyell was always found equal to the occasion. The Church knew his integrity of character and honesty of purpose, and had perfect confidence in his good judgment.

Deacon Stoyell was a zealous Anti-Slavery man. An Abolitionist when the very name was a reproach. Anti-Slavery societies were ridiculed and derided, and their lecturers insulted and mobbed in the streets. John Stoyell, believing slavery to be a wrong—a curse to the nation, and an abomination in the sight of God, labored earnestly to bring his neighbors and friends to the same conclusion, and so far as possible gave aid and comfort to those who came within his reach, in their endeavors to escape from bondage to a country which offered them the protection, security and liberty which the land of their birth denied them. He set his face as a flint against unjust legislative enactments and judicial dictums which set at defiance the Higher Law, outraged the conscience and consigned four millions of unfortunate people to inconceivable misery, degradation and despair. When the laws of God and the laws of men conflicted, there was no hesitation as to whom he would serve. He obeyed God rather than man. He fed, clothed and sheltered the fugitive, and often with his own conveyance, forwarded him on his way to the North at the risk of being himself arrested, and of receiving the fines and imprisonments which the laws in the interests of slavery demanded.

He enlisted as a private in Company F, 160th Regiment, and accompanied it to the field in Louisiana, and died at New Orleans, July 5, 1863, aged 61 years, giving his life to the cause which he had so early espoused and so earnestly labored for,—the Abolition of American Slavery. "Faithful unto death."

In political and social business life, he was actuated by religious principle, was kind and benevolent, honest and upright in all his dealings.

> " His life was gentle ; and the elements
> So mixed in him, that nature might stand up
> And say to all the world, *this was a man*."

CAPT. JOSIAH P. JEWETT.

When the 160th Regiment was being organized, Mr. Jewett volunteered, assisted in enlisting a Company, and was finally elected Captain of Co. F. He had lived several years in the family of the late Deacon Josiah Jewett, his grandfather, and was well and favorably known in the community as an upright and intelligent young man. Previous to his enlistment he became a member of the well known firm of "G. Jewett & Nephew," in Moravia Village, and was engaged in an extensive and profitable mercantile trade, which he left for the laborious and dangerous life of a soldier. This regiment as soon as organized was ordered to New Orleans. Co. F, on March 28th, 1863, was stationed at Brasheur City, whence about one-half of the company commanded by Capt. Jewett, were ordered to proceed (with other selected soldiers) up the Bayou, upon the gunboat Diana, to Grand Lake, for the purpose of discovering the whereabouts of the Rebel gunboat Cotton. Upon their return (disobeying orders) by another route, the Diana was obliged to pass a position occupied by the rebels, to the number of 7000 or thereabouts.— For two hours the Diana was at the mercy of the rebel batteries which were in easy range, and the men on board exposed to a terrible and incessant bombardment. Capt. Jewett being upon the upper deck was wounded upon the top of the head by a piece of shell, which exploded near him. He was afterward taken prisoner by the enemy, but shortly recaptured by the federal forces and sent home, where strong hopes of his recovery were entertained only to be crushed by the certainty of the rapid approach of death, whose footsteps cannot be stayed by a nation's necessities, or his purposes thwarted by the tears of friends. He died in his old home at "The Cottage," peacefully, another martyr in the cause of his country, and was buried in an honored grave, while his memory will be held in high respect as the years glide by bringing to the nation the fruits of the labors and the lives of those so nobly and so willingly sacrificed, "Peace and Good Will to men."

DORWIN F. WRIGHT.

Born and reared in this town, at the age of twenty-five years he enlisted under Capt. Salem Cornell in Co. E, 138th Regiment Infantry. Naturally of a kind disposition, genial and obliging, he had won the esteem of all who knew him. Well educated and a close observer of the political horizon, he understood and appreciated the importance of the struggle in which he was engaged, and the issues involved therein. That rebellion meant the dismemberment of the Union and the destruction of the principles of Government by the People, and that only in the complete success of the armies of the government could peace and prosperity be restored. Soon after its formation, the regiment was ordered to Washington, D. C., and stationed at Camp Morris, about five miles from the Capitol, where the men were engaged for several months in building military roads; the great design of the Government at that time being to protect Washington. Mr. Wright was a faithful soldier, and although the general experience of army life in camp was, on account of its immoral tendencies, distasteful to him, he never regretted the step he had taken, being buoyed up by the assurance that through the strife and turmoil of war, a lasting peace would be secured to those who should survive. He was a member of the Congregational Church of Moravia, and a teacher in the Sabbath School when he enlisted. He endeavored to avoid evil wherever met, helped to organize a prayer meeting and bible class in his company, in which he took an active part while he lived. He hoped to live to see peace restored, and to return home to enjoy the fruits of the labors which patriotism and fidelity to home and country always merit, and to engage in more desirable pursuits, but such hopes were never to be realized. He died in camp of typhoid fever, on January 11th, 1863, highly respected by his associates. His funeral services were held in the church of which he was a member, and his remains deposited in the "Old Cemetery," whither they were followed by a large concourse of sympathizing friends.

GEORGE C. STOYELL.

Lieutenant Stoyell was the eldest son of Loyal and Emily Stoyell, who are among the oldest and most esteemed citizens of this town. They were exceedingly indulgent to their children, and spared no pains to gratify their wishes when this could be done consistently with their best interests and permanent good. George was reared amid affluence and fine social position, and had excellent opportunities for acquiring an education. He was kind of heart, active, generous to a fault, and generally beloved by his associates.

On the 12th day of August, 1862, he enlisted in Company E, 138th Regiment Infantry, and upon the election of officers, received the office of Second Lieutenant. The regiment was stationed near Georgetown, D. C., where it remained for several months at work upon forts and other defenses. He was a capable officer, and liberal with his men. He was destined however, to share the fate of thousands of his fellow soldiers, and died at Georgetown, D. C., January 21st, 1863, aged twenty-three years. It will be remembered by those interested, that he was sick at the time of the funeral of Dorwin F. Wright, of the same company, where the welcome announcement was made from the pulpit that " Lieut. Stoyell was much better." But the apparent improvement was but temporary, and the next Sabbath but one, at the same church, almost the same assemblage of sympathizing friends were gathered at his funeral services. Upon that occasion, a sermon was preached by Rev. Henry Fowler, of Auburn, N. Y., from the text,— " Blessed are they that mourn." It was full of tenderness and sympathy, and love for the soldier, and overflowing with patriotic devotion to the principles for which they gave their lives

Mr. Stoyell was a member of the Congregational Church of Moravia, and its Sabbath School, and died trusting in God, and relying upon his unfailing promises.

LYMAN GOODRICH.

The subject of this sketch was born in Sempronius, but enlisted from this town in the 75th Regiment. He was the only son of Lyman and Roama Goodrich, had always lived upon the farm, and was in every sense a home boy, and disinclined theretofore to mingle in society beyond his own family and a few personal friends.

The announcement of his intention to enlist was therefore received with considerable surprise, and some expostulation on the part of friends. But he had quietly, yet determinedly come to this conclusion, and enrolled his name in the regiment above named, which was stationed at Fort Pickens, where he performed the duties assigned him promptly and cheerfully.

His character was above reproach. The home of his childhood from which he had theretofore scarcely been absent for a day, was left most desolate by his departure; but a desolation more deep and never to be dispelled overshadowed the future. After faithfully serving his country, he died at Fort Pickens, on March 20th, 1863, and was buried by his comrades in a soldier's grave, thousands of miles from the scenes of his childhood and youth.

FREDERICK ALLEN.

The above named enlisted in the 138th Regiment, on the 11th day of August, 1862. Doubtless some men enlisted during the latter part of the war to obtain the large bounties which were then offered to volunteers, and who cared very little for the success of the Union armies. A few, in fact, openly favored the rebellion, and declared that their only object in enlisting was the bounty. But at the date above mentioned, only a small government bounty was given, and volunteers were actuated by patriotic motives, duty to their country, and love of its institutions. Mr. Allen belonged to this class of soldiers. He sacrificed the comforts of home, family, and all else dear to him for this one loyal principle—the support of the government.

He was a member of the Methodist Church, and during his army life was a consistent christian soldier. He died in Camp, on May 1st, 1863, and was buried in the Old Cemetery south of Moravia village.

PROCTER MELLEN.

Enlisted in August, 1864, in Company M, 9th Regiment U. S. Heavy Artillery. He was the son of Jeremiah and Fanny Mellen, who have resided for many years in Montville, in this town.

This regiment did noble service throughout the time of their organization, and participated in several heavy battles and skirmishes, in all of which the men proved themselves to be soldiers, inferior to none in the army.

Mr. Mellen was in two severe battles—at Cedar Creek and Petersburg; in the former of which, he received a wound in the hand. He was a valiant soldier, a firm friend, and an agreeable comrade.—He died at Hampton, Va., June 22, 1865, his remains were brought home and interred in Indian Mound Cemetery.

JONATHAN JENKINS.

Mr. Jenkins enlisted in Company I, 111th Regiment, and saw considerable service, that regiment being from the first engaged in active operation against the enemy in Western Virginia. Though a hard working man of vigorous constitution, by the change of climate and army labor, he became broken in health, and finally died on the 18th day of February, 1863.

SANFORD BURLINGHAM.

He was also a member of Company I, 111th Regiment, and a son of Samuel Burlingham, and had always resided on the farm near the " Free Church." He was a young man respected by his neighbors, honest in business transactions, and a good citizen. The exact time or manner of his death could never be ascertained, although diligent search and inquiry were made by his comrades and friends. He was with his regiment during the battle of the Wilderness and was severely wounded and left upon the field, there being no time to attend to the wounded. The battle field upon which there was considerable timber, was very soon thereafter on fire and the flames sweeping with great fury over the ground where lay the dead and wounded soldiers of the Union army, among whom wounded and perhaps already dying, doubtless was the subject of this sketch.

EBENEZER PLATT.

He was an industrious, hardworking man, enlisted in Co. K, 111th Regiment. He performed the duties of a soldier well while he lived, and was killed at Bristow Station on Oct. 14th, 1863.

THOMAS HARROP.

The above named was the son of Thomas and Elizabeth Harrop, and although scarcely fourteen years of age, enlisted in Co. I, 111th Regiment, on March 10th, 1864. He was too young to endure the severe marches and labors, and the privations which necessarily followed, and under which even strong men failed. *But he did what he could.* He was in the battle of the Wilderness, and was wounded on June 17th, 1864. He died of typhoid fever, at Lincoln Hospital, Washington, and was buried at Arlington Heights.

WILLIAM SHIMER.

Another of the members of this regiment was the above named of Co. K, the eldest son of Daniel and Rachael Shimer. He was in several skirmishes in which the regiment was engaged, and was finally killed in a battle at Bristow Station, Va., while acting as sergeant, Oct. 14th, 1863. He was nineteen years of age, and had been in the army since July, 1862, and had the name of being a courageous and reliable soldier.

EDWARD STANHOPE MOSS.

He was by birth an Englishman, the son of Thomas and Eliza Moss of this town, and enlisted Aug. 8th, 1862, in Co. C, 7th Regiment Heavy Artillery, was elected Corporal on Sept. 1st, 1862, on Feb. 11th, 1864, he received his commission as 2d Lieutenant, was taken prisoner before Petersburg, Va., June 6th, and conveyed to Charleston, S. C., where he died Oct. 4th, 1864, of yellow fever.

William S. Moss was a brother of the above named. He enlisted in Co. M, and was transferred to Co. C, 7th Regiment, was captured by the rebels before Petersburg, June 6th, 1864, taken to Andersonville Prison, where he died of starvation in Sept. 1864. They were both very social, companionable men, and highly esteemed in their regiment, and by all who knew them as citizens. They were faithful and true men to the land of their adoption.

JOHN SLARROW.

Enlisted in Co. I, 111th Regiment. He was the son of Lorenzo Slarrow, also a member of the same company, and possessed of a good degree of courage and the other elements which go to make a capable soldier. He was in the battle of Boliver Heights, Harpers Ferry, Va., and was shot in the head and instantly killed on Sept. 14th, 1862.

DAVID GOULD.

Mr. Gould had lived in this town until he had established a good name. A farmer by occupation, he was industrious and frugal, a friend at all times to be depended upon; he had no enemies. He enlisted in Co. A, 111th Regiment, in 1861. He proved a very gallant and reliable soldier, was in several battles, and was finally, as hereinbefore mentioned, wounded in the attack upon Fort Bisland, from the effects of which he died at Brashear City, about May 22d, 1863.

SIMEON STODDARD.

He was a member of Co. E. of the 138th Regiment. He resided for several years upon a farm in the north part of this town. We have been unable to gather much of his history, except that he died of disease at City Point, Va., about July 1st, 1864.

JOHN S. CADY.

Capt. Cady was the son of Artemas and Lois Cady, who resided for many years in this village, where he was born on May 29th, 1836. His mother, a most estimable lady, died June 5th, 1850, when he was fourteen years of age, and his father, to whom reference is hereinafter made, a few years later. He had been carefully reared, and although at such an early age sustaining this irreparable loss, his excellent moral culture prepared him to meet the trials of life with a large degree of composure and firmness, and enabled him to establish a character for integrity and reliability, which made him a most useful and influential citizen and fearless soldier. After the death of his parents, he resided with his brother, A. S. Cady, Esq., in New York City, and attended Columbia College Grammar School, preparatory to entering college. By reason of poor health, with much reluctance he gave up his studies, and entered the Comptroller's office of that city under appointment of Hon. A. C. Flagg, where he remained until 1857, when his health again failed, and he removed to Anoka, Minn., where he engaged in business until 1862. "*The Home Missionary*" of February, 1864, contains the following very interesting sketch of his western life.

written by the pastor of the church in Anoka, of which he was a member, entitled "A Model Captain."

"The most important event in the history of this church for the three months closing the first of August, was the death of one of its most active and useful members. John S. Cady came from New York here in 1857, at the age of twenty-one years. Before coming here he indulged the hope that he was a christian, and soon after made a public profession of religion; being the first person who joined this church by profession, and the only young person here at that time a professor of religion. From the first till his death his hand has been in every good work here. By his honesty and faithfulness, his helpfulness and practical benevolenence, his manifest conscientiousness and exemplary piety, he won the respect and regard of every one who knew him. He was Superintendent of our Sabbath School, and held other important relations to our church and society. He had sustained two mission schools besides. A year ago he enlisted and was the principal agent in raising a company here; he was chosen Captain by acclamation; his company was detained in the state for service against the Indians. The last winter was one of leisure to his men, and he was most industrious in labor for their good. On the Sabbath he had a morning service for them in which he read a sermon; in the afternoon a bible class, and in the evening a prayer meeting; on Wednesday evenings he had a prayer meeting, and during the week he had classes in various studies. His good influence upon his men

19

was very obvious. He was often called 'The model Captain.' His men loved him of course; one of them said he believed 'more than half the men in Company A would be willing to step in and take a ball designed for his captain.' He spent a couple of Sabbaths with us in June, having business connected with his command to occupy the week. On Monday morning he left with a squad of his men, to return to his post on the frontier. On his way he learned that some horses had been stolen by the Indians, and started in pursuit. On Thursday morning he overtook them, and in the encounter, in which he seemed too little regardful of his own life, he was shot through the heart. Two of his bravest and best men rescued his body from savage mutilation. The sad tidings of his death reached us the next afternoon, and his body an hour or two later. The flag at half mast and the tolling bell spread the mournful inteligence. I never saw such universal grief in a community; every one had lost a personal friend. Our church assembled for its monthly meeting, and was like a family that had received tidings of the death of a son and a brother. The children at school wept as for a father. At a crowded meeting of the citizens the next week, the most touching tributes of respect and affection were paid to his memory. On the following Sabbath the funeral services took place, and though there was no relative present but his brother (the only person surviving him near of kin), there was a great concourse of mourners. The preacher sought to portray the amiable excellence and nobleness of Captain Cady's life, to win their imitation and to awaken a worthy ambition for a life of usefulness and true honor. There was no military display in connection with the service, but the two soldiers who rescued and brought home his body bore a furled and craped banner in the procession from the church to the place where for convenience the body was placed, under the canopy of a large flag, where bright stars were partially obscured by the folds of black. Under this the procession passed to bid farewell to the face where kind greeting in life had been so welcome to all. I have seen some splendid mourning pageants, but never more universal and sincere grief, on such an occasion. The mourning was not alone for the patriot soldier, the excellent officer, not alone for the young chieftain fallen in the heroic discharge of duty, but for the good man whose hand and purse, and influence were never invoked for a good object without success, and whose manly heart, always indignant at wrong, had a tender and helpful sympathy for suffering. The church, the Sabbath School, the Library Association, the community, had experienced what seemed an irreparable loss. Hundreds mourned for him as if he had been near kindred by blood.

When the sorrowful procession had passed around, it was drawn close about the pastor, who offered prayer and pronounced a benediction, and the congregation left the mortal remains of one so loved and honored to be in a few days taken east by his brother. On the evening of July 3d, at sunset, they were laid to rest beside those of his mother and father, in the burial place of his native town, Moravia, N. Y. It is rare that a church can lose so much in one man as ours lost in him."

JEROME PALMER.

Jerome Palmer was the son of Mrs. Mary A. Palmer of this town, where he was born. The following is an extract from the *Dundee Record* published at Dundee, N. Y.:

"When we first made his acquaintance, he was attending school at Lima, N. Y., where he pursued the classics with success. He had before been a student at Starkey Seminary, where he was a general favorite, from his frank, affable manners, and manly independence. At Lima he was beloved by his associates, and respected by all who knew him. In the fall of 1863 he was drafted, but was too young to be obliged to go; but his love for his country would not permit him to remain from the army, and in the winter he enlisted in the 8th N. Y. Heavy Artillery, and we remember how hopefully he spoke of the future as we accompanied him to Canandaigua, there to join his regiment and go immediately south. We never saw him again. He was assigned to the 2d Corps, Hancock's Division, and was killed on Monday, June 6th, 1864. The story of his death is thus related 'by a boy in blue.' It was a hot day in the trenches, and the landscape glimmered with the heat away toward Richmond while the thunder of cannon lazily tolled off the hours. The crack of a rifle would be heard at intervals, and yet the rifle pits were nearly quiet, for no general move was ordered, and nothing was to be done by either line but to grimly watch each other with keen sharpshooters' eyes. Dead bodies lay around, and the putrid smell of these decaying in the sun, almost over powered the senses of the little handful of brave boys that held one of the pits of that long line, that seemed the engirding of death slowly closing its folds about the doomed city. Five days they had cowered in the yellow sand and gazed at each other, and smelled that fearful stench, and tried to catch words of cheer in the distant roar of the cannon; but each throb of the heart only seemed to say 'wait.' At last one of them, a mere youth of nineteen, blue-eyed, open-faced and beardless, with light sunny hair hidden under his blue cap, said, as his voice faltered, and a vision of home and friends far away came up to his heart amid the wreck of the intrenchments, 'Boys, I can't stand this any longer, I must go from this place or I shall die.' 'No, no, Rome don't go out of this pit, the sharpshooters will kill you,' replied his friend, 'But I shall die here, and if I get away where there is fresh air, I can do good service; I must go, I might as well be killed by a bullet as to suffocate.' It may be that the heat and the oppressive deathly atmosphere had half turned the brain of the bright-eyed boy, for he staggered out of the pit, and started across an open space toward the woods. Keen, merciless eyes were on him, and hard steel

gleamed from the rebel thickets, when crack rang
the rifles of the sharpshooters, and—he was dead.

'Bury him where the sunlight shines,
In showers of gold the branches through,
And gilds the grave by the sighing pines,
Where sleeps the form of the boy in blue.

Far away in a northern land,
Hearts are sad that for him beat true,
Praying to Him whose guiding hand
Ever sheltered the boy in blue.

Mourn we not with a hopeless sigh,
Tears may darken our eyes 'tis true,
But the brave and loving can never die,
And such was the soul of the boy in blue.'"

CHAPTER XVII.

FIRST NATIONAL BANK—HISTORY OF ITS ORGANIZA-
TION — OFFICERS — CAPITAL STOCK — RULES AND
BY-LAWS.

This bank was organized under the National Banking Law, May 25th, 1863, with a capital stock of
Fifty Thousand Dollars, which was increased to
Eighty Thousand Dollars. For the purpose of giving a full history of its organization and the reasons
therefor, and the efficient though invisible machinery
by which it is controlled, we copy from its records
in full upon these points, deeming it a matter of considerable importance in the present and future interests of the town.

"The establishment of a bank in Moravia Villiage
having been a subject of frequent consideration and
discussion by the citizens interested in the welfare
and growing interests of the town, and it having occurred that the Congress of the United States had
passed and the President on the 25th day of February, 1863, approved an Act entitled 'An Act to provide a National Currency secured by pledges of
United States Stock, and to provide for the circulation and redemption thereof.' That this law had
been made by the government in view of the vast

amount of money made necessary for its use in successfully defending the government against the war of rebellion waged it against by southern rebellious states and men, and in establishing the federal authority over all its territory, and also in furtherance of the wise policy of the government of conducting the war, and supporting the government upon its own resources, giving to its own loyal people the opportunity to furnish the requisite supplies, and to receive the revenue arising therefrom in preference to foreign loans and purchases, thus rendering the government a self supporting institution ; and in all loyal portions of the country an unprecedented thrift in business and abundance of money as the wages of their loyalty and patrotism.

A consultation was held by Wm. Keeler, Austin B. Hale, and B. F. Everson, which embraced in its discussions the facts that there was much money in the country out of employment and seeking investment ; that at the present time the government would be benefitted by its use, that in the future, when war should end and business increase, the capital would be desirable for business purposes, and would especially be desirable to have available should a financial crisis occur, that in taking the provisions offered and establishing a bank under the national law, it might serve a mutual benefit, contributing material aid to the government, national aid and convenience to the community, and add an impetus to the growth and business importance of the town, and at the same time yield a fair compensation for the money invested.

The consultation resulted in the issuing of the following call:—

'We, the undersigned, feeling that the establishment of a Bank at Moravia, N. Y., with a capital stock of not less than Fifty Thousand Dollars, would direct capital into channels profitable to shareholders, serviceable to their friends and stimulating to public industry, hereby express our willingness to invest capital in such a bank, and request those interested to meet at Pressey's Hotel, on Saturday, April 11th, at 3 P. M., for the purpose of taking the matter into consultation.

Dated, Moravia, April 6, 1863, and signed by Hector C. Tuthill, James Thornton, Rufus W. Close, P. D. Livingston, Lucius Fitts, Thompson Keeler, S. D. Tabor, Wm. Keeler, Lyman Card, A. B. Hale, Lauren Townsend, Charles Chandler, B. F. Everson, E. E. Brown, W. W. Alley, Jr., W. C. Cramer, B. C. Goodridge, Joseph Dresser, Nathan Robinson, B. D. King, P. R. Robinson, S. B. Young, M. L. Wood, David Wade, Jr., Whitman Brockway, H. H. Alley, E. Hopkins, J. S. Paul, H. H. Tuthill, J. C. Odell, Reuben Rounds, and C. E. Parker.'

Pursuant to the foregoing call, a meeting was held and organized by the appointment of Hon. H. C. Tuthill, Chairman, and A. B. Hale, Clerk; whereupon, after discussion, it was thought advisable to organize a bank under the National Banking

20

Law ; and a committee appointed to obtain subscriptions to the capital stock.

At a meeting held April 25th, all of the capital stock being subscribed, B. J. Everson, A. B. Hale, and Franklin Goodrich, were appointed a committee to prepare and report Articles of Association and By-Laws.

On May 25th, 1863, a further meeting was held, and the Articles of Association presented by the committee, revised and amended were adopted, being as follows : —

'The subscribers hereby associate themselves together for the business of Banking in pursuance of an act of Congress entitled, 'An Act to provide a National Currency secured by pledge of United States stocks, and to provide for the circulation and redemption thereof,' approved February 25, 1863, and the acts additional and amendatory thereof, and for themselves, their personal representatives and assigns, they enter into and agree to abide by the following covenants and engagements.'

ARTICLE I.

SECTION 1. The name assumed to distinguish the Association, and to be used in its dealings, shall be 'The First National Bank of Moravia, N. Y.' and its place of business shall be the Village of Moravia, in the County of Cayuga, and State of New York.

SECT. 2. The amount of its capital stock shall be Fifty Thousand Dollars, divided into five hundred shares each, which capital stock may be increased with the written consent of shareholders holding two-thirds of the capital stock, and called in as they may determine, to the amount of One Hundred Thousand Dollars; but it shall not exceed that amount.

SECT. 3. Whenever any increase of the capital stock of the Association, and of the number of its shares shall be determined upon as provided for in the last preceding section, such increase of shares shall, as nearly as may be, be distributed to, and be subject to be taken by the then shareholders pro-rata in proportion to the number of shares then held by each, so far as they may desire the same, and in case all shall not desire to increase their number of shares, their pro-rata among such as shall in proportion to their number of shares by them held, so far as they may desire the same, and those then holding shares shall be entitled to take the whole of such increase of shares in preference to persons not then shareholders.

SECT. 4. The Association shall be authorized to commence banking business when its capital stock shall be subscribed for, and at least thirty per centum of each share of its capital stock has been paid in, and such other requisitions of the act aforesaid authorizing such banking associations shall have complied with, as that it shall be so entitled to commence its said business, and its said business shall terminate on the 25th day of February, 1883.

ARTICLE II.

SECTION 1. The object of the Association is the

business of banking, discounting bills, notes, and other evidences of debts, receiving deposits, buying and selling gold and silver, bullions, foreign coin, foreign and domestic exchange, loaning money on personal and other securities, issuing and circulating bills or notes, and the exercising of any powers necessary to conduct its business, not inconsistent with the said act of Congress.

SECT. 2.   The Association may purchase, hold and convey only.

1st, Such real estate as shall be necessary for its immediate transaction of the business.

2d, Such as shall be mortgaged to it in good faith by way of securities for loans made by such Association, and for monies due thereto.

3d, Such as shall be conveyed to it in satisfaction of debts previously contracted in the course of its dealings.

4th, Such as it shall purchase at sales under judgments, decrees, or mortgages held by such Association.

ARTICLE III.

SECTION 1.   The government of this Association and the management of its affairs are hereby vested in a Board of Directors which shall consist of nine persons, each of whom shall own at least five shares of its capital stock.

SECT. 2.   The Directors shall elect one of their number to be President of the Association, and he shall be vested with all the powers and authority which these Articles and the Act of Congress aforesaid, confer upon that officer until a successor shall be elected.

Sect. 3. The first election of Directors of the Association shall be held at the house of Wm. C. Pressey, in Moravia, on the first Monday of January, 1864, and the same day in January in each year thereafter, at such hour and place in the village of Moravia as the Board of Directors shall appoint; notice thereof shall be published in one or more public newspapers printed in the County of Cayuga, for at least thirty days immediately preceeding the time of such election. The said election shall be made by the shareholders either in person or by proxy, and shall be conducted by three Inspectors, to be elected by them at such annual election; but neither of such Inspectors shall be a Director or officer of the Association. The nine persons who shall have the greatest number of votes shall be Directors, and they shall enter upon the duties of their office on the day of their election; and if an equal number of votes shall be cast for any two or more persons, the shareholders shall proceed to a new ballot to fill any deficiency in filling the Board of Directors on account of tie votes, and so on until filled.

Within a week of such election, they shall proceed to organize and elect by ballot one of their number President of the Association.

If any Director shall cease to hold five shares of the capital stock, his office shall become vacant; and whenever any vacancy occurs it may be filled for the unexpired part of the term by such eligible person as the Directors may by ballot elect.

The failure of the Association to elect Directors at the times hereinbefore specified, shall not dissolve the Association, but in such case it shall be the duty of the Board to take immediate measures for an election as required by Sec. 40 of the said Act of Congress.

SECT. 4.   Each shareholder shall be entitled to one vote on each share of his or her stock, which he or she shall have held in his or her own name for at least thirty days prior to the time of voting ; but in organizing they shall be entitled to such vote regardless of the thirty days time of holding such shares before voting.

SECT. 5. The Board of Directors shall elect a President and Vice-President, and appoint a Cashier and such other officers, agents, clerks and servants, as are necessary to conduct the business of the Association. They may fix their salaries and change the same as they may deem advisable, but a majority of the whole number of Directors shall be necessary for that purpose.

SECT. 6.   The Board of Directors shall make such rules, regulations, and by-laws for the government of the Association and its officers, and the management of its affairs, as they may see fit.   Five Directors shall be necessary to constitute a quorum for the transaction of business.

SECT. 7.   Austin B. Hale, Silas D. Taber, and Cerebial S. Jennings, shall be Inspectors of the first election of Directors of this Association.

SECT. 8.   The Board of Directors shall require all payments to the capital stock of the Association to be made in certificates, drafts, or monies current at par value in the city of New York, or otherwise, in funds which shall be made equal to current funds at par value in said city by the shareholders paying the same; but nothing shall be taken in payment for which a greater sum shall be allowed than the par value thereof.   United States bonds bearing six per cent interest shall be taken at par value and accrued interest.

ARTICLE IV.

SECTION 1.   The President of the Association shall preside and may vote at the meetings of the Board of Directors, at which he may be present.— He is hereby indicated as the officer to whom conveyances of real estate shall be made, to take, hold and convey the same on behalf of the Association, according to law.   He is also authorized and empowered to collect, receive, and sue for any monies due or belonging to the Association, to cancel and satisfy any judgments, decrees or mortgages which it may hold, and to release and discharge the whole or any part of the property mortgaged or encumbered ; to sell and transfer any public debt, stock or other property belonging or pledged to the Association, and to receive any dividend arising therefrom under the direction of the Board of Directors, and he may appoint for any of these purposes an attorney in law or fact under him.

In case of his inability to act from any cause, the

Vice-President may exercise any or all of the powers of the President for the time being.

SECT. 2. The President and Cashier shall sign all the contracts made by the Association, and the notes, bills, or other evidences of debt, and certificates of stock issued by it; and no other officer, Director or shareholder unless specially authorized in writing by the Board of Directors, shall make any contract in any way binding upon it.

SECT. 3. Minutes of the proceedings of the Board of Directors shall be regularly kept and signed by the President and Cashier.

ARTICLE V.

SECT. 1. The Board of Directors shall cause suitable books to be kept for the registry and transfer of the shares of the Association, and every transfer shall be made on such books and signed by the shareholder or his Attorney duly countersigned in writing.

SECT. 2. Every transfer shall be made and taken subject to all the conditions and stipulations contained in these Articles, and the Act aforesaid under which this Association is organized.

SECT. 3. The Board of Directors may close the transfer books from time to time as the convenience of the Association may require.

ARTICLE VI.

SECTION 1. The Board of Directors may invest the funds of the Association as they may deem expedient in such property as they may lawfully hold, and may transfer to and deposit with the Treasurer of the United States, or other proper officer, any portion of such property to secure the payment of the notes or bills which the Association may issue and circulate as money.

ARTICLE VII.

SECTION 1.   Out of the funds of the Association, the Board of Directors shall defray the current expenses, and twice in each year may declare and pay to its shareholders or their attorneys, such dividends from its net profits of the business as they may deem expedient.   The expenses of the Association shall be borne by the shareholders in proportion to the number of shares of each, until such time as the whole capital stock shall be paid in, and until such time all shareholders who shall with the consent of the Directors, pay in on their capital stock a greater amount, and at sooner times than required by Section 7 of the said Act of Congress may so pay in, in advance of the requirements of said Section 7.

The Directors shall cause the same to be taken in as the corporation property of the Association, and the same shall be by them immediately invested in United States bonds bearing interest at the value of six per centum, and they shall cause an accurate account to be kept of the interest received on such bond, and the same shall be paid to the shareholders making such advanced payment in proportion to the amount and time of such advanced payment.   All dividends to shareholders shall be paid in the same kind of money received on interest on the bonds deposited with the United States Treasurer to the extent of such monies received, and any deficiency in current bank bills.

ARTICLE VIII.

SECTION 1. The Board of Directors may accept and exercise any necessary additional powers and privileges which may at any time be authorized by law.

SECT. 2. They may also by written consent of shareholders holding two-thirds of the capital stock, apply for and accept any act of corporation, and upon such conditions as shall be satisfactory to such shareholders may come to be transferred to the body corporate all the property of the Association.

SECT. 3. Two-thirds of the Board of Directors may at any time propose amendments to the Articles of Association, except for the purpose of increasing the capital stock beyond the amount of $100,000, the same shall be served upon such stockholders by enclosing either a written or printed copy thereof, and depositing the same in the Post Office at Moravia, and properly directed to such stockholders at their last known place of residence.

If, after twenty days notice to each stockholder, shareholders holding two-thirds of the capital stock shall consent in writing to such amendment or amendments, such written consent to be by them or their authorized agents duly acknowledged before any officer authorized to take acknowledgements of deeds, then such amendment or amendments on recording such consent in the manner provided by law for filing the certificates and Articles of Association, and upon the approval of the Comptroller of the currency, shall become a portion of these Articles of Association.

The first Board of Directors of this Association shall consist of the following persons who shall hold their office until the first Monday of January, 1864, and until others are elected in their places, viz:— Hector C. Tuthill, Daniel J. Shaw, Beriah D. King, Alvah Fitch, Austin B. Hale, William Keeler, Charles E. Parker, Thompson Keeler, and Benjamin F. Everson.

We, the undersigned, hereby assent to the foregoing Articles of Association, and severally agree to take the number of shares set opposite our respective names of, the capital stock of the Association, and to pay the same as may be required by the Directors thereof, according to law.

Dated, Moravia, May 2, 1863.

Daniel Goodrich, Hector C. Tuthill, Daniel J. Shaw, Beriah D. King, Cordial S. Jennings, Jeremiah Hunt, Benjamin Atwood, Thompson Keeler, William Keeler, Franklin Goodrich, James M. Thornton, Charles Chandler, Joseph Dresser, Silas D. Taber, John L. Parker, Lauren Townsend, Hiram Hunt, Wm. R. Richmond, Charles E. Parker, Elizabeth Barney, John C. Odell, Austin B. Hale, Hiram H. Alley, Morgan L. Wood, Peter R. Robinson, Benjamin F. Everson, Hector H. Tuthill, M. M. Greenfield, Wm. W. Alley, Jr., Erastus E. Brown, William Selover, Terry Everson, Alvah Fitch, Smith Hewett, H. W. Lockwood.

I hereby certify that the foregoing is a true copy of the Articles of Association adopted by the shareholders whose names are thereto subscribed, on the second day of May, 1863, as amended May 25, 1863."

B. F. EVERSON, Cashier.

Article 3. Section 3, was afterwards amended as follows :—

The name "First National Banking Association," was changed to "The First National Bank of Moravia."

Article 7. Section 1, was also amended by making the last clause thereof read as follows:

"All dividends to shareholders may be paid in current bank bills."

BY-LAWS ADOPTED MAY 25, 1863.

ARTICLE 1. The Board of Directors shall meet on the first week day of each month, at two o'clock P. M., and also at the call of the President, and shall be conducted, so far as practicable, by parliamentary rules.

ART. 2. All questions in the Board shall be determined by a majority of the Directors present, except as provided in the Act of Association and Law, and the ayes and nays shall be taken and recorded upon the call of any member of the Board.

ART. 3. All the Directors present when any question is taken shall vote unless excused by a majority, and in all cases when the vote shall be equal, the motion shall be lost.

ART. 4. The Cashier and all assistants shall give

each, bonds in the penalty of $10,000. for the faithful discharge of their duties.   The sureties to such bonds to be approved by the Board of Directors.

Art. 6.   A committee of three Directors shall be appointed by the Board quarterly to examine the vault, safe, count the bills, specie and funds of the bank, and report to the Board at their next meeting.

Art. 6.   A committee of five directors shall be chosen by a majority of the Board, any three of whom shall constitute a quorum, to allow discounts between the regular meetings of the Board.

Art. 7.   No one person or firm shall at any time be a debtor to the bank as principal in a sum exceeding five thousand dollars, or as principal and surety in a sum exceeding ten thousand dollars.

Art. 8.   No paper shall be discounted when any one of the committee absolutely dissents thereto, nor shall any reason be assigned to the party offering the paper, when they decline to discount it, unless by consent of the Committee.

Art 9.   The transfer books shall be closed thirty days before any dividend is declared, also thirty days before the annual meeting of the stockholders.

Art. 10.   All salaries shall be paid quarterly.

Art. 11.   All officers, agents, and attorneys of the bank, shall be subject to the control and direction of the Board of Directors.

Art. 12.   The Teller shall make up his account daily after the close of the bank, and test by the balance of cash on the ledger, and in case of deficieney or excess, report the same to the Cashier and he to the Board at their next meeting, unless in his judgment, a sooner report is necessary.

ART. 13. The Cashier shall exercise the power and perform the duties usually pertaining to said office, subject to Act 11 of these By-Laws.

ART. 14. Banking hours shall be from 10 o'clock in the forenoon to 3 o'clock in the afternoon.

ART. 15. No paper or note shall be renewed more than once without consent of the Board.

ART. 16. The Cashier shall give notice of all special meetings of the Board of Directors by immediately depositing such notice in the Post Office at Moravia, properly directed to each Director.

ART. 17. No Director shall have any voice as a committeeman in deciding upon any paper offered for discount in which he is interested as principal or surety.

ART. 18. These By-Laws may be altered or added to, by a majority of the Board of Directors at a regular meeting, upon notice being given at the last previous meeting ; but all Directors shall have at least ten days notice, personal or by mail, directed to their post office address, specifying the alteration or addition to be made.

I hereby certify that the foregoing is a correct and true copy of the By-Laws adopted by the Board of Directors, on the 25th day of May, 1863.

BENJAMIN F. EVERSON, *Cashier.*"

To the men who originated and so firmly established this public institution, their fellow citizens should be truly grateful. While it was in accordance with, and pursuant to the laws of Congress and consistent with the great primary object of the organization of National Banks, to give aid and support to the government in its extreme peril and financial embarrassment, it was also an organization of which the public and private interests of the community stood in need. The safe and speedy transfer of moneys from the soldier upon the camping ground to the friends and family at home; the depositing in safe custody under legal protection of the funds received, from bounties and pensions; the commercial interests of the town all combined to render such an organization desirable and almost absolutely necessary for the transaction of business.

The men to whom we are indebted for this organization were fortunately of the first business talent of the town, honest, reliable, and capable, they possessed the confidence of the people, who knew that both their interests and those of the government would be consulted and secured. A bank gives an impetus to all kinds of business; its accommodations to business men can hardly be overestimated.

Since its establishment this bank has been conducted wisely and honorably. Its officers have been men of ability with a goodly knowledge of financial affairs. Upon its first organization, A. B. Hale was chosen President, and B. F. Everson, Cashier. In 1864 Mr. Everson resigning, Leander Fitts was made Cashier, and has held the position to the present time. Mr. Fitts is peculiarly adapted to the business of banking, is familiar with the business men of this vicinity and their financial standing, is kind and ,courteous, yet possessed of those essential elements of character so desirable in such an office—firmness and decision.

We give herewith some interesting statistics, to wit: Average yearly deposits, government taxes, &c.

1864—$74,380 18	1868—$123,823 76
1865— 94,288 25	1869— 91,491 20
1866— 84,389 93	1870— 69,515 68
1867— 90,766 29	1871— 68,604 31

Average deposits during eight years, $87,157 45.
Taxes paid to the government, $14,554 65.
Amount of dividends paid to shareholders, $78,300.
Capital stock, - - - - $80,000 00
Present surplus, - - - 18,000 27
____

Total capital and surplus, $98,000 27

CHAPTER XVIII.

WILLIAM WADE—CORNET BAND—NEWPAPERS FIRST PUBLISHED IN CAYUGA COUNTY—THE LAVANNA GAZETTE IN 1798—CAYUGA TOCSIN—NORTHERN CHRISTIAN ADVOCATE—AUBURN JOURNAL—CAYUGA CHIEF—FIRST PRINTING PRESS IN THIS TOWN —THE CAYUGA COUNTY COURIER—MORAVIA VALLEY REGISTER--ITS "STAFF"—MORAVIA WEEKLY NEWS-ITS "RESERVE" CORPS.

WILLIAM WADE.

Mr. William Wade was born in Dighton, Mass., on the 28th day of April, 1811, and was a resident of this town for about fifty-five years. Greatly interested in the subject of education, and possessed of a good practicable knowledge of the English branches and mathematics, he very often engaged in teaching the District Schools in this vicinity, and invariably with success.

In 1840 he was Commissioner of Common Schools for this town. He was a Keeper in the Auburn States Prison for several terms, and was appointed Enumerator for the towns of Moravia, Niles and Sempronius in 1840, and also in 1860.

In 1867, he was elected Justice of the Peace for a term of four years, although at that time the town was largely Republican, and in 1870, was chosen a Justice of Sessions for Cayuga County.

In 1835, he became a Free Mason, and in the Lodge and Chapter, took a prominent position. Unlike a majority perhaps, of the masonic order, he made Masonry a study, and was familiar with its origin and history, and all the business relations of the Order, and was zealous and efficient in all its rites and ordinances.

For many years previous to his death, he was a Knight Templar. Politically a Democrat, strong in his adherence to party measures, intimate with the machinery of the political parties of the past, he was no weak antagonist in private debate or on the rostrum. Socially, he was friendly to all, without regard to political, religious, or secular views or preferences. He was a member of St. Matthews' Church, of this village. He died on the first day of May, 1871, at the age of sixty years.

The following is an extract of the address of Rev. G. Williams, Grand High Priest of the State of New York : —

"Companion William Wade, for many years a member of this Grand Chapter, died at Moravia, on the 1st of May last. In all matters pertaining to our Institution, he was devoted, full of zeal, and every duty devolving upon him he discharged with fidelity."

CORNET BAND.

The Moravia Cornet Band was organized in 1859, their instruments having been purchased by subscriptions from the business men of the village, to the amount of one hundred and twenty dollars, or thereabouts. The Band consisted of the following members : —

William Jones, 1st E flat Cornet ; G. R. Huff, 2d E flat Cornet ; A. K. Clark, B flat Cornet ; J. A. Wright, 1st Alto ; W. G. Wolsey, 2d Alto ; George Beebe, Baritone ; Benjamin T. Avery, Tuba ; Fred. Tallman, Tenor Drum ; Smith Harter, Bass Drum.

They did good service through the political campaign of 1860, making perhaps, more noise than harmony ; but that was expected of them, and is a component part of campaign gatherings.

Since that time the Band has passed through many changes, until now it is composed of the following members,—some of them of many years practice :—

G. R. Huff, Leader, 1st E flat Cornet ; W. D. Bennet, 2d E flat Cornet ; A. Colony, 1st Alto ; Jas. Wolsey, 2d Alto ; A. K. Clark, B flat Baritone ; Smith Sawyer, B flat Tenor ; Fred. B. Heald, Tuba ; E. D. Greenfield, Bass Drum ; J. Lewis, Tenor Drum ; J. Parker, Cymbals.

They are well organized and thoroughly drilled, and make much better music than the majority of bands in the country. It cannot be expected that men who have other daily business which demands their attention, and who can only obtain practice after such business has been attended to, can attain to perfection in this or any other art. Constant and severe practice is required, a natural ear for harmony, a delicate perception of the sentiment of music, combined with fervent love for it, can alone constitute a musician worthy of being heard and patronized.

This Band under its present organization, gives general satisfaction, and should be sustained and encouraged. People unacquainted with the facts, are apt to think that a Band is a kind of public property, and should be ready at all times to entertain them gratuitously.

It should be remembered that its members devote time and money in order to be prepared when called upon. It should also be remembered that they are business men to whom " time is money," and when their services are required they should be well remunerated.

There may be occasions and doubtless are, when they, like all other men or organizations, should contribute to the public interest. There are public ceremonies to be performed without money and without price, and with willing hearts and hands. But aside from these we believe the Band should be employed and paid, not only for their services rendered, but as tending to encourage and keep intact an organization which is almost indispensible to the town, and a source of much gratification to the citizens.

NEWSPAPERS.

The first newspaper published in Cayuga County was *The Levanna Gazette*, at Levanna, on July 20th, 1798, by R. Delano, and which naturally had a limited circulation ; southern Cayuga had at that time comparatively few settlers. In 1799 *The Western Luminator*, a small weekly paper, was published at a place called Watkins Settlement, in Scipio. The *Aurora Gazette* was published the same year at Aurora, by H. & J. Pace. *The Cayuga Toesin* was first published at Union Springs in 1812, and was afterward removed to Auburn, and held an influential position in the County. The publication of *The Northern Christian Advocate* was commenced in April 1841, by Rev. John E. Robie, as a religious weekly, in the interests of the Methodist Episcopal Church. The *Auburn Daily Advertiser* and *Weekly Journal* were first published in 1846, by Henry Oliphant ; in 1850 he sold to Messrs. Knapp & Peck, who have continued their publication to the present time, twenty-three years, during which time the papers have been greatly improved in size and general appearance ; the *Journal* having a large circulation throughout the county among families by whom it is regarded as an old reliable friend. From 1849 to 1857, *The Cayuga Chief*, devoted to the temperance cause, was published by Thurlow W. Brown, at Auburn. Mr. Brown was an enthusiast in the matter of temperance reformation, an able writer and lecturer, and had a large circle of friends in this town, where his paper was extensively circulated.

Moravia of course had to rely upon Auburn papers for county and local news ; but for several years before it became a "newspaper town," attempts were made to start a paper, which signally failed for want of funds, subscribers, or other causes; it is however, a very long road that has no turn. On February 20th, 1860, H. H. Alley purchased a "Jones Press" which printed a sheet 4 by 5 inches in size, and soon afterward one which printed a sheet 12 by 18 inches; for several years he printed tickets for town meetings. Finally in October, 1863, the *Cayuga County Courier* was published in the office in Smith's Block, by A. O. Hicks, who continued its proprietor until the summer of 1864, when he died; the paper however, was continued by his brother, A. J. Hicks, for another year, when A. J. Hicks and Wm. M. Nichols formed a co-partnership, the latter shortly afterward purchasing the interest of Mr. Hicks, and continuing the proprietor until March 10th, 1867, when Mr. A. J. Hicks and Abner H. Livingston became the owners and publishers until December following, when Mr. Livingston purchased the interest of Mr. Hicks, and became sole proprietor and continued as such until January 1st, 1871, when he sold out to Mr. M. E. Kenyon, who improved the general appearance of the paper and changed its name to *The Moravia Valley Register*; it is a seven column paper, 24 by 36 inches, and is issued every Friday morning, from No. 4 Shimer Block, on Mill Street. Mr. Kenyon is a man in the prime of life, of business qualifications, well informed, a ready writer, and has held several offices of trust; in 1870 he was appointed Enumerator for the town of Moravia.

The *Register*, according to the American Newspaper Directory, had in 1873, a circulation of 750 copies.

In politics it is independent. The assistant "staff" of the *Register* consists of Miss Ida M. Green, James Keeler, Dorr Thomas, and Charles E. Tallman.

The *Weekly News* was first published on January 25th, 1872, in the building situate on the corner of Main and Cayuga Streets, by Uri Mulford. The size of the first volume was 19 by 24 inches, and in politics was neutral, until July 18, 1872, when its influence was given to the Republican party, to which it has since adhered. On April 1, 1873, the office was moved to the brick block owned by Messrs. Small & Jennings, and on May 15th, the paper was enlarged by the addition of one column to a page. On August 7, 1873, it was again enlarged to a seven column paper—size 24 by 36 inches. The present volume commenced with Uri Mulford as editor, and L. & U. Mulford, proprietors. Mr. Mulford claims to be the youngest editor in the State of New York, and is under twenty-one years of age. He learned to set type in the office of the *Valley Enterprise* in Laurenceville, Pa., and also the general business of a country printing office. The proprietor of the *Enterprise* having failed, the encouraging advice of M. M. Pomeroy, formerly a printer in an office in Corning, N. Y., was taken, and Mr. Mulford "struck out for himself." He is active and ambitious, and means to become "master of the situation."

The "reserve corps" of the News is composed of Miss May Mulford, Ami F. Mulford, E. Nye Sturdevant, and Ed. Mulford.

CHAPTER XIX.

Union Free School—Its History—School Buildings—Names of Teachers.

On or about December 1st, 1868, the following petition, signed by many of the prominent men of the
town, was presented to the Trustees of School Districts Nos. 1 and 2:—

"We the undersigned, freeholders and persons
having a right to vote at any school meeting held in
School Districts 1 and 2, in the Town of Moravia,
N. Y., do hereby unite in a call for a meeting of the
inhabitants, legal-voters of said Districts, to determine whether such Districts shall be consolidated by
the establishment of a 'Union Free School' therefor
and therein, in conformity with the provisions of
Title 9, Chapter 555, Laws of New York, and the
acts amendatory thereof."

In pursuance of such petition, after due notice
given by the Trustees of said Districts, a meeting of
the inhabitants thereof was held at Smith's Hall, in
Moravia Village, December 19, 1868, at which Leonard O. Aiken was elected Chairman, and John L.
Parker, Secretary.

The names of the legal voters in each of said School
Districts having been called, the Chairman an-

nounced that a quorum of each District was present, more than one-third of said voters having answered to their names.

Mr. Leander Fitts then offered the following :

"*Resolved*, That a Union Free School be established within the limits of School Districts Nos. 1 and 2, in the Town of Moravia, pursuant to the provisions of Chapter 555, of the Laws of 1864, and the amendments thereof."

Which resolution was duly voted upon and declared passed by the following vote: Ayes, 151. Nays, 8.

On motion of J. L. Parker, the meeting proceeded to ballot for a Board of Education for said District, consisting of six Trustees, resulting in the election of the following named as Trustees, to wit. :

C. C. Jewett, Wm. Titus, S. Ed. Day, Leander Fitts, Terry Everson, and John L. Parker.

At a subsequent meeting of the Board of Education, Terry Everson was chosen President, and Leander Fitts, Clerk of the Board.

On the 13th day of January, 1869, a special meeting was held at Smith's Hall, when on motion of L. O. Aiken, it was voted, "That the Moravia Institute grounds, together with lands adjacent thereto, proposed to be purchased of Enoch Lacey, be designated as a site upon which to build a school-house.— Ayes, 92. Nays, 29.

This meeting was adjourned until February 10, 1869, at which time J. L. Parker submitted the following resolution :

Resolved, That Fifteen Thousand Dollars be

raised by tax upon the taxable property of the district, for the purpose of erecting a suitable building for a school house, the same to be levied and collected by installments, as follows:—$3,000 on September 1, 1870; $3,000 two years from said date; $3,000 three years from said September 1, 1870; $3,000 four years from September 1, 1870; $3,000 four years from September 1, 1871.

Without coming to any conclusion, however, the meeting was adjourned to February 20th inst., at which adjourned day a vote was taken upon Mr. Parker's resolution, with the following result:— Ayes, 75. Nays, 88.

Mr. Parker then moved to make the amount to be raised, $12,500, to be paid in five equal annual installments, commencing on the first day of September, 1870, which was carried. Ayes, 82. Nays, 66.

A motion was also made and carried, that the Legislature be petitioned to pass a law authorizing the Board of Education to issue bonds of the district to meet the payments with interest of the installments aforesaid.

In accordance with said resolution, a petition was sent to the Legislature, and on April 16, 1869, an act was passed thereby, entitled, "An Act to authorize the Board of Education of Union Free School, District Number One, of the Town of Moravia, in the County of Cayuga, to bond said district for the purpose of building a school-house, and to legalize certain acts of the inhabitants therein, and of the said Board of Education."

"SECTION 1. The Board of Education of Union Free School, District Number One, of the Town of Moravia, in the County of Cayuga, is hereby authorized and required to procure suitable blanks, and to issue the bonds of said district signed by the President and Clerk of said Board, with interest coupons attached in the form to be adopted by said Board, for the sum of $10,000, which has been voted by the inhabitants of said district to be raised bearing interest at the rate of seven per cent per annum from the date thereof, payable semi-annually, on the first day of October, and the first day of April in each year, at the First National Bank of Moravia. Such bonds shall be issued in sums of not less than one hundred dollars each, and be made payable with the interest thereon as aforesaid, in four equal annual installments from the first day of October, 1869.

SECT. 2. The Board of Education of said district is hereby directed and required to levy upon the taxable property in said district in the manner provided by law for the collection of school district taxes, each year hereafter for four years from the first day of October, 1869, the sum of $2,500, and the interest as aforesaid on the whole amount of bonds unpaid in each year.

SECT. 3. The taxes in this act directed to be levied and collected, shall be paid to the Treasurer of said district, and by him be applied to the payments of the bonds of said district herein directed to be issued, and the interest thereon as aforesaid, as the same shall become due and payable.

SECT. 4.   The Board of Education of said district are hereby directed to add to their tax list for the year 1869, an amount sufficient to pay the interest which will become due at the end of the first six months on said bonds, and to levy and collect the same in the same manner as other school district taxes are levied and collected.

SECT. 5.   The clerk of said Union Free School District, or any other person authorized by the Board of Education thereof, shall negotiate at not less than their par value the bonds provided to be issued by this act, and the avails thereof shall be applied by the said Board of Education towards the erection of school buildings for said district, and to supply the same the necessary furniture.

SECT. 6.   The said Board of Education are also hereby required to issue the bonds of said district for such further sum or sums of money payable at such times as the inhabitants of said district may by resolution at any general or special meeting direct, not to exceed, however, the sum of $10,000; said bonds to be so issued in accordance with the provisions of this act.

SECT. 7.   The acts and proceedings of the inhabitants of said Districts Nos. 1 and 2, and the Board of Education, in forming a Union Free School, in procuring and locating a site, and raising money for the erection of buildings thereon, are hereby confirmed.

SECT. 8.   This act shall take effect immediately.

In accordance with the foregoing act, bonds were

issued by the Board of Education in the following form :

STATE OF NEW YORK, CAYUGA COUNTY.

MORAVIA SCHOOL BOARD.

KNOW ALL MEN BY THESE PRESENTS:

That Union Free School, District Number One, of the Town of Moravia. is jointly indebted and promises to pay to the holder hereof, on the presentation of this bond, the sum of ——— dollars, payable on the first of October, 18—, at the First National Bank of Moravia, together with interest thereon, payable semi-annually on presentation of the annexed coupons at said Bank.

This bond is issued in pursuance of a resolution passed by the legal voters of said district, at a meeting held February 20, 1869, and of an act of the Legislature of the State of New York, entitled " An Act to authorize the Board of Education of Union Free School, District Number One, of the town of Moravia, in the County of Cayuga, to bond said district for the purpose of building a school-house, and to legalize certain acts of the inhabitants therein, and of the said Board of Education, passed April 17, 1869.

In witness whereof, the President and Clerk of the Board of Education of Union Free School. District Number One, of the Town of Moravia, here set their hands and seals, this ——— day of ———, 18—.

——————————, *Clerk.* ——————————, *President.*

Union Free School, District No. 1, of the town of Moravia, will pay to bearer, ——————— dollars, on the first day of ————, 18—, at the First National Bank of Moravia, for six months interest on bond. No. ———, for ———— dollars.

——————————, *Clerk of the Board of Education.*

A substantial and commodious brick building has been erected, under the management of a very efficient and faithful Board of Education, who have devoted much time and personal attendance to the general work of securing suitable building materials, furniture and fixtures for the school rooms. The school building is an ornament to the town, and bespeaks a healthy, moral, and intellectual growth of public sentiment.

The first term of school commenced on the 25th day of April, 1870, with about 150 pupils in attendance, and the following term this number was increased to 250, under charge of the following teachers:—

Principal Hosea Curtis. Assistants—Miss Grace A. Wood, Miss Sarah M. Cole, Miss L. Annie Brownell.

The Board of Education have been fortunate in their selection of instructors, if we may judge from the present appearances of the school, and the rapid advancement made by a large proportion of the pupils.

It must be admitted that when this school was opened, the status of a majority of the pupils was very unsatisfactory. This was owing not to their inability to receive instruction, but largely to an aversion to study, which had been caused by the incompetent and unsatisfactory manner in which the district schools had been conducted. Nor was this the fault entirely of the teachers of these schools. They taught for the paltry wages which they received, and earned their money. The educational atmosphere had become impure and obnoxious. The patrons of the schools had been penurious. The outlay small, and the returns proportionally scant. "As ye sow, that shall ye also reap," as a spiritual maxim, is as truly applicable to temporal things. Men gather not grapes of thorns, or figs of thistles; neither can it be rationally expected that children subjected to shabby school buildings, unfinished and repellant, with instructors uninteresting and inapt to teach, parents giving little if any encouragement to teacher or scholar, can be other than backward, undisciplined and unpromising pupils. As our churches, schools and homes are made attractive and interesting, in such degree shall we find the former well attended and prosperous, the latter a protection against vice, and in all, the security of personal and religious liberty and happiness.

It is therefore with justifiable pride that we behold the work accomplished by this community, by their deputed officers, the Board of Education, in the erection of a beautiful school building, the furnishing of the same attractively, and the ornamentation and beautifying of the grounds.

The cost of these amounting to about $16,000, including the enlarging of the grounds, is being paid in installments as the same become due, as set forth in the act of the legislature herein before referred to. The estimated annual expenses including teachers' wages, fuel, incidentals, &c., are $3,600.

With its present favorable prospects, the school will be nearly self-sustaining after the liabilities for building, &c., shall have been cancelled.

CHAPTER XX.

CEMETERIES—OLD BURIAL GROUNDS—THE FLOOD
OF 1863—PARTIAL DESTRUCTION OF THE OLD CEM-
ETERY—INDIAN MOUND—COLD SPRING AND PUB-
LIC PARK—NAMES OF RESIDENTS OF THIS TOWN
OVER 75 YEARS OF AGE—ALSO OF PERSONS WHO
HAVE DIED RESIDENTS, OVER 75 YEARS OF AGE.

BURIAL GROUNDS.

" The dead are there ;
And millions in their solitude, since first
The flight of years began, have laid them down
In their last sleep ; the dead reign there alone."

While the deepest philosophy cannot reach beyond
the grave, or remove the veil which shuts from our
limited vision the life which is to come, or revelation
lead our finite minds into the wondrous mysteries of
the Infinite, death is accepted by all as a certainty
fixed and inexorable. The end of *this* life we know,
and prepare ourselves as best we may for the putting
off of this mortal coil. While in point of fact,
when that time comes, it may matter little where
the body shall be laid, there is yet an instinctive
shrinking from a burial in a strange land, or apart
from friends dear to us in life.

Even in the early ages, the family tomb and burial
place was selected and kept with care, and protected
from generation to generation.

How expressively mournful, yet urgent the request of Abraham to the sons of Heth:

"I am a stranger, and a sojourner with you: give me a possession of a burying-place with you, that I may bury my dead out of my sight."

"And the field of Ephron which was in Machpelah, which was before Mamre, the field and the cave that was therein, and all the trees that were in the field, that were in all the borders round about, were made sure."

"And the field and the cave that is thereon were made sure unto Abraham for a possession of a burying place by the sons of Heth."

Nearly one hundred years after this, the last words of the patriarch Jacob to his children, express an affectionate longing for a grave in the burial grounds of his ancestors:

"And he charged them, and said unto them, I am to be gathered unto my people: bury me with my fathers in the cave that is in the field of Ephron, the Hittite. In the cave that is in the field of Machpelah, which is before Mamre in the land of Canaan, which Abraham bought with the field of Ephron, the Hittite, for a possession of a burying-place."

"There they buried Abraham and Sarah, his wife. There they buried Isaac and Rebekah, his wife, and there I buried Leah."

This feeling was also evinced by Joseph, who, dying in Egypt, took an oath of the children of Israel: "God will surely visit you, and ye shall carry up my bones from hence." More than two hundred years thereafter, this was literally fulfilled, and the bones of Joseph, which the Israelites had carried with them throughout their journeyings, were buried in Shechem, in a piece of ground which Jacob bought of the sons of Hamor, the father of Shechem.

The old-time benizen.—"May you be buried among your kindred," expresses the natural desire of the heart.

While the labors and the duties of life often of necessity require the separation of the dearest family relations, there is yet satisfaction in the thought, that when these labors are ended, and we shall have filled up the measure of our days, we may as families and friends, rest together in one sepulcher, awaiting in hope the morning of the Resurrection.

A few of the early settlers were buried on East Hill, near the Brick Yard. At a later day, a piece of land lying one-half mile south of the village was purchased by the "First Congregational Church Society," of Moses Little, for burial purposes. The grounds were never properly prepared, and graves have been made without regard to regularity or space. Grass and weeds have often covered the entire enclosure. Laterly, however, the grounds, together with an half acre purchased of Jesse Cole, have been conveyed to "The Moravia Cemetery Association," which has made great improvement in their general appearance by building new and substantial fences, subduing obnoxious weeds, and arranging the newly purchased portion into lots of uniform size. Notwithstanding the undesirable location of the grounds and the wretched condition in which they have been kept, there are many of the older families now living, who have attachments for the "Old Burial Grounds" which are too strong and sacred for severance. Their friends rest beneath its rough exterior. The spot whereon they sleep is hallowed ground. There the tears of affection have been shed, fond memories awakened, and resolutions made for future usefulness.

There, too, are buried some who were the pioneers of civilization in this region, of Puritanic blood and principles, who possessed within themselves the elements of moral strength and worth little realized by those who to-day casually read their histories only by the humble monuments which mark their graves. For these reasons, the old burial ground has its attractions, and its sacred memories. But it has become unsafe and undesirable for burial purposes. "Dry Creek," the name of which is certainly a misnomer, flows along its southern and western boundaries, and may at time of high water, renew the terrible scenes of the past, the remembrance of which still thrills our hearts with horror.

On the morning of July 21, 1863, the people of this village were greatly alarmed by the continuous heavy rains of the day and night previous, and the rapid rising of the waters in the creeks.

Their fears were more than realized, at ten o'clock. A. M., when a vast volume of water came rushing down from the north and east, carrying away every mill dam and bridge in its course, uprooting trees, and destroying several buildings. As a consequence, a large part of the village adjoining the creek was inundated to the depth of two or three feet, and all communication between the two sections of the village entirely suspended.

"Dry Creek," within a few hours, became a foaming torrent, filled with trees and logs. About eleven o'clock its banks were overflowed, and the main current of the stream turned against the western bank of the cemetery, the lower stratum of which, on a level with the creek, being composed of gravel and quicksand, was quickly undermined, and within an hour the western portion of the grounds containing from thirty-five to forty graves, carried away.

The writer, in company with G. L. Wright and John Storms, apprehending danger from this source, reached the cemetery by a circuitous route, east of Morses' Grove (the highway being impassable) in time to find a small portion of the bank caved off, and the coffin of Lieut. George C. Stoyell exposed to view. A rope was immediately procured from the house of Philip Ercanbrack, and an attempt made to secure the remains, but before this could be done the embankment again went down, and they were precipitated a distance of twenty-five feet into the flood below.

It is impossible to describe the feelings of the witnesses of this terrible scene, who, powerless to save, saw the remains of one who a few months previous, was their associate and friend, so ruthlessly unearthed and swept wildly down the watery current. The box in which the coffin was enclosed, was however, firmly built, and without receiving material injury, was cast upon a bank of sand which had been thrown up in the midst of the stream just above the plank road. Here another attempt was made to rescue the body, by the aid of a rope, one end of which was firmly held by two of the party and grasped by the other who plunged into the waters, but was instantly swept away from the rope and down the stream with great force, and only escaped destruction by catching and clinging to the willow branches overhanging the creek, until rescued.

Meantime several coffins were carried down the stream, while some were thrown upon the adjoining fields and door-yards. Bodies long interred, were torn from their tombs, and seemingly with out-stretched, fleshless arms, plunged into the watery abyss.

Although at this time assistance had arrived from the village, it was found to be impossible to save any from this terrible devastation, except by exhu-ming and removing the bodies to a remote part of the grounds, which in many instances was done.

The remains of Mr. Stoyell were afterwards dis-covered near the mouth of "Dry Creek," and re-moved to the village through the water, which was from three to four feet in depth over the flats.

The scenes of that terribly eventful day aroused the feelings of the whole community, and proceed-ings were immediately had to procure grounds in a more suitable and safe location.

The following is an extract from the Historical account of the origin of "Indian Mound Cemetery," by S. Edwin Day, Esq.

"The demand for a new Cemetery was felt to be imperative. Immediately, a committee of citizens, consisting of Messrs. Guernsey Jewett, Rufus Warren, Norman Parker, Gideon F. Morey, C. A. Conant, E. A. Mead, and others, having in view the formation of a Cemetery Association under the general law of the State, volunteered to visit most of the lands in or near the limits of the incorporation of the Village of Moravia, which were deemed fit and suitable for cemetery purposes. Their duties were not a little arduous and perplexing. The desideratum was a place of security, easy of access, pleasant as to situation and scenery, with appropriate surroundings, and a soil naturally adapted to the digging of graves. The grounds most nearly embodying perfection in all these qualities, were found in a piece of land then owned by Samuel E. Day, Esq., lying but a few rods east of the limits of the corporation, and between it and the village of Montville,—a place at once inviting and singularly suited to the purpose intended. The preliminary steps having been taken, the following named citizens of said town assembled at the office of Mr. G. Jewett, on the 17th day of August, 1863, and proceeded to organize and establish a Cemetery Association, pursuant to law, viz. :

Hector H. Tuthill, Dr. Charles C. Jewett, Loyal Stoyell, James H. Jewett, Rufus W. Close, Guernsey Jewett, Hector C. Tuthill, Thompson Keeler,

24

Chauncey Wright, Lauren Townsend, Joseph Dresser, Rufus Warren. Cordial S. Jennings, S. Edwin Day, and Charles E. Parker.

Hector C. Tuthill was made Chairman, and Chas. E. Parker, Secretary of the meeting. The corporate name determined upon. was, "The Indian Mound Cemetery Association." It was deemed the fittest appellation for many reasons, not the least of which was, that, by an old tradition. the lot, the purchase of which was contemplated. had, many years before been the depository of the remains of the deceased sachems, chieftains and warriors of the brave Cayugas, whose spirits had long ago entered upon the felicities of the happy hunting grounds. Mounds indicative of graves beneath, were still there to be seen.

The trustees were to be nine in number, and the following named persons were duly elected:

Rufus W. Close, Gideon F. Morey, Guernsey Jewett. Cordial S. Jennings. Austin B. Hale. Charles E. Parker, Hector H. Tuthill, Charles C. Jewett, and William Keeler.

By law, these are required to be divided by lot into three classes. Those in the first class to hold their offices for one year. Those in the second class to hold their offices for two years, and those in the third class to hold their offices for three years.

This was done, and the classification resulted as follows: *First Class.*—Hector H. Tuthill, Charles C. Jewett, and William Keeler. *Second Class.*—Cordial S. Jennings. Austin B. Hale. and Charles E.

Parker. *Third Class.*—Rufus W. Close, Gideon F. Morey, and Guernsey Jewett.

It was determined that the future annual election of Trustees should be held on the first Tuesday of October. On the 20th day of the same month, the Trustees met and appointed from their number the first officers of the Board, which were as follows:

President.—Guernsey Jewett. *Vice President.*—Rufus W. Close. *Secretary.*—Hector H. Tuthill. *Treasurer.*—Gideon F. Morey.

At a meeting of the Trustees held September 22, 1863, the President was authorized and empowered to enter into a contract with Samuel E. Day, Esq., for the purchase of the premises herein-before mentioned, which he did verbally. Intermediate the time of the making of this part of the agreement and next meeting of the Trustees, to wit: On the 13th day of October, 1863, Mr. Day died.

At the special instance of the Trustees, although the grounds had not yet been surveyed or plotted, his remains were on the 15th day of October, buried in the new cemetery, it being deemed fit that the late owner of the premises being dead, should be the first to be interred in 'Indian Mound.'

On the 24th day of October, aforesaid, a warranty deed was duly executed by the widow and heir at law of the said deceased, conveying the fee simple of said lands unencumbered to the Trustees of the Association and their successors in office forever.

About the same time formal possession of the premises was taken by the Trustees, who proceeded at once to cause the same to be laid out into lots, plats. &c., with suitable walks. avenues and paths. under the direction of Fred. E. Knight, C. E. The task of the engineer was performed in the most thorough and perfect manner."

The conveyance to the Association as above stated, consisted of ten and sixty-three one-hundredths acres of land. Thereafter, and on the 26th day of December, an additional piece of land containing one-half acre or thereabouts, was also conveyed to the Association, by Charles E. Parker, and Harriet G., his wife.

ORDINANCES OF THE ASSOCIATION.

The Board of Trustees of Indian Mound Cemetery Association, do by virtue of the power and authority in them vested, hereby ordain and establish the following Rules and Regulations for the government of the Association. and the management of the property and affairs thereof, viz. :—

First. All the business of the Association shall be managed by a Board of nine Trustees. one-third of whom shall, after the expiration of the terms of the first and second classes already designated, be elected annually. by the proprietors of lots in the Cemetery, for the term of three years.

Second. An annual meeting of the proprietors of lots in the Cemetery for the election of Trustees, and the transaction of such other business as may be lawfully submitted to them, shall be held at such place as shall be designated by the Trustees. on the first Tuesday of October. of which it shall be the duty of the Secretary to give at least six days notice in a local newspaper published in this village, or by a conspicuous notice at the Post Office, or both.

Third. From the Trustees of the Association there shall be chosen immediately after each annual election, a President, Vice-President, Secretary and Treasurer, who shall hold their offices respectively for one year, and until successors shall assume the duties of the said offices, and appointed by the President two standing committees, to wit: a Committee on Finance, and a Committee on Improvements.

Fourth. It shall be the duty of the President to preside at all meetings of the proprietors and Trustees, to call special meetings of either or both, at his option, or when thereunto requested by the Trustees. To appoint the Standing Committees required by the preceding ordinance to sign deeds of burial lots, to recommend to the Board by annual communication or otherwise, such measures for improving, protecting, beautifying and enlarging the cemetery grounds as he shall deem expedient and proper, and in general to supervise the affairs of the Association. In his absence the duties of his office shall be discharged by the Vice President, if he shall be present, and if not, by a President *pro tempore.*

Fifth. It shall be the duty of the Vice President to discharge the duties of President whenever the latter shall be absent, or from any cause be unable to occupy the chair.

Sixth. It shall be the duty of the Secretary to record the proceedings of all meetings of the Board of Trustees and stockholders, to keep a registry of the sale of lots in the Cemetery, and of interments reported by the Superintendent; to sign licenses for interments whenever thereto requested by any person who shall require the right to inter in the Cemetery, from the President of the Board of Trustees.

Seventh. It shall be the duty of the Treasurer to receive and safely keep the funds of the Association, to disburse the same only on the order of the President, countersigned by the Secretary, to report all funds in the Treasury, and the financial condition of the Association to the Board whenever thereunto requested, and before entering upon his office to execute a bond to the Association with such sureties and in such penalties as shall be approved by the Board of Trustees, for the faithful performance of his duties.

Eighth. All monies which shall be derived from the sale of lots, from bequests, and from other sources, shall, except so far as they may be necessarily applied to the payment of the consideration money for the lands which constitute the Cemetery ground, be faithfully and economically expended upon the said grounds, or otherwise devoted to the purposes and objects of the Association, and shall in no event be paid to, or be permitted to enure to the individual benefit of any member of the Association.

Ninth. It shall be the duty of the Board of Trustees to appoint a Superintendent of the Cemetery, who shall hold his office during their pleasure, and receive for his services such compensation as the Board shall prescribe.

Tenth. It shall be the duty of the Superintendent to attend at the Cemetery from time to time, and at such times as the Board of Trustees shall direct, and particularly during funeral ceremonies and interments, to report to the Secretary the name, place of nativity, late residence, age, and occupation of every person whose remains shall be interred or entombed in the Cemetery, together with the date of his or her demise.

Eleventh. All interments in lots shall be made under the direction of the Superintendent, and shall be restricted to the remains of members of the family and relatives of the owner of the lot in which such interment shall be made, except special permission for the interment of the remains of other persons upon a particular lot be obtained from the Board of Trustees.

Twelfth. Whenever application shall be made to the Superintendent by any person whom he does not know to be the proprietor of a lot, for the opening of a grave in the Cemetery, he shall before, complying with such request, require the applicant to produce to him a permit, signed by the Treasurer.

In all cases of interments in lots, there shall be immediately due from the owner of such lot, and payable to the Treasurer of this Association for each interment, the following sums or prices, to wit :

For opening and closing a grave less than three feet in length, three dollars ; for opening and closing a grave of three feet or more in length, four dollars.

Thirteenth. The Superintendent shall, before he suffers disinterment to take place, require the production of a written permit to that effect, signed by the Secretary of the Association.

Fourteenth. In order to preserve uniformity and symmetry, and to prevent the introduction of noxious or objectionable plants, all improvements to lots, grading, ornamenting and planting of trees, shrubs, or flowers, are to be done after consultation with, and under the direction of the Superintendent of the Committee of Improvements.

Fifteenth. The proprietor of each lot may enclose the same with a fence or railing, as may suit his taste, not exceeding three feet in height, provided such fence or railing except the posts, which may be of some durable timber or stone, shall be of iron, and shall be light, neat and symmetrical, and the gates thereof shall swing into the lot.

Sixteenth. All vaults or tombs shall be constructed of durable material and fitted up with catacombs, and with the exception of the receiving vault of the Association, shall be sealed up with hard brick or cement immediately after the deposit of bodies therein, and the entrance protected with stone or metal doors.

Seventeenth. If any monument, vault, tomb, effigy, railing, or structure whatever, or any inscription be placed in or upon any lot which shall be determined by four of the trustees for the time being to be offensive or improper, the trustees shall have the right, and it shall be their duty to enter upon such lot and remove the said offensive or improper objects, provided, however, that if such structure or improvement shall have been made with the consent of the Board for the time being, the same shall not hereafter be removed except with the consent of the owner thereof.

Eighteenth.   In the erection of monuments, vaults, tombs, railings, or other obstructions, a place will be designated by the Superintendent for the deposit of the stone, or other material which shall not remain longer on the ground than is actually necessary for their construction, and which shall be conveyed to, and the rubbish consequent therein removed from the grounds upon hand-barrows or vehicles with broad wheels.

Nineteenth.   If any tree or shrub situated in any lot shall by means of its roots or branches become detrimental, dangerous, or inconvenient to the adjacent lots, walks, or avenues, the Trustees shall have the right, and it shall be their duty, to cause the removal of said tree, or shrub, or such part or parts thereof, as may be deemed detrimental, dangerous, or inconvenient.

Twentieth.   It shall be the duty of the proprietor of each lot to place and keep in repair, permanent landmarks of the boundaries of their respective lots.

Twenty-first.   Proprietors of lots are requested to provide themselves with a copy of the ordinances

25

and recommendations of the Board of Trustees before erecting any structure, or planting any trees, or shrubbery upon their lots, that they may be advised not only of the peremptory rules of the Association, but of the suggestions of the Board presenting the kind of structures which are the most durable and tasteful, and the species of shrubbery and flowers the most appropriate to the place of graves.

Twenty-second. Visitors properly admitted to the grounds, may have access to every part of the Cemetery, provided that they ride or drive in the carriage-ways, and walk in the avenues and paths laid out for those purposes, and abstain from all disturbing and unnecessary noises; that they ride or drive no faster than a walk, if they have with them hearses or carriages; that they bring upon the grounds no fire-arms, fire-crackers, or other explosive substances, refreshments, other than water, and abstain from smoking during ceremonies of interment; that they leave no horse or horses on the grounds unattended without fastening; that they refrain from entering any lot which is occupied, without the special leave of the proprietor, and abstain from plucking any flowers, either wild or cultivated, or breaking, or injuring any monument, railing, shade-tree, shrub, or plant whatever; that they refrain from writing upon, marking, or in any respect marring or defacing any tablet, monument, tree, head-stone, or structure used in or belonging to the Cemetery; that if they are under twelve years of age, they are attended by some person who will be responsible for their conduct, and that they observe in all respects such rules of decorum and propriety as shall be harmless to the Cemetery, inoffensive to other visitors, and befitting well-bred visitors to the resting-places of the dead.

Twenty-third.   Any person who shall violate any of the foregoing rules in regard to visitors, shall be expelled and thereafter excluded from the cemetery grounds, and subject to the severe penalties which the law in such cases imposes.

Twenty-fourth.   All applications for the sale and purchase of lots shall be made to the President.— The purchase money on any sale is to be immediately paid to the Treasurer, or secured to him by an approved note, when the Treasurer will deliver to the purchaser a good and sufficient deed of the premises so sold ; and no interment will be permitted until the purchase money of the lot on which any burial shall be sought to be made, has been paid or secured.

Twenty-fifth.   It shall be the duty of lot owners to cause all bases of head-stones to be set upon sub-bases or cobble-stone at least two feet in depth, and the setting shall be done under the direction of the Superintendent.   All head-stones having no bases, shall be set under like directions in a base of cobble-stones and hydraulic cement.   The time of the Superintendent occupied in or about such setting, shall be paid for by the person for whom such services are rendered, at the rate of twenty-five cents per hour. Where the cement used is furnished by the Association, such person shall pay a reasonable price therefor.

Twenty-six. Upon the purchase of a lot by any person, the Association undertakes and agrees to see that the same is kept in order forever thereafter; that the mounds of any grave therein shall be retained in shape, that any monument or head-stone thereon be carefully attended to; that the grass be always neatly cut, the trees and shrubs suitably pruned and cared for; and generally to do and perform such necessary and proper things in and about the care and management of said lots, and the mounds, monuments and erections thereon, as by right should be done.

Twenty-seventh. Any person who may be desirous of having a bed of flowers made and cultivated upon any lot of which he may be the owner, may give notice thereof to the President, who thereupon and after the payment of a reasonable compensation to the Treasurer for the work to be laid out, shall cause the flower bed to be constructed by and under the direction of the Superintendent; the bed shall be carefully kept, and shall be maintained from year to year on like payment of a small annual consideration.

Twenty-eighth. Alterations or additions to these ordinances shall be proposed in writing, to the Board of Trustees, and shall lay over until a subsequent meeting, when, if they receive a vote of a majority of the Trustees elected, they shall take effect as ordinances of the Association.

Indian Mound Cemetery, with its location and natural scenery, will soon compare favorably with any burial grounds in this portion of the country.

The evergreens, of which there are many varieties,
under careful management and culture, are assuming beautiful form and proportions. Maples and
elms, the most beautiful of forest shade-trees, are
set at stated distances along the carriage roads.
Choice shrubbery and flowers have been placed by
loving hands upon nearly every occupied lot. At
this writing, many costly and elegant monuments
have been erected.

The officers of the Association are deserving of
great credit for the very efficient manner in which
their labors have been conducted, and for the beautiful and tasteful appearance which the grounds now
present. A local pride is naturally felt by all in
the great improvements which have been made, in
fitting up desirable, and above all, secure burial
grounds, which shall for all time be safe from floods
and devastation, and which, under the care and control of a legally organized and established body corporate will be permanently maintained and protected, with all the sacred reverence and respect which
the living owe to the silent dwelling-places of the
dead.

COLD SPRING.

This valuable spring is located on the "Morse
Premises," near the eastern boundary of the corporation, three-fourths of a mile distant from, and
perhaps two hundred feet above the village ; and
with its present dimensions, contains from six to
eight barrels of water, which is very pure and cold,
and possesses a sweetness rarely to be found in the
waters of this part of the county of Cayuga.

From its location, the waters of this spring could, without difficulty, be conducted in iron tanks to all portions of the village, and would furnish an abundant supply for each building, by having a reservoir of suitable dimensions, at some convenient point on East Hill.

Such a "water power" would be of great value as a protection against fire, and much cheaper and more reliable than fire engines. With hydrants and hose stationed at convenient distances, the principal streets could be kept free from dust, and lawns, yards and gardens watered at pleasure.

Thus far, we have shown simply some of the pecuniary advantages to be derived from this project. But there are others equally desirable. Moravia needs a "Public Park,"—a place for recreation, promenades, social gatherings, and innocent amusement. Doubtless in a few years, the premises known as "The Grove Park Grounds," could be purchased or leased (the former would be preferable), for a term of years at a reasonable valuation or rental, for such purposes. Properly laid out, with carriage-roads and walks, and tastefully arranged with fountains, flowers, shrubbery, &c., in addition to the beautiful natural scenery, these grounds would be an ornament to the village, and an attractive and desirable place during leisure hours.

Trout ponds could be added to the above with profit. By a small admission fee to the grounds, the project would be self-sustaining; but it should be light, that none need be excluded on the plea of poverty ; and better yet, if, by any reasonable means no entrance fee should be charged.

These suggestions in regard to "Cold Spring" and the Public Park, are offered with the hope that they may ere long lead to the accomplishment of such desirable objects.

AGED PERSONS.

Of the persons who died residents of this town, of the age of 75 years or upwards, we have been able to gather the following names, and regret that it has been impossible to obtain a complete list, either of the dead or the living of such an advanced age :

Jane Berean, died March 19th, 1853, aged 96.

William Bowen, aged 96.

David Wright, died August 19th, 1869, aged 95.

Dorcas Card, died 1849, aged 93.

Daniel Wood, aged 92.

Dudley Loomis, died December 31st, 1869, aged 90.

Daniel Goodrich, Sen., died April 29th, 1855, aged 89.

Rhoda Smith, died May 24th, 1836, aged 88.

Sarah Camp, died February 7th, 1859, aged 88.

Laura Wright, died January 22d, 1852, aged 87.

Charlotte Childs, died October 25, 1863, aged 87.

Sarah Warren, died February 9th, 1829, aged 86.

Capt. Alexander Stark, died September 18th, 1864, aged 86.

Deacon Josiah Jewett, died February 24th, 1860, aged 86.

Leah Cortwright, aged 86.

Lucy Cady, died January 21st, 1854, aged 85.

Gad Camp, died March 27th, 1840, aged 84.

John Dennis, died September 2d, 1856, aged 84.

Harriet S. Loomis, died March 26th, 1864, aged 83.

Moses Little, died March, 1839, aged 82.

Zadoc Cady, died March 6th, 1846, aged 82.

John Stoyell, Sen., died October 23d, 1842, aged 82.

Polly Ames, aged 82.

Richard Smith, aged 82.

Silas Lincoln, died October 22d, 1864, aged 82.

Jerusha Wright, died April 15th, 1860, aged 80.

Prudence Skinner, died December 1st, 1844, aged 80.

Sophia Johnson, aged 80.

Thankful Rogers, died January 14th, 1837, aged 80.

Eunice Powers, died September 3d, 1838, aged 80.

John H. Parker, died 1874, aged 80.

Peleg Gallop, died March 26th, 1858, aged 79.

Tryphena Cole, died September 9th, 1858, aged 79.

Catharine Dennis, died April 21st, 1849, aged 79.

Daniel Goodrich, Jr., died March 28th, 1869, aged 78.

Aaron Parsons, died August 21st, 1870, aged 78.

Mehetable Taber, died November 27th, 1864, aged 77.

Squire Robinson, died March 29th, 1858, aged 77.

Joseph Wilson, died April 22d, 1860, aged 76.

John White, died June 21st, 1867, aged 76.

Ruth Shimer, died March 24th, 1859, aged 76.

Elias Rogers, died December 20th, 1863, aged 75.

Sarah Tuthill, died March 30th, 1866, aged 75.

Jeremiah Sabin, died August 6th, 1847, aged 75.

Gershom Morse, died September 27th, 1843, aged 75.

Ebenezer Smith, died May 22d, 1853, aged 75.

Chauncey Wright, died January 15th, 1872, aged 75.

Names of residents who are of the age of 75 years and upwards:

Eleazer Carter, aged 97 ; Belinda Carter, aged 90 ; Lois Mosely, aged 90 ; Sally Hough, aged 87 ; Lucy Wood, aged 84 ; Matilda Rogers, aged 82 ; Luman Barber, aged 81 ; Daniel Seed, aged 81 ; Daniel Stewart, aged 80 ; William Everson, aged 79 ; Loami Adams, aged 78 ; Catharine Everson, aged 77 ; Naomi Goodrich, aged 77 ; Hector C. Tuthill, aged 77 ; Henry P. Harter, aged 77 ; Abisha Morse, aged 76 ; Oliver Davenport, aged 76 ; Laura Goodrich, aged 75 ; Peter VanTuyl, aged 75 ; Stephen Lilley, aged 75 ; Rebecca Platt, aged 75.

CHAPTER XXI.

MEMBERS OF ASSEMBLY—SKETCHES OF ARTEMAS
CADY, JOHN L. PARKER, AND HECTOR C. TUTHILL
—GOVERNMENT OFFICIALS—STATE, COUNTY, AND
OTHER APPOINTMENTS FROM THIS TOWN.

MEMBERS OF ASSEMBLY.

This District has been represented in Assembly by
the following named gentlemen from this town:

William Satterlee, in 1810; Rowland Day, in
1818; Artemas Cady, in 1839, and John L. Parker,
in 1865 and 1866. They were all able representatives. and among the leading and most influential
members of their times.

Artemas Cady was the brother of Isaac Cady, and
the father of A. S. Cady, of New York city, and
Capt. John S. Cady, who was killed by Indians on
the western frontier, in 1864.

At the time of his election, Mr. Cady was engaged
in mercantile business in this village. He was a man
of integrity. and highly respected at home and
abroad. In the Assembly. he was a quiet. unobtrusive, but very intelligent member, carefully scruti-
nizing every bill which came before that body, understanding fully its meaning and import before ex-
erting his influence or casting his vote for or against

its passage, and then laboring and voting accordingly, conscientiously and effectively.

JOHN L. PARKER.

Mr. Parker was forty years of age when first
elected member of the Assembly, and always resided in this town. The following article is copied
from "Life Sketches of State Officers, Senators, and
Members of Assembly," written by S. H. Harlow,
and H. H. Boone, and published by Weed, Parsons
& Co., in 1867.

"The birthplace of Mr. Parker, is Moravia, Cayuga County, N. Y., where he was born on March 25,
1823.

On his mother's side, he is a descendant of John
Locke, whose name is familiar to almost every one.
Mr. Parker has natural and acquired qualifications,
which have placed him among the most influential
members of the House. As a parliamentarian, he
has few superiors, and his knowledge in this regard,
with his naturally quick intellect and intuitive
shrewdness, have rendered him one of the best tacticians in the Assembly for several years. This fact
caused him to be selected by a party caucus in his
first year (1865), to engineer the Metropolitan Paid
Fire Department Bill through the House; and he
did it, although the opposition was strong and un-
scrupulous. His skill in this respect received a
striking illustration in 1867, when in the first few
weeks of the session he brought to a third reading
in the House, and passed by a unanimous vote a bill
to require the rail road companies of this State to

give equal freight and express facilities to all (a bill designed to reach the case of the Merchant's Union Express Company). The bill passed through all the stages of legislation openly, yet so quietly, that its presence was scarcely known before it had passed beyond the jurisdiction of the House.

Mr. Parker has also eminent qualifications as a presiding officer, having the requisite knowledge and promptness for that position. His qualifications in that respect caused him to be selected in 1865, by a party caucus, as Chairman of the Committee of the Whole on the Metropolitan Health Bill, and the Buffalo Police Bill. In 1866, he was frequently called to take the Chair, by Speaker Tremain.

He is also an effective debater. In 1865, he delivered a speech on the Constitutional Amendment; and in 1866, on the Health Bill, and the resolutions indorsing Congress against the President; and, in 1867, an impromptu argument on the Constitutional Amendments, all of which were deservedly and highly praised, and widely read.

In his general course as a legislator, he has sought the best interests of the State, the keeping down of taxation, and the overthrow or crippling of monopolies. He has been Chairman for two years of the Committee on Railroads, serving in that delicate position with true credit to himself, honor to his constituents, and the true interests of the State."

HECTOR C. TUTHILL.

Hector C. Tuthill, a well known and highly respectable gentleman, represented the District in Assembly in 1848 and 1849. He was at that time a resident of the town of Sempronius, where he settled as a farmer in 1827. He was born in Goshen, N. Y., where he was reared upon a farm and received a thorough practical education in agriculture. When he settled in Sempronius, nearly all of his neighbors were heavily in debt, and only able to make the ends of the year meet by the most rigid economy and arduous labor. None of the houses between Nonesuch and Kelloggsville were painted. Mr. Tuthill's farm consisted of two hundred acres of land, which, like the lands in that section, had been used for grazing. He saw that farming in that way was not profitable, and being familiar with the dairy business, purchased a number of cows, and commenced making and packing butter for the New York market. His neighbors ridiculed the idea of farming in that way. They had been accustomed to make but little butter, and that was sold to the nearest store-keeper at six or eight cents per pound, *store pay* at that.—The merchant packed the different varieties and different qualities of butter thus gathered together, and shipped it to New York, or some nearer market, where it brought but an inferior price, and helped to give to Western New York its unenviable reputation for second-rate butter, which it has taken years to overcome.

Mr. Tuthill, however, could well afford to submit quietly to the notions of his neighbors, so long as the business was profitable, and his increasing prosperity did not fail to have its influence; and one after another of his neighbors followed his example, until that section of country became famous for its large dairies, and excellent quality of butter marketed.

Mr. Tuthill also brought with him from Orange County, the castings for a machine for churning with a dog, which excited considerable curiosity at that time.

In the Assembly, he was a practical, honest, cautious legislator. During his first session, 1848, the following laws were passed which had reference particularly to Cayuga County.

"An Act to incorporate the City of Auburn, giving its boundaries, and dividing it into four wards."

Also, "An Act to declare the public use of a rail road from Auburn to Ithaca, through the town of Fleming and Scipio, and down the valley of Salmon Creek."

The men who conceived the idea of this road, among whom were Leonard Searing, Slocum Howland, Worthington Smith, Alfred Avery, John H. Chedell, George Rathbun, and Thomas Y. How, Jr., were considerably in advance of the people of Southern Cayuga, at that time, and the road for various reasons was not built, although surveyed and partially graded; but the idea was a good one, and now after more than twenty years later, a rail road occupies for a considerable distance the track then graded, and will doubtless shortly connect the city of Auburn and Ithaca for all practical purposes as thoroughly as the road contemplated in 1848.

It was also during the session of 1848, that the following concurrent resolution was passed :

"*Resolved*, That the thanks of the Legislature of the State of New York be tendered to Ex-Governor William H. Seward, for the eloquent eulogium on John Quincy Adams, delivered at the request of both Houses of the Legislature, on the 6th day of April, 1848, and that a copy be requested for publication.

Resolved, That twenty times the usual number of copies be printed."

Twenty-four years later, the distinguished orator upon that occasion, himself had joined

> " The innumerable caravan that moves
> To the pale realms of shade."

While Charles Francis Adams stood before the Legislature of this State, and pronounced a suitable and fitting tribute to his memory.

But, perhaps the most important measure upon which Mr. Tuthill was called to vote during the session, and which became a law, was an act which revolutionized the rights of property of married women in this State, known as, "An Act for the more effectual protection of the property of married women," and which gave any female who should thereafter marry, owning real or personal property, the right to hold and use the same, as her sole and separate property, not subject to her husband or liable for his debts. Also, the right to receive by gift, grant or devise, from any person except her husband, real or personal property, to hold and use the same and the rents thereof, the same as if unmarried. This law marked a new era in the "rights of women," and has doubtless done more substantial good than all the "woman's rights associations" or parties, or movements led by "strong minded" women amalgamated with weak minded men of questionable morals and doubtful associations.

This law gives to women substantial rights and protection of incomparable greater value than all the theoretical, nonsensical plans which such parties have originated, and endeavored to force upon the people.

In the session of 1849, Mr. Tuthill was exceedingly interested in the bill which finally became a law, establishing free schools throughout the State, giving the children of the poor an opportunity of acquiring a common school education without expense. The law has doubtless been beneficial to the entire people of the State.

Mr. Tuthill removed from Sempronius to this town in 1856, where he now resides, at the age of 75 years.

27

CHAPTER XXII.

MONTVILLE.

This is a hamlet one-half mile north-east of Moravia Village, and contains a population of about one hundred and seventy souls. It is a quiet, peaceable mind-its-own-business sort of a place, possessed of considerable wealth, a fair average of brains, industrious, practical mechanics and business men. Its water power is excellent, and has been put to good use for over seventy years. "Goodrich Creek," always in good running order, flows through the centre of the village, and at its extreme western boundary, after having been as serviceable as possible to its inhabitants, leaps over a rocky precipice one hundred feet in height, and forms a junction with "Pierce Creek" which flows from the north, whence both, having fallen to such low estate, as if by common consent bury themselves in the oblivious waters of "Sylvan Lake."

Montville was settled at an early day, and its first inhabitants are all dead. Very few now living remember even who they were, and yet they lived and moved and had a being, while some occupied positions of honor and trust which required intelligence and business capacity.

Daniel Goodrich, Sen., bought out the Carding Machine (the property since owned by Mr. Mellen,) in 1805. He was by trade a carpenter and joiner, and one of the best mechanics in the country. He afterward built the Congregational Church in this village, and several private residences. Previous to this, however, and in 1816, John Stoyell had erected the saw mill, and in 1818, the grist mill. In 1800, a tavern was kept by Zadoc Cady, in a frame building, one-half of which (since somewhat remodeled,) is now occupied by Frank Williamson, and situate near the Spoke Factory. This house has the honor of being the oldest in Montville.

Walter Wood (an uncle of Charles P. Wood, Esq., of Auburn,) came to Montville about the year 1810, and in 1812 built the house on the corner, now owned by Russell Green; and in 1814, the "Hotel Building," since owned by Franklin Goodrich. He was a lawyer of extensive practice, dealing largely in real estate, and in his prime, retained in nearly every case upon the Calender of the Court of this County, a large portion of the cases involving the title to real estate. He was also at one time County Judge. He owned nearly the whole of Montville, the only exceptions being the Shove and Goodrich places, and the premises of Thomas Hunt, now "Indian Mound Cemetery," and Mrs. Jenkins' residence. Mr. Hunt's Tannery was located near the head of the Gulf, there being no highway there at that time, but farther to the east. Mr. Wood also in 1811, built the "store" since rejuvinated into the dwelling house of William Richmond. Isaac Wood, his son, was also a lawyer of fair abilities, but his father died soon after he began practice, leaving a large estate, from which Isaac received a competence, making his profession no longer desirable. Later in life, he was proprietor of the Montville Hotel.

Millard Fillmore commenced the study of the law in Judge Wood's office, having first served an apprenticeship in the Woolen Factory; while a student, he obtained his first notoriety by the delivery of a Fourth of July address in a grove upon the premises now owned by Wm. Walker, near the Gulf.

Some of his hearers then prophesied that he would "make his mark," and perhaps *become a Judge;* but he went far beyond their expectations, and doubtless his own brightest fancy never anticipated the high estate to which he was to arrive at last.

"There were giants in those days," in Montville. Jerry Sabin was celebrated for his great strength. Also his son of the same name, and the father of Walter W. and Lyman Sabin. He was a man of large stature, and possessed of immense strength, and according to report, could easily carry two barrels of cider at once, by placing two fingers in the bung-hole of each. Of course, he had considerable notoriety in the neighborhood as a very smart man; the current meaning of the word "smart" being well illustrated by one of his admirers in the following incident, which occurred in "Tune" Barhite's blacksmith shop.

It seems that the character of Rowland Day was being discussed, when some one present remarked, that Rowland was a "smart man." "Tune" was busy shoeing a horse: but amid the din of the shop overheard the above expression, let go of the foot of the horse, straightened himself up, gave the anvil a stroke with the hammer by way of emphasis, and exclaimed: "Wall, Rowland Day *is* a pretty smart man, but then, Jerry Sabin *can lick him in a minit!*"

Another illustration of *greatness*, although differing somewhat in tenor, is found in the *summing up* by Captain Crosby, of Captain Whipple and himself — both of whom were old New Hampshire men.

Captain Whipple being a wonderful self-conceited man who told all he knew, and generally a little more, as his neighbors thought, while Captain Crosby was always observing and commenting upon the traits of the former. Says Captain Crosby, "That Captain Whipple, is an *awful* smart man. He's a wonderful man. He knows most everything. *Captain Whipple and I do know everything.* In fact, *he* knows everything except *one* thing, and that *I* know. *That is, that he's a d——d fool!*"

A small foundry was built at an early day, by Messrs. Rogers & Skinner, on the bank of the creek in Moravia, near the premises of Henry Fox; but was shortly afterward removed to Montville, and located near the junction of the creeks below the Falls. At this establishment, plows were also manufactured. Another foundry was erected just below the "Big Dam" (Selover's); but with the dam, was carried away by a flood soon thereafter, and was never rebuilt.

Near "Parker's Grist Mill," were a Nail and Scythe Factory, and Trip Hammer, and on the opposite side of the creek, an Oil Mill.

There are now in Montville, about thirty-five dwelling houses, one grist mill, two saw mills, a spoke factory, planing and matching mill, one woolen factory, a blacksmith and cooper shop, and grocery store. These indicate an enterprising and industrious population.

SCHOOL HOUSES.

In addition to the above, and not the least in importance, Montville has a commodious and comfortable Brick School House, capable of seating from forty to sixty pupils, according to size and circumstances, and which has generally been well filled, for Montville, like the unsophisticated father of "Ginx's baby," is married, &c., though unlike him, if the innocent *thirteenth* should be born, no unseemly threats of drowning would be heard from *pater familias*, but in an almost incredible brief space of time, the urchin would be swinging his toes from a seat in the school house, puzzling his brains over " B-a Ba ; B-e Be ; B-i Bi ;" giving the boundaries of the United States, and otherwise preparing himself for Post Master, or some other lucrative office in the gift of the Government, or the people.

The "Old Red School House," which, like its builders, has disappeared, being too decrepit for further use, was situate across the road from its more pretentious successor. What a contrast in the two. The former was erected, apparently without the least idea of the "eternal fitness of things." The seats certainly never "fitted" any scholar of the hundreds who from time to time did penance upon them six hours per day. Imagine a narrow seat two feet high from the floor, for a boy of six or eight years of age to adapt himself to, meantime, to be thankful that he was born in a Christian land, where school houses were accessible, and education comparatively free to all. But it consumed the four months school term to educate his legs and back to an even balance, and get his little body properly adjusted to the seat, which consisted of a slab with the rounded side uppermost, smooth as glass from constant wear, with two long legs of the same material at each end. Balancing upon a tight-rope, or upon the top of a pole, at an angle of forty-five degrees, is secured by a rigid application of muscle, close study, and strict attention to the laws of attraction and gravitation. But to maintain an exact poise and position upon the rounded surface of those smooth slabs, with no support for the legs or back, was a feat which, with no knowledge of the sciences, boys could never with any certainty accomplish.

though it were often sought carefully and with tears. But there are pleasant memories associated with the old house, barring the *sittings*. Who of the pupils will ever forget the faces or the manners of the pedagogues who taught their young ideas how to shoot. Where are they all ? Like their pupils, scattered,—some dead and gone. But one here and there of those teachers remain. And yet, that was only twenty-five years ago.

Memory goes back to the first experiences of that school house, when Miss Sophia Wright (since Mrs. Cady,) successfully presided within its portals over fifty boisterous scholars, some of them almost men grown or was that the imagination of the "smallest boy." The Woods, of the "Hollow District," the Vosburgs, Berrys, Tidds, Pierces, Whites, Lockes, Sellecks, Mellendys, Oakleys, Coopers, Sabins, Chandlers, and others. And who will forget poor Lester Sabin,—kind and generous hearted when in his right mind, but a terror to the children when attacked with the terrible malady which finally terminated his life: but even at such times, perfectly harmless. And there was black Hiram Wheatly, very black outside, but good withal to the boys and girls, and with pockets generally supplied with candies ; he lived at Wood's Hotel.

Another of the teachers was Miss Rowe, a mere girl of sixteen or seventeen years, a teacher of the summer school, pleasant, laughing and merry, romping and singing when out of school. Her kind heart won the affections of her pupils, and all wept when school was dismissed and she bade them good bye.

One of the most efficient teachers was Miss Arminda Heald (since Mrs. M——), she had that peculiar firmness of character so desirable in that position: controlled the school, which was large and called theretofore unruly, with perfect ease apparently, taught her pupils thoroughly whatever studies were pursued. Under her teachings and discipline the school made marked progress, not only in books but in general conduct and appearance. She was employed for two or three terms to the satisfaction of the district. The pupils "didn't see why she could not teach longer;" but she was even then, if memory is not at fault, otherwise engaged. A most estimable woman and teacher, her old pupils have cause to remember her with gratitude.

Alfred Hawk taught one winter in the old school house. He was a well meaning man, but we have doubted, or did in those days, whether teaching was his peculiar forte. He was a hard worker, and intended to make his scholars improve. His manner was stern, his government oftimes severe, and his pupils seemed in constant fear of trouble. He was at heart a kind and conscientious man, and all that he did was meant for the good of the school. His voice was heavy and well adapted to the reading of tragic verse, in which he took great delight.

Franklin Goodrich had charge of the school during two winters, and was really one of the most thorough and practical of the common school teachers of his day.   He was perfectly familiar with the branches which he taught, and no sum was done or problem demonstrated, until it was fully ascertained whether it would *prove*.   He was a good disciplinarian, tho' at times his quick temper led him to extremes ; but a more conscientious man never conducted a school, and none more anxious to correct himself if he made a mistake in judgment or otherwise, in fact he disciplined himself as much as his pupils and apologized to the school when convinced by his own sense of justice that he was in error.   His pupils not slow to judge character, greatly respected the high moral principle by which he was actuated, and learned from him lessons of justice and honorable dealings which were never forgotten.

At a later period came other teachers, prominent among whom was Peter VanArsdale, who labored industriously and with marked effect.   He was always ready to "set a copy," "do a sum," or give an unruly boy a "good licken," at the shortest possible notice, and would go through either of said operations with *neatness and dispatch*.   A good hale, hearty teacher, he enjoyed a joke as well as any of his scholars.   But he was the master and they the pupils, *that* was well understood.

Oh, the old school house with its shattered frame and shabby outside, saw much of jollity, shy amusement, and comic scenes, intermingled with sorrow, pain and penalties within.   The old stove and desk, and even the uncomfortable, homely benches, from long acquaintance were respected as old friends, and

the *ferule, that always held a commanding position.*
Some of the teachers' whose experiences include the
"Old Red School House," reside hereabouts, but
the school companions seem scattered to the four
winds.   How changed to-day from those early days
of childhood.   To some the school of life below is
dismissed ; others are involved in the busy session,
unmindful of the approaching terminus, when with
opportunities improved or otherwise, the great lesson
of life well learned or neglected, the books shall be
closed, and the Great Master announce the final roll
call.   When that time comes who of us all can answer "Perfect?"

CHAPTER XXIII.

Plutarch records that at the building of Rome, "Romulus took a plow, to which he fastened a colter or plowshare of brass, and so yoked in an ox and cow, he himself holding the plow, did make round about the compass of the city a deep furrow." The ancients ploughed with an instrument which was but a crooked stick, with a sharp projection to stir the ground.

"The Rotterdam Plow,* used in England one hundred and fifty years ago, was a heavy, unwieldy implement, made entirely of wood except the colter or knife depending from the beam, to cut through roots and soil, and two shoes on the under side of the share, which were of wrought iron. But in 1870 James Small, a Scotchman, introduced a revolution

---

*Copied from an unknown author.

in husbandry by producing a cast iron mold-board. That was the beginning of a new era. Then there was no marked change until nearly fifty years afterward, when Robert Ransom of Ipswick patented an iron plowshare.

Until after the revolution the history of agricultural instruments in America was nearly the same as in England. Yankee inventativeness did not assert itself, till the Colonies threw off the yoke of the mother country. But as the United States struggled out of the gloom in which the war left, improvements in agriculture and manufactures began to occupy the keenest minds of the country. In 1797, Newhold of New Jersey, obtained a patent for some improvement in plow making, which was purchased by David Peacock, who afterward produced a plow having both mold-board and land-side of cast iron, with share of sharpened steel or wrought iron. So important were improvements in plows considered, that the versatile and philosophic Jefferson was greatly interested in them, and in 1798 he wrote a long, elaborate treatise on the construction of mold-boards. His theory was, that as at the bottom of the furrow is or ought to be flat, the breast of the mold-board, where it comes in direct contact with the soil, should be flat also. But the plow still continued in a very imperfect state. As late as 1820, according to the testimony of old farmers now living, the kind best known and most commonly used bore the name of the "Bull Plow." It was made principally of wood and iron, and ordinarily cost $40 to

$50; the mold-board was of wood fitted bunglingly to the irons, and the action of the rude implement "might be illustrated by holding a sharp pointed shovel back up and thrusting it through the ground." The share was of steel, and frequently had to be sharpened by a blacksmith at a charge of from ten to twenty shillings. The plowing season, especially when land was stony, proved very expensive to the husbandman.

In 1814 John Wood, a farmer of ample means and large intelligence, living in Cayuga County, New York, took out a patent for an improved plow.—From early childhood he had shown remarkable ingenuity in the construction of agricultural implements. When only a few years old he molded a little plow from metal, which he obtained by melting a pewter cup. Then cutting the buckles from a set of braces, he made a miniture harness with which he fastened the family cat to his tiny plow and endeavored to drive her about the flower garden. The good oldfashioned whipping he received for this mischief was such as to drive all desire for repeating the experiment out of his juvenile head. But when he grew to manhood, the ruling passion asserted itself, and for years the improvement of the plow was his darling project. His chief desire was to invent a new mold-board, which from its form should meet the least resistence from the soil, and which could be made with share and standard entirely of cast iron. To hit upon the exact shape for the mold-board, he whittled away, day after day, until his neighbors, who thought him mad upon the subject, gave him the sobriquet of the "Whittling Yankee." His custom was to take a large oblong potato and cut it till he obtained what he fancied was the exact curve.

The plow which he patented in 1814 he found defective, and destroying his first patterns he set to work again. In 1819 he took out a patent for his perfect plow. It covered five distinct improvements. 1st. The new shape of the mold-board to raise and turn the soil with the least resistance. 2d. The cast iron standard, which is a projection of the mold-board, connecting it with the beam. 3d. The cast iron edge or share, and the manner of catching it to the upper side of the mold-board. 4th. The fastening of the handles to the land-side and mold-board by notches or loops, cast with the land-side and mold-board respectively. 5th. The manner of connecting the land-side and mold-board without the aid of screw bolts. He obtained his patent for a period of fourteen years, and his invention received the name of the "Cast Iron Plow," from the entire abandonment of wrought iron in its construction. He immediately began to manufacture his plows and introduce them to the farmers in his neighborhood.

The difficulties which he now encountered would have daunted any man without extraordinary perseverence and a firm belief in the estimable benefit to agriculture sure to result from his invention. He was obliged to manufacture all the patterns, and to have the plow cast under the disadvantages usual with new machines.   The nearest furnace was thirty miles from his home, and baffled by obstacles which unskillful and disobliging workmen threw in his way, he visited it day after day, directing the making of his patterns, standing by the furnaces while the metal was melting, and after, with his own hands aiding in the casting.

When at length samples of his plow were ready for use, he met with another difficulty in the unwillingness of farmers to accept them.   "What," they cried in contempt, "a plow made of pot metal! You might as well attempt to turn up the earth with a glass plowshare.   It would hardly be more brittle." One day he induced one of his most sceptical neighbors to make a public trial of the plow.   A large concourse gathered to see how it would work.   The field selected for the test was thickly strewn with stones, many of them firmly imbedded in the soil and jutting up from the surface.   All predicted that the plow would break at the outset.   To their astonishment, and Wood's satisfaction, it went around the field, running easily and smoothly, and turning up the most perfect furrow which had ever been seen. The small stones against which the farmer maliciously guided it to test the "brittle" metal, moved out of the way as if they were grains of sand, and it slid around the immovable rocks as if they were icebergs.   Incensed at the non-fulfillment of his prophecy, the farmer finally drove the plow with all force upon a large boulder, and found to his amazement that it was uninjured by the collision.

It proved a day of triumph to Jethro Wood, and from that time he heard few taunts about the "pot-metal." It was soon discovered that his plough turned up the soil with so much ease that two horses could do the work for which a yoke of oxen and a span of horses had sometimes been insufficient before; that it made a better furrow, and that it could be bought for seven or eight dollars. No more running to the blacksmith either to have it sharpened. It was proved a thorough success. Thomas Jefferson, from his retirement at Monticello, wrote Wood a letter of congratulation, and although his theory of the construction of mold-boards had differed entirely from the inventors, gave him most hearty appreciation to the merits of the new plow.

During the same year, Jethro Wood sent one of his plows to Alexander I, Emperor of Russia, and the peculiar circumstances attending the gift and its reception formed a large part of the newspaper gossip of the day. Wood, though a man of cultivation intellectually as well as agriculturally, was not familiar with French, which was then as now the diplomatic language. So he requested his personal friend, Dr. Samuel Mitchell, President of the New York Society of Natural History and Sciences, to write a letter in French to accompany the gift. The autocrat of all the Russias received the plow and the letter, and sent back a diamond ring, which the newspapers declared to be worth $7,000. to $15,000. in token of his appreciation. By some indirection, the ring was not delivered to the donor of the plow.

but to the writer of the letter, and Dr. Mitchell instantly appropriated it to his own use. Wood appealed to the Russian Minister at Washington, for redress. The Minister sent to his Emperor, and Alexander replied that it was intended for the inventor of the plow. Armed with his authority, Wood again demanded the ring of Mitchell. But there were no steamships or telegraphs in those days, and Mitchell declared that in the long interval in which they had been waiting to hear from Russia, he had given it to the cause of the Greeks who were then rising to throw off the yoke of their Turkish oppressors. A newspaper of the time calls Mitchell's course "an ingenious mode of quartering on the enemy," and the inventor's friends seem to have believed that the ring had been privately sold for his benefit. At all events, it never came to light again, and Wood, a peaceful man, a Quaker by profession, did not push the matter further. In truth, he had little time to devote to side issues. His patterns had cost him some thousands of dollars. For the past year or two, he had given away his plows to the farmers in all directions, that their value might be thoroughly tested. Now, when he began to look around for some benefit to accrue to himself, he found the plow makers everywhere manufacturing them in defiance of his rights as patentee and inventor. In fruitless suits and vain struggles against the inefficacy of the law, the fourteen years for which the first patent was granted expired. But in 1833, he succeeded in getting a renewal for fourteen years more. In the mean time, however, he had spent a large private fortune, and became heavily involved. His invention had brought him literally nothing but a plentiful crop of lawsuits, which seemed to spring up in every furrow his plow had traced.

In 1834, he died pecuniarily ruined. Notwithstanding all his disappointments, his life was singularly bright and genial. His serene, equitable disposition was proof against all trials. Many persons yet living remember him as one whose beautiful, sunny nature no adversity could cloud, and whose good, loving philanthropy no ill treatment could sour. In the event of reaping the deserved reward for his invention, he had resolved to establish a fund for a system of public schools in the State of New York, and he seemed to feel as much disappointed at the failure of this scheme as at his own losses. He always wore the garb and manners of the community of Friends, was of benignant and winning presence, courtly grace of manner, and a tender, affectionate heart.

After his death his son Benjamin, who received the invention as a legacy, continued his efforts to wrest justice from the unwilling hands of the law. Nearly all his father's failures had proceeded from the inadequacy of the patent laws, which were almost worthless to protect the rights of the inventor.— Even now a patent is worth little until it has been fought through the Supreme Court of the United States. In those days so many obstacles were thrown in the way of inventors, and the combinations against them were so formidable, that Eli Whitney, in trying to establish his right to the Cotton Gin in a Georgia Court, while his machine was doubling and trebling the value of lands through the State, had this experience, which is given in his own words: "I had great difficulty in proving the machine had been used in Georgia, although at the same moment there were three separate sets of this machinery in motion within fifty yards of the building in which the court set, and all so near that the rattling of the wheels was distinctly heard on the steps of the Court House."

Similar difficulties had met Jethro Wood in his suits, so his son resolved to strike at the root of the evil, by securing a reform of the laws. He accordingly went to Washington, where he remained thro' several seasons, always working to this end. Clay, Webster, and John Quincy Adams, all of whom had known Jethro Wood and his invention, aided his son powerfully with their votes and counsel, and he succeeded in securing several important changes in the patent laws. Then he returned to New York, and commenced suit to resist encroachments on his rights, and the wholesale manufacture of his plow by those who refused to pay the premium to the inventor.— The "Cast Iron Plow" was now used all over the country, and formidable combinations united their capital and influence against Benjamin Wood.

William H. Seward, then practicing law at Auburn, N. Y., was retained as Wood's counsel, and the plow makers engaged all the talent they could muster to oppose him.   Heretofore it had never been contradicted that Jethro Wood was the originator of the plow in use; but now the right to the invention was denied, and it was alleged that his improvements had been forestalled by other makers.   Again and again the case was adjourned, and Europe and America were ransacked for specimens of the different plows which were declared to include his patent. Wood also obtained from England samples of the plows of James Small and Robert Ransom.   He searched New Jersey to find the Peacock plow, which was said to have a cast iron mold-board, of exactly similar shape to his father's.   Everywhere in that State he found "Wood's Plow" in use, but he could hear nothing of the one he sought.   At length riding near a farm house he discovered one of the old "Newbold-Peacock Plows" lying under a fence, dilapidated and rust eaten.   "We don't use it any more," the farmer replied to his inquiries.— "We've got one a good deal better."   Will you sell this? asked Wood.   "Well, yes," and Wood, glad to get it at almost any price, paid the keen farmer, —who took advantage of his evident anxiety—two or three times the price of a new plow, and added the old one to his specimens.

This motley collection of implements was brought into court and exhibited to the Judges.   At last, after the case had dragged its slow length along through many terms, and the plaintiff was nearly worn out with the law's delay, the time for final trial and decision arrived.

The combination of plow makers feared that the case would go in Wood's favor, and made every effort to keep him out of Court, that he might lose it by default. During his long entanglement in the law, he had contracted many debts, and one of his opponents had managed to purchase several of these accounts.

Just before the case was to be heard for the last time, this worthy plow manufacturer, attended by a sheriff, and armed with a warrant to arrest Wood for debt, appeared at the front door of his house. Fortunately, Wood had a few moments warning, and slipped out at the back door. He made his way under cover of approaching darkness to the house of a friendly neighbor. There he procured a horse and started for Albany, 150 miles distant, hearing every moment in fancy, the clattering of hoofs at his heels. As if fortune could not be sufficiently ill-natured, his horse proved vicious and unmanageable, and thrice in the tedious journey, threw his rider from his saddle upon the frozen earth, so injuring him that he was barely able to go on.

On arriving at Albany, he found himself not a moment too soon. The case had an immediate hearing, and after three days trial, the Circuit Court decided unequivocally, that the plow now in general use over the country was unlike any other which had been produced; that the improvements which rendered it so effective were due to Jethro Wood, and that all manufacturers must pay his heirs for the privilege of making it.

This was a great triumph, but it was now the late autumn of 1845, and the last grant of the patent had little more than a year to run. Wood again repaired to Washington to apply for a new extension, but the excitement of so long a contest had been too much for him. Just as he had commenced his efforts, they were forever ended. While talking with one of his friends, he suddenly fell dead from heart disease, and the patent expired without renewal. The last male heir to the invention was no more. On settling the estate, it was found that while not a vestige remained of the large fortune owned by Jethro Wood when he began his career, less than five hundred and fifty dollars had ever been received from his invention.

The after history of the case is a brief one. Four daughters of Jethro Wood alone remained to represent the family. In the winter of 1848, the two younger sisters went to Washington to petition Congress that a bill might be passed for their relief, in view of the inestimable services of their father to the agricultural interests of the country. Webster declared that he regarded their father as a "public benefactor," and gave them his most efficient aid. Clay warmly espoused their cause, and the venerable John Quincy Adams, with his trembling hand then so enfeebled by age that he rarely used the pen, wrote them kind notes heartily sympathizing with them.

On one memorable day while they were in the House gallery, Mr. Adams at his desk on the floor wrote them briefly in relation to their case. A few minutes later he was struck with the fatal attack under which he exclaimed,—"This is the last of earth; I am content;" and was borne dying to the Speaker's room. The tremulous lines, the last his hand ever traced, were found on his desk and delivered to Miss Wood.

A bill providing that in these four heirs should rest for seven years the exclusive right of making and vending the improvements in the construction of the cast iron plow; and that twenty-five cents on each plow might be exacted from all who manufactured it, passing the Senate unanimously. But Washington already swarmed with plow manufacturers. The city of Pittsburgh alone sent five to look after their interests. Money was freely used, and the members of the House Committee who were to report on the bill, were assured that during the twenty-eight years of the patent, Wood's family had reaped immense wealth, and wished to keep up a monopoly. The two quiet ladies, fresh from the retirement of a Quaker home where they had learned little of the world, were even accused of attempting to secure its extension through bribery. It was the wolf charging the lamb with roiling the water. So ignorant were they of such means that though the chairman of the committee plainly told the younger lady in a few words of private conversation, that a very few thousand dollars would give her a favorable verdict, she did not understand the suggestion

30

till after an unfavorable report was presented, and the bill killed in the House.

When they were about to leave Washington, some friendly members of Congress advised them to deposit the valuable documents which had been used in their suit, including the letter from Thomas Jefferson to Jethro Wood, in the archives of the House, where they could only be withdrawn on the motion of some member. They did so, and left them for some years uncalled for. When at last they applied for them they could not be found ; nor from that time to the present has any trace of them been discovered by any of the family. Thus perished the last vestige of proof relating to this ill-fated invention. A few public attempts were made in later years to obtain redress, but Jethro Wood's contemporaries and friends, public and private, were nearly all gone. The "Cast Iron Plow" was everywhere in use, but the name of the inventor was forgotten. Even the New American Cyclopedia, in its history of the plow, does not mention it. But ancient wooden plows unused and falling to decay upon thousands of American farms, yet remain to show by contrast the exceeding service which Jethro Wood performed for the country. His invention is in universal use through the length and breadth of the land, but his few surviving heirs are living lives of poverty and struggle.

The United States Agricultural Report for 1866, says truly : "Although Wood was one of the greatest benefactors to mankind by this admirable invention, he never received for all his thought, anxiety and expense, a sum of money sufficient to defray the expenses of his decent burial."

Mechanical inventions are our national shame.—Jethro Wood served his country more effectually than many a man to whom we have given wealth and fame, and monument of enduring brass.

"Wood's Patent Plow" was first manufactured in Moravia, near the Selover Mills, by Rogers & Skinner, under a written agreement, a copy of which is here given:

"This agreement, between Jethro Wood of the first part, and Elias Rogers and Isaac W. Skinner of the other part, witnesseth. That whereas Letters Patent were issued to said Jethro, under the seal of the United States, for an improvement in the plough, dated 1st of July 1814. And whereas other Letters Patent were also issued to said Jethro, under the seal as aforesaid, for other new and useful improvements in the plough, dated 1st of September 1812; and whereas the said Elias Rogers and Isaac W. Skinner, are desirous of obtaining under conditions herein contained, certain rights and privileges under said patents.

Now Therefore, it is agreed by the said Elias Rogers and Isaac W. Skinner, that they will not, during the continuance of said Wood's patents, or either of them, make or sell, or authorize to be made or sold, any Ploughs or Plough Castings, or rights in regard to Ploughs, containing the improvements or any parts thereof specified in said Wood's Letters Patents, or

either of them, except under and by authority of this
instrument, and on the following conditions. And it is
further agreed by said Elias Rogers and Isaac W.
Skinner, that they will, during the continuance of
said Wood's last Letters Patents, use every reasonable exertions to procure men in different parts of
the country to make and vend Ploughs under said
Jethro's patent, by virtue of a license signed by said
Jethro Wood.   *   *   *   *   *   *   *
And said Jethro doth further agree that one equal
half part of all monies received by him or his representatives, as premiums on Ploughs or Plough Castings by virtue of said contract, shall be by him or
them paid over to said Elias Rogers, and Isaac W.
Skinner, and to that end the said Jethro or his representatives, will meet the said Elias Rogers and Isaac
W. Skinner at the house now owned by Platt Titus, in
Troy, or some other place to be agreed upon, the first
Monday in May in each year, during the continuance
of said Wood's Letters Patent, and will render unto
them a just and true account in writing of every
Plough sold by him or any person acting under him,
up to the first day of January then preceding, and
will then and there pay over to said Rogers & Skinner, or to their order, one equal half part of all monies that may have been received by the said Jethro
or his representatives ; and in case said Jethro shall
fraudulently withhold rendering such account, and
paying over as above provided, then he will forthwith pay to said Elias Rogers and Isaac W. Skin-

ner one thousand dollars as stated damages, expressly agreed on by the parties hereto.

Dated this 7th day of August, 1823.

JETHRO WOOD.   [SEAL]
ELIAS ROGERS.   [SEAL]
I. W. SKINNER.   [SEAL]

In the presence of B. H. WOOD."

Annexed to the foregoing agreement is a Deed over the signature and seal of Jethro Wood. dated August 7th, 1823, giving Elias Rogers and Isaac W. Skinner the right to make, use and vend "Wood's Patent Plough" in the States of New York, Pennsylvania, and elsewhere; Mr. Wood agreeing to furnish "at some furnace not more distant than the town of Sempronius in the State of New York, a set of patterns for said improved Plough."

Messrs Rogers & Skinner manufactured a large number of plows, and sold the same in the States above named.

Moravia has the honor of being the headquarters for the manufacture of the first Cast Iron Plow manufactured in the United States.

CHAPTER XXIV.

It was not intended that these Sketches should "smell of the shop whence they were turned out." One's business is apt to become a hobby which he rides into the face of every one he meets. The bar however, from their well known innate modesty and delicacy of public notice, may not be subject to this general accusation.

Since the greater portion of this volume was written, it has been suggested by authority which it would be unreasonable to doubt, much less to contradict, that without at least brief reference to the bench and bar of the town, this work would in an historical point of view, be incomplete.

Of the former, Walter Wood once held the office of Judge of this county.

The offices of Justices of the Peace were filled formerly by appointment by the Governor, and latterly by election. Doubtless some inaccuracies have crept into this portion of this chapter, as the old records are not very reliable or complete. Of the latter, difficulty has been experienced in ascertaining the history and residences of several of whom it would be interesting to have a true and full history, but from these brief sketches the future historian of this town may be enabled to form a basis for a complete and impartial work.

THE BENCH.

Justices of the Peace in and for the old town of Sempronius, so far as their names can be ascertained from the old records, are given below:

1798—John Stoyell, Jacob T. DeWitt.

1799— "   "   "   "

1800— "   "   "   "

1801— "   "   "   "

1802—John Stoyell, Jacob T. DeWitt, Charles Kellogg.

1803—John Stoyell, Jacob T. DeWitt, Charles Kellogg.

1804—Abel Sabin, Jacob T. DeWitt, Charles Kellogg.

1805—Abel Sabin, Jacob T. DeWitt, Charles Kellogg.

1806—Seth Burgess, Cyrus Powers, Aaron Stark, Charles Kellogg.

1807—Charles Kellogg, Seth Burgess, Levi H. Goodrich, Gershom Morse, Aaron Stark, Cyrus Powers.

1808—Charles Kellogg, Levi H. Goodrich, Aaron Stark, Cyrus Powers, Gershom Morse, William Satterlee.

1809—Gershom Morse, Levi H. Goodrich, William Saterlee.

1810—Cyrus Powers, Nathaniel Fillmore, Zadoc

Rhoads, Seth Burgess, Gershom Morse, William Satterlee.

1811—Nathaniel Fillmore, Zadoc Rhoads, Seth Burgess, Cyrus Powers, Gershom Morse.

1812—Gershom Morse, Zadoc Rhoads, Nathaniel Fillmore, William Satterlee.

1813—Nathaniel Fillmore, Zadoc Rhoads, Seth Burgess, Cyrus Powers, Gershom Morse.

1814—Same as 1813.

1815—William Satterlee, Cyrus Powers, Nathaniel Fillmore, Thadeus Histed.

1816—William Satterlee, Ebenezer Smith, Zadoc Rhoads, Nathaniel Fillmore, Gershom Morse, Cyrus Powers.

1817—Same as in 1816.

1818—Charles Kellogg, Gershom Morse, Zadoc Rhoads, Nathaniel Fillmore, Ebenezer Smith.

1819—Same as 1818.

1820—William Satterlee, Zadoc Rhoads, Charles Kellogg, Ebenezer Smith, Jonathan Hussey.

1821—Ebenezer Smith, Asaph Stow, Gershom Morse, Cyrus Powers, George H. Brinkerhoff.

1822—Bliss Forbush, Matthias Lane, Gershom Morse, Asaph Stow, George H. Brinkerhoff.

1823—Same as 1822.

1824—Same as year previous.

1825—Same as year previous.

1826—Same as year previous.

1827—Same as year previous.

1828—Same as above.

31

1829—Asaph Stow, Matthias Lane, Jonathan Hussey.

1830—John Rooks.

1831—George H. Brinkerhoff.

1832—Ebenezer Smith.

Gershom Morse held the office for twenty-one years, and did a vast amount of civil and criminal business, generally holding his courts at Cady's Tavern.

Cases were often commenced in Justice's Court, and upon joining of issue, "left out" by consent of parties to arbitrators, who generally managed by "hook or by crook" to satisfy all concerned. This is contrary to the experience of arbitrators in these latter days, for they seldom, however good their intentions, have the luck to please either party.—But times have changed. Then, arbitrations were generally had at Cady's Tavern, where the surroundings were most favorable, and the elements of a satisfactory settlement generally forthcoming in the flowing bowl. This subdued the savage breast and moistened the eyes of the most hostile forces. "Yer Honors," counsel, jurors, officers and attendants, thirsted for an amicable reconciliation, and several drinks all around. Routs and riots might ensue, but for the nonce at least, in the words of Sergeant Buzfuz, "All was confidence and reliance."

The high and the low, the rich and the poor, sipped from the same cup and joined in the universal satisfaction,

> For all men by whiskey, are brought to a level,
> Where each is to all, good lord and good devil.

While Isaac Wood and H. B. Hewitt were doing business as merchants in Montville, they had considerable experience in litigation ; among others they brought an action in Justices Court against Wm. Smith for damages sustained in a horse trade, and Mr Smith in retaliation, sued them upon some trade in grain, &c. Both cases were finally left to arbitrators, of whom Squire Morse was one. By agreement the horse case was tried one day and the and the grain case the next. The evidence was taken by the arbitrators in full, in both cases, and in the latter concluded in the evening, when upon retiring from the "long room" in Cady's Tavern, where the trial was had, Squire Morse touched Mr Hussey upon the shoulder and innocently inquired : "Hussey, Oh–Ah–what became of that hoss?"

It is said that Mr. Morse once asked the following question : "Mr. Crippen, what is it worth by the hundred to saw lumber, where you saw at the halves?"

Scene in Court. Justice Morse presiding.

Court.—Mr. Stocking, what is David Churchell's given name?

Mr. Stocking.—David Churchell, you old fool you.

Court.—No contempt of court, Mr. Stocking, no contempt of court.

Mr. Stocking.—Oh, no, course not, you old fool you."

Squire Morse upon one occasion decided a case which was before him, adversely to John Keeler, one of the parties, who never forgave him, and endeavored to harrass and ridicule him whenever opportunity offered. Mr. Morse was one day holding Court, the room being filled as usual with attendants, among whom was Mr. Keeler, pretty "blue," who at intervals ejaculated, directing his remarks to the Court, "You old pumpkin head." After several such interruptions, "the Court knew herself," and told Mr. Keeler squarely that the Court would commit him. Keeler becoming frightened, duly apologised, meanwhile edging along to the door, upon reaching which, he darted out, exclaiming, "Well you are an old pumpkin head anyhow," and went on his way rejoicing, believing himself beyond the jurisdiction of the Court.

Another story is told of the early experiences of the Squire. Immediately after he received his appointment and before he had sworn in, he had some doubts as to his competency especially in performing the marriage ceremony, which devolved very often upon the magistrate, in the absence of local preachers. Therefore to test his own capabilities in that line, he went out into the grove near his house for practice. After going out alone several times, he invited his wife to go along and witness the ceremony. Upon arriving at the chosen place, where were two young trees standing close together, he began: "Mr. Hickory and Miss Whitewood join hands. Mr. Hickory you take Miss Whitewood as your wife do you?" Answer (sotto voice by the Squire,) "I do." "Miss Whitewood do you do the same by Mr. Hickory?" Answer by the Squire, "I do."   "Then in the name of Squire Morse, Justice of the Peace of the County of Cayuga, I call you man and wife, according to the Constitution of the United States.   Mrs. Morse would you qualify?"

Jerry Sabins used to claim that he overheard this marriage ceremony, as he was returning home through the grove, but it was conjectured that the whole thing was a fiction, but he told the story so often in the presence of the Squire that finally when Jerry began the story the Squire would immediately ask him, "what he would have to drink?" which had the effect to direct the attention of Jerry to the more interesting matter, and the story would be left untold.

In 1833, when the Town of Sempronius was divided, John Rooks, Mathias Lane, George H. Brinkerhoof and Ebenezer Smith were acting Justices. At the first Town Meeting held for the Town of Moravia, ballots were cast for Justices of the Peace which resulted as follows:

William VanOrder, 204; Andrew Dibble, 203; Jonathan Hussey, 174; Leonard O. Aiken, 133; Thomas Morey, 109; Thomas Hill, 105. The first three named being elected.

Justices were elected thereafter as follows:

1834—Beriah Curtis.	1835—Samuel E. Day.
1836—Ebenezer Smith.	1837—William VanOrder.
1838—Beriah Curtis.	1839—Samuel E. Day.
1840—Rufus W. Close.	1841—William VanOrder.
1842—Wm. B. Stoddard.	1843—Samuel E. Day.
1844—Walter W. Sabin. Rufus W. Close.	

1845—Walter W. Sabin.   1846—Daniel M. Brown.
1847—Samuel E. Day.   1848—William H. Price.
1849—Franklin Goodrich. 1850—Alfred Lester.
1851—Thomas Loomis.   1852—William H. Price.
1853—Franklin Goodrich, Silas D. Taber.
1854—Alfred Lester, Samuel E. Day.
1855—Bradford Shirley. 1856—Jeremiah Mellen.
1857—Samuel E. Day.   1858—John L. Parker.
1859—Dwight Lee.
1860—Terry Everson, Alfred Lester.
1861—John M. Stoddard.
1862—John L. Parker.   1863—Alfred Lester.
1864—Terry Everson.
1865—Charles E. Parker, John M. Stoddard.
1866—John L. Parker.
1867—William Wade, Loyall Stoyell.
1868—Lauren Townsend.
1869—James A. Wright, Seth R. Webb.
1870—Lorenzo D. Sayles. 1871—Rowland D. Wade.
1872—Seth R. Webb.   1873—Franklin Goodrich.

Samuel E. Day held the office for nineteen years. He became perfectly familiar with the practice and jurisdictional questions of this Court, presided with dignity and firmness, and made his decisions with fairness, and in accordance with his own views of what was right and just upon the testimony in the case before him. He held that the law was founded on common sense, and acted accordingly, and but few appeals to a higher Court were taken from his decisions.

William Van Order held the office for twelve years.

Alfred Lester eleven, and John L. Parker for twelve years. Several of the others were elected for two terms. While the town has not in all cases elected its most capable men to this office, by reason of the unavailability of such, or their unwillingness to accept office, or strength of party ties, or personal prejudice, yet it has been as fairly represented in this particular, as in other town offices, in the gift of the people.

THE BAR—LEONARD O. AIKEN.

Mr. Aiken was born at Antrim, New Hampshire, September 5th, 1805. His parents moved to the town of Locke in 1806. After receiving other education, he studied law one year with Jonathan Hussey, and afterward entered the law office of Judge Reed, in Homer, N. Y. He was admitted to practice in the Court of Common Pleas in 1828, and shortly thereafter to the Supreme Court at a General Term held at Utica. Of those admitted at that time with Mr. Aiken, were Henry R. Selden and Preston King. His first law partner was Judge Reed, of Homer, N. Y., with whom he established an office at that place, and where he had his first case in 1830, which is reported in 5th Wendall, he appearing for the defendant, and Freeborn G. Jewett, of Skaneateles, for the plaintiff. Judgment was entered for the plaintiff, and notice of the taxation of costs at Utica, served upon defendant's attorney. Upon the day noticed for the taxation, the defendant who was sued as administrator, by his attorney, claimed that he was not liable for costs. The Clerk so held and declined to tax them, whereupon a motion was made by the plaintiff's attorney for a rule or order directing the Clerk to tax his costs. The only point upon the argument of the motion was whether the defendant as administrator was liable for the plaintiff's costs. After an elaborate discussion by counsel the Court held "that as it did not appear that the claim upon which the action was brought, was presented for payment six months after the notice of the administrator requiring all persons having claims against the deceased to present them, and that the payment of such claim was unreasonably neglected or refused, or that defendant refused to refer his claim, the plaintiff was not entitled to recover his costs in the action."

Mr. Aiken first came to Moravia in August, 1831, and commenced business alone, but afterward formed a co-partnership with   a grandson of Judge Wood. He was also a partner with N. T. Stephens, (who studied law with him) until the latter went to California in 1850. After this S. Edwin Day entered his office as a student, and upon being admitted to practice, formed a co-partnership with him, which continued until 1869.

E. M. Ellis was also with him for nearly two years thereafter. Several other young men in addition to the above named, have studied law in his office, to wit: George Cutler, who is now practicing in Pennsylvania; Mr. Branch, in Michigan; Samuel Alcox, in Wisconsin; Clinton Fitch, who removed to the West, and has since died.

When Mr. Aiken first commenced business in Moravia, Jonathan Hussey was the leading lawyer in this part of the country, but he soon became incapacitated for business and Mr. Aiken was for several years the only lawyer in town. His opponents in those days were generally Seward and Beardsley, and John I. Porter, of Auburn, and Jewett and Sanford of Skaneateles, all of whom came to Moravia to try causes. From 1842 to 1846, Jared Smith, a lawyer of fine legal ability, was a resident of this town. He died during the latter year.

In 1835 an action was brought in Supreme Court by one Samuel Baker as Administrator, &c., of David Bradley deceased, against "The Owl Creek Company," composed of Elias Rogers, Jonathan Hussey, Isaac Wood and Christopher Morgan.

The action was brought to set aside a Sheriff's Deed of premises bid off by the defendants several years previous, on the ground of fraud in the sale. The premises in question consisted of about 300 acres, situate in East Lansing, Tompkins County, N. Y. The plaintiffs attorney was Benjamin Johnson. Jonathan Hussey appearing as the attorney for the defendants, with Mr. Aiken and David Woodcock as counsel. A large amount of testimony was taken in the case before an Examiner in Chancery, at the hotel in East Lansing. The parties and their counsel occupied a week at that place taking testimony. During the examination of the widow of David Beardsley, deceased, and while she was giving a history of all the proceedings at the time of the Sheriffs' Sale of the premises, Isaac Wood, had been sitting in his chair apparently sound asleep. As she concluded her statement the plaintiffs attorney remarked, "Just twenty years since this tragedy was enacted." At that moment Mr. Wood awoke with a grunt, exclaiming, "Yes, just twenty years between the tragedy and the farce."

This case was argued at Binghamton, N. Y., before Judge Monell, by Hon. John Collyer, for defendants, and a decision rendered in their favor.

Soon afterward an action was brought by "The Bank of Ithaca" against Gilbert Honeywell, to set aside a Sheriff's Deed of premises, purchased by Mr. Honeywell, of about 200 acres lying south of Summerhill Village. The attorneys for plaintiff were Messrs. Bruyn & Dana, of Ithaca, and Mr. Aiken and and John I. Porter, of Auburn, were retained for the defendant. The testimony in this case was taken before Thomas Y. How, Esq., of Auburn, at Barber's Tavern in Summerhill. This examination lasted for several days. Mr. Bruyn was a very nervous, but gentlemanly man, and as they were busily engaged one evening upon this examination, by the aid of tallow candles, which at their best threw but little light upon the transactions in question, Mr. Bruyn suddenly jumped up, looked under the table upon which they were writing, remarking "that a dog (which had been quietly resting himself unmindful of laws or lawyers) had bitten his toe." The dog was accordingly turned out of doors without a hearing, and the suit went on for half an hour, when again Mr. Bruyn jumped up as before and looked under the table exclaiming, "d——n that dog, he has bitten me again." The poor dog however, was half a mile away at his home, beside the fire-place, enjoying the sweet and undisturbed repose of innocence, which comes only to dogs of good moral characters, and who are worthy of confidence in any Court of Justice.

The suit in question was never finished, for after a weeks experience at litigation in Summerhill, all parties were satisfied, and compromised.

Mr. Aiken was also the attorney for the plaintiff in an action in Supreme Court in which Wm. Keeler was plaintiff and Dudley Loomis defendant, concerning the right to the use of the water of Mill Creek; George Rathbun, Esq., was counsel with Mr. Aiken for plaintiff. B. D. Noxen, of Syracuse, was counsel with Paris G. Clark, the defendant's attorney. A large amount of testimony was taken in the case, before Judge Maynard. The case was finally settled without arriving at any decision of the legal points involved.

Mr. Aiken's practice has been to a great extent connected with real property in this and adjoining towns. Very many of the farms were held by defective titles, or merely by possession, and hence many litigations arose concerning them, which involved intricate and interesting questions of law and arduous labor. He has been in practice in this town for forty-three years, during which time he has obtained a fair competence, and held several offices of trust. His old associates are nearly all gone.

JOHN L. PARKER.

Mr. Parker was born March 25th, 1825, received his education chiefly at the Moravia Institute, read law in the office of Jared M. Smith, a practitioner in this town, and after his removal, with L. O. Aiken, Esq., and was admitted to the Bar on July 4th, 1848, and has continued in practice since that date. He held the office of Justice of the Peace for twelve years, was appointed Superintendent of Common Schools, for the years 1851 and 1852, was elected President of the Village in 1870. In 1863 he received the appointment of Engrossing Clerk in the Assembly, which office he also held the following year. He was Member of Assembly in 1865 and 1866, was appointed Agent of United States Pension Department of the Special Service Division, in 1873, which office he still holds. In politics he is a Republican.

S. EDWIN DAY.

Mr. Day was born in this town, January 20th, 1840; was educated at the Moravia Institute, studied the law in the office of L. O. Aiken, Esq., and was admitted to practice at Auburn, on June 6th, 1861. He soon went into the office of Mr. Aiken, and afterward formed a co-partnership with him, which continued until 1869, since which time Mr. Day has been in practice alone. He has held the office of Supervisor for the years 1869, 1872 and 1873, running largely ahead of his ticket, which was otherwise generally defeated. He was elected President of the Village in 1868. Politically he is a Democrat and received the nomination of his party for District Attorney of this county in 1868.

ROWLAND D. WADE.

Mr. Wade was born Feb. 21st, 1840, and graduated at the Moravia Institute. He entered the Army and remained in service until July 22d. 1862, and upon his return home, commenced the study of law with John T. Pingree, Esq., of Auburn, N. Y. He was admitted to the Bar at Rochester, N. Y., on June 7th, 1867. In 1868 he formed a co-partnership with E. E. Brown, Esq., which continued until the removal of Mr. Brown to Nebraska, in 1869. Although a Democrat, he was elected Justice of the Peace in 1871, being the only candidate who was elected, upon his ticket.

WING T. PARKER.

The above named is the son of John L. Parker, and was born December 13th, 1849. He also received his education at the Moravia Institute. He studied law with his father, and was admitted to the Bar at Buffalo, N. Y., on June 9th, 1871. He afterward engaged in business for a year with L. O. Aiken, Esq. Since which time he has formed a co-partnership with his father, under the firm name of J. L. & W. T. Parker. He is a Republican.

MORTIMER V. AUSTIN.

He was educated in Moravia, and commenced reading law in the office of E. E. Brown, in 1865. He removed to Auburn in September, 1867, and entered the law office of Messrs. Cox & Avery, and was admitted to the Bar at Rochester, N. Y., in June, 1868.

He remained in the office of Messrs. Cox & Avery as chief clerk until 1869, when he opened an office and commenced business for himself. He was admitted to practice in the United States District Court, at Buffalo, in August, 1873.

ERASTUS E. BROWN.

He studied law in the office of Messrs. Wright & Pomeroy, in Auburn, N. Y. Was admitted to the Bar, and came to Moravia in 1861, where he commenced the practice of law, in which he continued until 1868, when he formed a co-partnership with R. D. Wade, which was dissolved by the removal of Mr. Brown in 1869 to Nebraska City, of which he has since been elected Mayor, and which office he still holds.

HULL GREENFIELD.

The above named was educated at Moravia Institute, studied law with S. Edwin Day, and was admitted to practice at Syracuse in November, 1871. Soon after this he removed to the City of New York where he obtained a position as clerk with the well-known law firm of Weed & Parsons, where he still remains.

JAMES A. WRIGHT.

He was born May 4th, 1838 ; was educated at the Moravia Institute ; studied law with E. E. Brown, Esq., and afterward with Wright & Waters, of Cortland, N. Y. Was admitted to the practice of law at Binghamton, N. Y., June 6th, 1864 ; removed to Waverly, N. Y., where he remained until April, 1868, when he returned to Moravia, and formed a co-partnership with J. L. Parker, Esq., which continued until 1870, since which time he has been in practice alone. He has held the office of Justice of the Peace since 1870. Politically he is a Republican.

The first lawyer of any notoriety in this town was Jonathan Hussey. The writer however has not been able to obtain sufficient facts concerning him for a biography. It is said that he had a very large and lucrative practice, connected with the titles of real estate in Southern Cayuga. He built the stone mansion on Main Street, and owned a large tract of valuable land at the time of his becoming irrational.— He relied, we are informed, more upon the opinion of other lawyers than upon his own in difficult cases, but was a careful manager, and quite successful.

Nelson T. Stephens was also a well-known lawyer of this town for several years prior to 1862, when he entered the Army as Captain. He was a man of acknowledged legal ability and ranked with the best lawyers of Cayuga County.

COLLEGE GRADUATES.

Of the young men who have graduated at College, and who had previously graduated at the Moravia Institute, are the following named:

Andrew D. White,	Yale College.
Leonidas Dibble,	"
Robert T. Mitchell,	"
Julius Townsend,	Hobart College.
Smith Townsend,	" "
Frank D. Wright.	Union College.

George Dunbar.

William Sutphen.

George L. Wright.   Yale College.

Fay Royce.

Thomas Bell.   Hobart College.

Aaron Phelps.

In addition to the above who graduated at the Institute, and entered the professions, are the following:

Lawyers.—John L. Parker, Adolphus E. Hughitt, S. Edwin Day, Rowland D. Wade, Wing T. Parker, James A. Wright, Hull Greenfield, William Slade, Jr.

Physicians.—Arthur B. Aiken, Harmon Royce, Rollin Goodell, William Bennett.

Clergymen.—John G. Webster, Manson Brokaw.

In addition to the names of the teachers of Union Free School, given in Chapter XIX, we notice the following: Prof. Charles A. Rowndy, Principal, formerly of Syracuse, where he had been successful in conducting an Academy for the past eighteen years, he assumed the position vacated by Mr. Curtis, and has proved himself a very competent teacher. His assistants have been Miss E. Bertha Smith, Miss Adele Cuykendall, Miss Carrie Freese, Miss Adell Rowndy.

CHAPTER XXV.

The following list of business men and their places
of business may be interesting in the future as a
matter of reference:

Attorneys.—Leonard O. Aiken, John L. Parker,
S. Edwin Day, Rowland D. Wade, Wing T. Parker,
James A. Wright, Main Street.

Physicians.—Cyrus Powers. Elias A. Mead, Aurora Street; Arthur B. Aiken, Congress Street; W.
W. Alley, Wm. Cox, Main Street.

Dentists.—Edward A. Huntington & William Cutler, Main Street.

Hotels.—Milton Goodrich, Main Street, Charles
Shimer, Main Street.

Merchants.—Everson & Tuthill, G. Jewett & Sons,
Jennings & Parker, Wm. D. Bennett.

Government Officers.—E. A. Mead, Post Master,
Main Street; John B. Strong. Assessor; David Wade,
Assistant Assessor.

Book Store.—L. M. Townsend. Main Street.

Saloons.—H. A. Walden, James Wolsey. Main
Street; James Wallace, Mill Street.

Flouring Mills.—M. C. Selover & Co.. Cayuga

Street; Alley & Cuykendall, Mill Street; Otis G. Parker, Montville.

Tanneries.—G. F. Morey.

Marble Works.—H. Baker, Main Street.

Meat Market.—Butler & Smith, Main Street.

Lumber, Coal, &c.—Titus & Foster, Parker & Nostrandt.

Sewing Machines.—Wm. Westfall, James M. French.

Jewellers.—Charles Ball, M. Downing, Main St.

Planing Mills.—J. & H. McCredie, Main Street; Wm. Selover & Co., Levi White, Montville.

Bakery.—Christian Rhamb, Mill Street.

Furniture.—Wm. Walden, Geo. Furguson, Main Street.

Butter and Produce.—Daniel Butler, M. L. Williams, P. D. Livingston.

First National Bank.—H. H. Tuthill, President; Leander Fitts, Cashier, Main Street.

Printing.—M. E. Kenyon, Moravia Valley Register; Uri Mulford, Moravia News, Main Street.

Hardware.—Hale & Greenfield, Small & Jennings, Main Street.

Clothing.—M. P. Collins & Son, Benjamin Alley, Thomas Green, Rufus W. Close, Main Street.

Grocers.—Alexander Colony, M. L. Everson, D. Hall, Main Street.

Harness.—L. D. Sayles, Defendorf & Foote, Main Street.

Carriage Shops.—W. G. Wolsey, Main Street; H. P. Parker, Mill Street; S. L. Tice, Aurora, Street.

Boots and Shoes.—B. J. Lumbard, J. D. Clark, Andrew Perry, Wm. Glover, M. Downing, A. Goodell, Main Street.

Daguerreian Hall.—T. T. Tuthill, Main Street.

Brick, Lime and Tile.—A. B. Caldwell.

Barbers.—Henry Paul, Earl Blakely, Main Street.

Coopers.—A. Lansing, W. Peck, Aurora Street; Daniel Lilly, James White, Montville.

Foundry.—J. & D. McCredie.

Saw Mills.—Wm. Selover & Co., Joshua Rosecrans, Smith M. Bowen, Ezra Baker.

Woolen Factory.—J. Mellen & Son, Montville.

Blacksmiths.—John McGeer, Aurora Street; R. T. McGeer, Mill Street; H. P. Parker, Mill Street, Chas. Brigden, Aurora Street; W. G. Wolsey, Main Street; E. Lacy, Aurora Street.

Livery.—VanEtten & Cutler, John Signor, Main Street.

Mortar.—Henry Fox, Mill Street.

In addition to the above, there are the following named establishments conducted very successfully by ladies:

Millinery.—Mrs. H. M. VanEtten, Mrs. P. D. Livingston.

Dress Makers.—Miss Susan Foster, Mrs. G. R. Huff, Main Street; Miss Adelia Bartlett, Cayuga Street.

SOUTHERN CENTRAL RAILROAD.

Moravia Village was for many years after its first settlement a very inaccessible point to reach save in a southerly direction, but as the surrounding country

became more settled, additional roads were surveyed
and built, and access made more pleasant and comfortable.   A public conveyance, in other words, "a
stage," was put upon the road, and made weekly
and thereafter tri-weekly trips from Auburn to Skaneateles and Ithaca, via of this Village.   Then came
another change, from Auburn to Cortland with
"coach and four" via Owasco, Dutch Hollow, Milan and Summerhill, changing teams and drivers at
Moravia.   The driver of "ye olden times" was an
illustrious character ; not only was he invested with
the authority of the Government, which though
sometimes brief, was none the less potent, but he
was the general news monger of the day ; no need to
peruse the official organs, or local items which were
enclosed within the sheep skin receptacle tuck-
ed away with care beneath the seat, with double
padlock, and glaring letters U. S. M. portentious of
untold importance.   He knew and was not slow to
relate all matters of importance, at every station on
his route ; and his ready inventive imagination never
failed to supply any deficiency, when there was a
dearth of actual facts, and he never failed to find
ready and anxious listeners, and believers, as there
always have been, and doubtless will be, in the
marvelous and the supernatural.   The driver's horn
announcing the approach of this very important
branch of the Government service, was the signal
for suspension of all other horns, until the passen-
gers were duly looked over or unloaded, when the
driver was ushered in to partake, if in winter, of

something "warmin'," and if in summer, of something "coolin'" to wit : rum and molasses, at both seasons. But stages have had their day ; the coach and four no longer runs the "Hollow Road." The drivers and their horns have ceased to blow. Serviceable in their time, but none would have their days of service lengthened.

The Auburn and Moravia Plank Road opened a new and direct route from Moravia to Auburn, being one of the most beautiful and picturesque drives in the county, along the shores of the Owasco Lake, for its entire length. For several years this road was maintained, and kept in good repair. But the plank wore out, by incessant travel over them. Stone and gravel were substituted, but these in turn were ground to powder. Extensive repairs were made, at large outlays of money and materials. Expenditures left small margin for profits. To maintain the road in good order would not pay : less repairs were made, the road became bad, and almost impassible ; the people grumbled. Rates of transportation of merchandise advanced, and general dissatisfaction prevailed. But is it not darkest just before day ?

For many years people had hoped, almost against hope, that at some time a Rail Road through the Valley would connect the towns of the Southern Tier with the City of Auburn. Adjoining towns were almost equally anxious for a road which they could reach by coming to Moravia. Meantime enterprising men had deliberated, engineered, and calculated the costs, and as a most glorious result we have the Southern Central Rail Road.

The population of the town in 1870 was 2169, and of the village 1131.

Farming land is worth from $35 to $100 per acre, according to location and improvements upon the same. The farm of Thomas VanArsdale upon the lake road is valued at $90 per acre; that of Hiram Hunt near Free Church, at $100 per acre; the Lawrence Vosburgh farm on East Hill, at $80 per acre; while the farms south of the village are held as high as $100 to $125 per acre. While these are not over-estimates for the farms named, the larger proportion of farm lands will fall much below in value.

The total assessed valuation of real estate in the town is $556,855. The town is bonded to aid the construction of the Southern Central Rail Road for $84,000, which is the total town debt.

The village is the natural business center for the towns of Moravia, Locke, Summerhill, Sempronius, Venice, and portions of Genoa, Niles, and Scipio.— Situated in one of the most beautiful valleys of Central New York, with natural scenery unsurpassed in the State, with excellent churches, and schools and easy of access, it must be conceded that Moravia is destined to become a place of no inconsiderable importance. Its wealth and population are steadily increasing; enterprising business men are here fixing "a habitation and a name."

Public institutions which tend to elevate the morals of community are well patronized, and liberally sustained. Liberality in any community is a mark of healthy and prosperous growth. Moravia a few years since, seemed encrusted with a class of tolerably wealthy, but selfish, penurious and narrow minded citizens, an element sufficient in itself to stunt the growth of any town, and prostrate all its business interests. Churches were but grudgingly supported in a cheap way ; schools and school houses shocked the feelings of every passer by, and were but guide boards which pointed too truthfully the course we were pursuing, while other public affairs were in the same unfavorable and dilapidated state. It is not pleasant to refer to those times, save for the encouraging contrast which is now presented.

Old things are passed away, and all things are become new. An important era in our history has commenced. Let by-gones be by-gones. Let animosity cease. Let petty quarrels, over more petty objects, unfair dealings between neighbors, malice and all ill-will be cast aside. And let us all strive in unison to promote the general good, the best interests and prosperity of the town. It cannot be expected that all will think or act alike. Different by nature and by education, warped by the circumstances in which we have been living, by peculiar surroundings and influences, it would be irrational to expect, that in all the minutiae of business relations, and all the characteristics of social life, there would be perfect harmony, or oneness in opinion or preferences. And it is a very easy matter to look upon the peculiar traits of our neighbors, with critical and disapproving eye. Their faults are so glaring to our fastidious taste that it is hardly possible to possess our souls with any degree of patience, as we contemplate them. One possesses peculiar temperament and disposition the very counterpart of the amiable and self-sacrificing Mrs. Caudle, another forbearance (when forbearance ceases to be a virtue), the humble submissive spirit of her husband. One is a spendthrift, another miserly. Some dress too richly; others outlandishly. All in our opinion, biased and warped associations, have some peculiar faults, which we ourselves do not possess.

So apt are we to act the part of the unjust Judge. This may be illustrated by an incident in the history of a lady who was continually finding fault with other people. No matter how many *good* qualities a person possessed, they were hidden from view by this woman whose chief delight seemed to consist in dwelling upon the errors of others. Upon one occasion the character of a certain well known lady was being discussed by a circle of her acquaintances, a majority of whom decided that she was the most perfect of any lady they ever knew; of amiable disposition, kind to the poor, tender hearted and forgiving, possessing all the womanly virtues, in fact they could not remember a single fault; but this *faultfinding* woman, from long and careful attention to others faults, thinking she had discovered an imperfection even though of the smallest kind, and unwilling that *any* one should pass from her hands spotless, remarked: "Well, she is a very good woman, *but I do think she is very absent minded.*"

How different appears the character of the old

lady who had a good word for *every* one, and who when informed of the death of a notoriously bad man, whose life had been one continuous round of wickedness, unwilling to speak of his frailties but wishing in the kindness of her heart to say something in his favor, remarked: "*Well, he was a very spry man.*"

Oh, how noble thus to throw around the character of even the most erring, the broad mantle of charity, shrouding from the gaze of the inquisitive and unfeeling the weaknesses which are a part and parcel of each ones daily life. Solon's well known motto, "Know thyself," was written in golden characters over the door of Apollo's Temple; let it be written in living characters upon our hearts, that with a knowledge of our own frailties we may be mindful of those of others, knowing that *we all* are fallible. Let us be charitable, while differing honestly in opinions, having respect for the opinions of others.

The business in which we are each engaged should be conducted to the injury of none, and for the good of all. Political affairs should be so controlled that the greatest good to the greatest number should be obtained. Local quarrels, insignificant in the object, but often productive of great mischief and discord in the attainment, should be abandoned as a disgrace to society, and as relics of barbarism, which tend to hinder and obstruct the progress of reformation.

A house divided against itself cannot stand. The interest of one party or faction, is the interest of the whole town. All receive injury from the misconduct

of any. So all are benefited by the reformation, or
by the high morality of a portion of community. If
one member suffers, all suffer. And in the improvement of one, all are improved.

But a few days, or years, and we all step off the
stage of action, having acted our parts. We make
our own records, and are responsible, each for himself. Let those records be worthy of the privileges
which we enjoy, and the times in which we live.
Let us be united, and endeavor to build up our town
upon a broad, liberal, moral, and intelligent basis,
and upon the principles of brotherly love and esteem.
Let us

> " Be just and fear not,
> And may all the ends we aim at
> Be our Country's, God's, and Truth's."

CHAPTER XXVI.

[According to tradition, the Owasco Lake once covered that portion of the valley known as the "Flats," and including the present site of Moravia Village.]

On the shores of the Owasco,
On its Eastern shore and Western,
Dwelt the Irroquois in safety,
Sovereign of the land and water,
Roaming through the field and forest,
In the freedom of his nature,
For the centuries unnumbered
Up and down these rugged hillsides,
Drinking of these flowing brooklets,
Sleeping neath these giant oak trees ;
In these fields around our homesteads,
Once their bark huts nestled closely
And their Villages were scattered
Here and there throughout the country,

On this hillside dwelt Cayugas
Of the Irroquois the foremost,
With their chieftan On-ten-e-ga,
Now bowed down, old and decrepit
In his wigwam, lived his daughter,
La-wa-ne-ta, fairest maiden
Of the daughters of Cayuga,
Well beloved by all the nation,
Most beloved by Me-na-ah-tha,
Their young chief, who in life's vigor,

By the will of On-ten-e-ga,
All the reins of State assuming,
All its heavier burdens bearing,
Guided by the riper counsel,
And the wisdom of his senior.

Thus the years in peace and plenty
Passing lightly o'er this people,
But increased their strength and numbers,
Fitted them to meet the future.

Ah ! who to-day can tell what sorrow
May await them on the morrow,
The past and present no sign giving,
Or aught of future things revealing.

Unheralded there came a time
Which involved the entire nation
In a war of self protection ;
Bloody, cruel, yet victorious,
But at cost of valiant warriors,
Ranking high among Cayugas.
From the Westward swift advancing
Came the Al-le-ghans their foemen.
Subtle, fleet of foot in warfare,
Striking quickly and returning.
But without the valiant spirit,
And the dreadful furious valor,
Which the Irroquois possessing,
With their craftiness and wisdom,
Made them terrible in battle,
All their deep felt wounds revenging.

Then began a fearful warfare,
Waging years without cessation,
Alleghans without succeeding,
Irroquois were yet unconquered.

Then forsaking all their wigwams,
Leaving them to care of women,
And combining all their forces,
The Cayuga's and Oneida's,
Seneca's and On-on da-gas,
Mohawk's and the Tus ca-ro-ras.
Roused to fury, all uniting,
With renewed and deadly onslaught,
Forced their foes from out their strongholds,
Swept them from within their borders.

But while victory crowned their armies,
And the enemy retreated
From before them to the Westward,
Near the homes of the Cayugas,
Near their camp, along the Was-kough,
In their absence unprotected,
Stealthily and quick in movement,
Came an Al-le-ghan in silence,
Through the dense and darkened forest,
Spying out where dwelt the maiden,
Plighted long to Me-na-ah-tha,
Then as silently departed.

In his heart revenge was rankling,
Bitter, deep, and full of hatred,
For the chief of the Cayugas
Who had fought and won their battles,
Who had met him, Wah-wah-no-kee,
Of the Westward, and in combat,
Oft' defeated all his forces,
Routed oft' his bravest warriors.

But again in haste returning,
Ere another sun was setting
Near the home of La-wa-ne-ta.
Near the path where oft' she wandered,
Hidden 'neath the low pine shrubbery.
Watched the coming of his victim.
35

Ah ! what shriek is that which sounding,
To the Westward, o'er the waters,
To the Eastward, o'er the hill-tops,
Backward, forward, through the welkin,
Echoing like answering voices ;
'Tis the cry of La-wa-ne-ta,
La-wa-ne-ta, bound and struggling,
In the arms of Wah-wah-ne-ka,
Fiercely clasped and hurried onward.
As she quickly scans the waters,
And the hillside to the Northward,
Where in evening twilight often
Neath the silent pines and hemlocks,
On the brow of Os-ke-o-la,*
La-wa-ne-ta and her chieftan.
Me-na-ah-tha strong and fearless,
Lingered, till the lengthening shadows,
Faded in the evening darkness,
While her heart in joyous lightness
Heeded naught but loves securenes.

Now a captive she is carried,
By a foe of all her nation,
And into a boat cast helpless.

Out upon the placid Waskough,†
Shoots the fragile bark of birchwood,
Forced by arms rough ridged with sinews.
Cunning in the arts of boatcraft,
Laden with this mourning wild dove,
Parted from its mate thus ruthless,
While so near sat Wah-wah-no-kee.
Hated Al-le-ghan, and cruel,
Gloating o'er the trembling maiden,
From the camp of Me-na-ah-tha,
From the wigwam of her father,
On-ten-e-ga lone and aged.

-----
*Os-ke-o-la, Indian name for Indian Hill.
†Waskough, Indian name for O-was-co.

Ah ! Cayugas on the war-path,
Spake the warrior, Wah-wah-no-kee,
Following the fleeting shadows,
Leave the pride of Me-na-ah-tha,
To the care of Al-le-ghans-es,
To the storm cloud of the westland.
Wah-wah-no-kee is a chieftan,
In his wigwam scalps be plenty,
As the deer upon the mountain ;
As the beavers in the river's
To their number Me-na-ah-thas,
The Cayugas shall be added,
While the fair eyed La-wa-ne-tah,
Is the bride of Wah-wah-no-kee.

Hark ! from out among the pine trees,
From the banks of Os-ke-o-la,
Comes the shrill whoop of the nation,
Comes the loud cry of the warriors,
Home returning, flushed with victory.

Quickly down the rugged hillside,
Sprang in hot haste the Cayugas,
And across from Northern headland,
To the Southward, and the Westward,
All their boats in haste were flying,
For the rescue of the maiden,
For the blood of Wah-wah-no-kee.
For the pride of the Cay-u-gas,
And their chieftan. Me-na-ah-tha.
Swiftly o'er the sparkling waters,
Sped the Al-le-ghan retreating,
Swifter yet the boats pursuing,
And the shouts rang fierce and loudly.
As the foremost gathered nearer,
Hedging in all ways of 'scaping ;
While erect sat Wah-wah-no-kee,
Now his boasting changed to fury.

And his glitering eyes flashed vengeful,
As he turned them on the maiden,
Bound and helpless in the boat's end,
Then upon his belt of buck-skin,
From whence hung a glistening knife blade.

Then was heard the twang of bow string,
And the whizzing of the arrows,
Tipped with limestone from the quarry,
Winged with feather from the eagle,
O'er the waters flying thickly,
Yet the Al-le-ghan unharming,
Till at last from out the quiver,
Me-na-ah-tha drew an arrow,
Quickly to the south he pointed,
Drew the bow string to its utmost,
And from an unerring aiming,
Darted forth the deadly missile,
Pierced the side of Wah-wah-no-kee,
Turning out a crimson streamlet.

From his seat, e'en with death battling,
To the bound and captured maiden,
Leaped he, and with last endeavor,
Pierced her breast, deep to the knife hilt,
And with savage vengeance sated,
Joined the spirits of his fathers.

While the dying La-wah-ne-tah,
With her eyes fixed on her lover,
And her bound hands outstretched toward him:
O'er the boatside, frail and shallow,
Sank amid fair Waskough's stillness,
Sank deep down amid the pebbles,
Mid the lake grass and the lillies,
From the sight of Me-na-ah-tha,
Down into the deepest soundings,
And the birch boat drifting onward,
Left unmarked her place of resting,

And the darkness of the twilight,
Settled down o'er lake and valley,
But the darkness of death's shadow,
Chilled the heart of Me-na-ah-tha.

Shoreward to the east returning,
To the hillsides where their wigwams,
'Mong the oak trees, nestled closily,
Whence their camp-fires smoke ascended,
High above the topmost branches,
Came these grim and stoic warriors,
Came in silence to their comrades,
While their chieftain Me-na-ah tha,
To the pine crowned Os-ke-o-la,
Turned him in deep desolation,
And upon its lofty summit,
Laid him down in bitter anguish,
Prone upon his face in darkness,
Heeding not the damps of midnight,
Nor the chill winds from the northward,
For his heart was buried deeply,
In the depths of Waskough's waters.
Hours passed by—unbroken silence
Reigned o'er all the lake and forest,
When from out amid the darkness,
Spake the voice of Me-na-ah-tha.

Oh, Great Manito the mighty,
Ruler of the winds and waters,
Speaking in the clouds above us,
Walking in the depths beneath us,
Dwelling in the clearest sunlight,
Ever present in the darkness ;
In thy hands are all the rivers,
All the rivulets and fountains,
And the streams and flowing brooklets,
And the great lakes and the small ones ;
Oh, look down on Me na-ah-tha,
Pitying his lone condition,
36

For his eyes are dim with watching,
And his ears are pained with listening,
And his voice is faint with calling,
Yet no answering voice replies.

All his love too weak to rescue,
From the cold embrace of Waskough,
La-wa-ne-tah dead and silent,
Out of sight and out of hearing.

Oh, behold the bitter sorrow,
Weighing down his soul in darkness,
Oh, Great Spirit stretch thine arm out,
And remove from out its boundaries,
All the waters of the Waskough,
From the southward to the northward,
Let the waters be as dry land,
And from out its deep recesses,
Free the spirit of the maiden,
Now within its depths imprisoned,
Give once more unto the Indian,
La-wa-ne-ta his beloved ;
Let him clasp her to his bosom,
Let his eyes again behold her,
Though in death—in death's pale shadow.

Oh, thou waters part asunder,
Oh, depart far to the northward,
Speed thee in thine onward coursing,
And from out thy deep, dark confines,
From among the grass and lillies,
Give him back poor La-wa-ne-tah,
Ere his heart is dead within him.

Thus he spake in earnest pleading,
With his hands uplifted westward,
While his eyes looked into darkness,
Waiting silently and trembling.

Thus in the hours silent watching,
Passed away, to him long lengthened,
And the clouds above sped onward,
All the beauteous heavens unveiling,
Till the gray dawn of the morning,
Dimly in the east appearing,
Faintly, yet each moment brightening,
While beneath the mountain's summit,
Naught but thickening fogs were seen,
Hiding all beneath their mantle.

But anon from out the northwest,
Blew the winds, the mists dispelling,
And a vision strange and wondrous,
To all natures sight revealing,
For the Indian's prayer was answered,
And beneath him lay a valley,
Where before was Waskough's surface :
All its waters had departed,
To the northward far from hearing,
All the waters were as dry land.

Quickly down from Os-ke-o-la,
To the south ran Me-na-ah-tha,
Half across the valley's distance,
To the spot where wreathed in lake grass,
Dew drops sparkling in her tresses,
La-wa-ne-tah lay as sleeping,
Sweetly as in childhoods slumber,
But a sleep which knew no waking,
And a slumber without ending.

In his arms he bore the maiden,
Back upon the mountains summit ;
There a grave he dug in sorrow,
Deeply down among the gray sand,
'Neath a hemlock's sheltering branches,
And therein spread softest mosses,
Spread a couch of natures sweetness.

There upon the pines and mosses,
'Mong the evergreens and oak leaves,
Laid his loved one, La-wa-ne-ta,
All unconscious of his presence.

Down beside the grave he sat him,
Guarding well his lifeless treasure,
While three suns arose and setting,
Marked the time of faithful watching ;
Then a bird he caught at day dawn,
Golden crested, swift in flying ;
Down within the grave then kneeling,
By the side of La-wa-ne-tah,
Murmured in her ear his sorrow,
And a fond farewell repeated.
Then the bird he loosed to westward,
And his voice the silence breaking,
Uttered forth his last.

Go, oh wild bird on swift pinions,
To the lands beyond the sunset,
To the unseen world of future,
La-wa-ne-tah's spirit bearing,
Out beyond the realms of darkness,
Out upon the plains of beauty,
To the pleasant lands of summer,
There to linger in the sunlight,
Till the morn shall break which welcomes
Me-na-ah-tha to her presence,
Till the Great Chief beckons to him,
Bids him enter on his journey,
Leads him to the land of spirits.

When three days and nights were ended,
Which by custom of the nation,
Were devoted to their burials,
And held sacred to their chieftain,
To the burial place to meet him,
Came his warriors slow and silent.

In the grave beneath the hemlock,
In the grave of La-wa-ne-tah,
Found they also Me-na-ah-tha.

He had heard the voices calling,
He had seen the welcome signal,
And had entered on his journey.

There amid the quiet forrest,
Scores of years ago they buried
These two children of Cayugas,
In one grave beneath the hemlock ;
And e'en now at stated seasons,
If faith in legendry be strong,
May be seen their flitting shadows,
And be felt their spritely tappings,
And be heard their mystic whispers,
Round about Old Indian Mountain.